ICY GAZE

By: Margaret Yoder

Order this book online at www.trafford.com
or email orders@trafford.com

Most Trafford titles are also available at major online book retailers.

This is a work of fiction. All of the characters, names, incidents, organizations, and dialogue
in this novel are either the products of the author's imagination or are used fictitiously.

Printed in the United States of America.

ISBN: 978-1-4269-5496-2 (sc)
ISBN: 978-1-4269-5497-9 (e)

Trafford rev. 02/09/2011

 www.trafford.com

North America & International
toll-free: 1 888 232 4444 (USA & Canada)
phone: 250 383 6864 ♦ fax: 812 355 4082

I would like to dedicate this book to my grandma,
Anna, who helped raised me when I was growing up,
and my mom, Helen, who said I could do anything
as long as I believed in myself.

I love you both very much.

TABLE OF CONTENTS

ICY GAZE

Prologue…

The open world has always been my home but that can no longer be my haven. Running from everything to go into hiding, looking more like a wolf with its tail between its legs. Even though it was my order I felt shameful. Hating the city where I now had to take refuge from those who wish to capture me and use me against those I loved.

To hide with creatures who have hunted my kind for thousands of years. Falling in love with us only to damn us on sight after realizing what we truly were. Humans disgusted me. My father believed that everything could change for the better but then again he practically became what he was to avenge my mother's death before trying to end his life when he was saved by a woman. He found love twice and with the second he refuse to let anything happen so I'll go for now so they won't worry.

When it came to humans attacking us we were never worried, but now that some of our own brothers and sisters were commanding humans as slaves to get to us made us more worried. It wasn't often that a werewolf went after another but it was a confrontation others stayed out of unless they were called as a witness to what happened.

Why werewolves were coming after me was far from being within reason. All we knew was that they wanted to strike at my father because he was the first. He had created all that our race held dear. Maybe this was something that they silently feared as well. If he gave it then he could take it away? He might've been a great warrior but just because he had grown up battling in wars it didn't mean he didn't have a soul. He fought to protect what was important. Had personally knew how hard it was to find happiness therefore I could not see him taking it from others so easily unless there was reason for it.

Why I had to go all the way to America and leave my home I had no idea. The ocean in front of my eyes looked more vast now then ever so the doubt of not reaching my destination was weighing heavily on my mind.

The clouds rolling in the sky heading towards us predicted a storm coming. I silently hoped it was the only kind of storm heading in my direction. What would it be like in America? What would the humans be like there? Out of every continent, America was the only one where hunters held company with our kind. They helped destroy creatures that had gone rogue so that all creatures could be protected.

I was slightly interested of the people I'd meet there.

Chapter 1

Elaina sat in her chair staring into her mirror trying to find any flaw possible with how she looked. She was eighteen years old now and went to University High School were the only thing good there were the teachers, prom, and sports programs. The food made a lot of people question on the fact of whether they wanted to really be an omnivore. Since it made a lot of people picky most girls preferred the salad bar while some just ordered from local restaurants… that or they went into town which was a five minute walk and ate there. Elaina was never one to turn down a hamburger but when you're in the mood for a chicken fajita and you open it to put taco sauce and find wilted lettuce in it, it's no longer appetizing.

Elaina was about five-foot-eight although one could never really tell, she had a curvy yet well toned frame because she played basketball and swam, she was slightly on the fair side but it must've added something to her charm, her hair was tawny and utterly unmanageable with all the fly-away hairs, and her eyes were almost bronze in color but they had a bit too much brown in them.

Seeing no problem whatsoever she smiled brightly before heading down the stairs were their guests would soon be arriving. They were traveling here from Rome, she'd always wanted to go there. So much was there that she wanted to see but that would never happen. She had limited mobility. Elaina was paralyzed from the waist down from a car crash that had killed her mother. She'd never known her father either so she stayed with her aunt.

"Elaina hurry up, I see the cab coming down the road!" her aunt called only to smile as Elaina came down in the seat which was hooked to the stairs. "You look very cute."

"The hair is still as bad as ever." Elaina grumbled as she pointed so her aunt smoothed it out making it stay put. "Thanks Aunt Tricia."

"Are they here!?" Daisy piped as she held out two flowers in her little fists. Daisy was Tricia's four year old daughter.

Elaina smiled at Daisy and how adorable the little girl was. Her uncle was over in Iraq fighting in the war. He would be coming home for leave during Christmas before going back for another couple years. She admired at how strong her Uncle David was, he had seen strangers and friends alike die but he held so much hope.

"They *are* here." Tricia said before there was a polite rapping on the door. Tricia opened the door with a bright smile as Elaina felt her heart start skipping so fast she thought it would jump right out of her chest so she took a calming breath. "Welcome to our home, please come in."

"Hi! I'm Daisy!" Daisy piped cheerfully and held out the flowers only to receive a frown from both making her burst into tears.

"Jerks." Elaina found herself saying making them look at her.

"Elaina please don't…" Tricia started only to see Elaina's eyes spark as Daisy wailed even harder.

"What did you call me?" The one she'd been looking at ever since her aunt had opened the door feel her icy personality come out.

"A jerk, making a little girl cry. If she is showing respect by welcoming you here then you can at least acknowledge it." Elaine bit out seeing them looking stunned as Elaina wheeled over. "I think they're very pretty Daisy."

"Really?" Daisy sniffed as she started wiping her face so Elaina helped.

"Of course, they're the prettiest flowers ever." Elaina replied with a bright smile, "You can even put them in my room."

"Elaina you're allergic to those kinds of flowers." Tricia reminded her after Daisy had ran upstairs.

"I can put up with sneezing for a couple nights, that or I'll just pick up some Benadryl… maybe Zyrtec even." Elaina said as she waved it off with her hands before looking back at their guests.

"I am Talon Roberts and this is my cousin Torrin Cauldwell." he said as he tried to figure out the girl in front of him. "We didn't mean to be rude."

"But it was obviously interpreted that way. You could've at least accepted the flowers." Elaina said before Tricia could say anything.

"You speak of manners and not being rude to others yet you don't *stand* to greet your guests." Talon bit out only to watch her eyes darken. She wasn't afraid of him at all, not one bit.

"I *can't* stand you idiot, I'm paralyzed form the waist down." Elaina bit back causing him to look at her legs and then at the chair.

"Paralyzed?" he asked causing her to look at him like he *was* an idiot before leaving.

"Elaina was in a very bad wreck when she was only Daisy's age, only four years old, the doctors said it was a miracle that she even lived at all. The wreck had damaged her spinal cord and paralyzed her from the waist down. She'll never walk or stand ever again. It doesn't bother her anymore though, she makes up for what she can't do." Tricia informed proudly making them nod understandingly.

"Why don't her parents take care of her?"

"Elaina's mom died in the crash and she had never told anyone who Elaina's father was." Tricia explained seeing Torrin accept the answer.

"Hey Aunt Tricia! Tell me when Julie gets here! I'm helping her rehearse today!" Elaina called right before a horn honked as a little red car pulled in.

"Julie's here!" Tricia celled before Julie shot in with a furl of bright blond hair and nearly tripping over the carpet. "Julie no running!"

"Sorry Mrs. Miller!" Julie called without looking over her shoulder. "Elaina guess what!?"

"Would it have to do with the reason why you're yelling?" Elaina asked lamely as the others came in with her aunt.

"I'm getting married!" Julie squealed only to see Elaina frown instantly. "Don't start Ellie, just let me celebrate okay?"

"Fine." Elaina grumbled only to get pulled into a big hug.

"You *have* to be my maid-of-honor."

"More like the maid-of-horror." Elaina replied simply making Julie snort but nod in agreement.

"Great! We can take pictures of you running down the best man." Julie improvised and Tricia couldn't help but laugh as Elaina put on a sly yet impish face.

"I can read the headline now '*Paraplegic on the roll, no deaths but injuries resulting in tread marks*'." Elaina said causing Julie to laugh hysterically. "Now that I have ideas lets practice."

"Umm…who are they?" Julie asked and pointed to the guys.

"Our live in guests, Julie meet *Dracula* and *Lestat*." Elaina introduced sarcastically seeing the guys gawk at her.

"ELAINA!"

"What!?" Elaina yelled back at her aunt as she frowned. "They're brooding so much that they're practically *sucking* all the fun out of the house. I might go Emo just by looking at them."

Elaina could see Julie clamping her hands over her mouth and shaking with silent laughter. "Is there any time when you aren't brutally honest?" Tricia asked only to see Elaina shake her head and hurry to the music room. "Sorry about her, she doesn't like seeing people acting like that."

"At least she's honest." Torrin voiced causing Talon to shrug. "What are they practicing?"

"Singing for their school. Elaina is also a pianist, she sings in the choir but only to keep herself busy." Tricia said before the haunting melody began so she started on dinner having no problem with the music. "You can go watch if you want, they don't mind any audiences."

"Ah! I can't hit the pitch!" Julie yelled in frustration as they walked in so Elaina played again. "Why didn't you take the solo?"

"I didn't want it." Elaina replied only to hear Julie miss again. "You're taking a breath too soon. Besides, if I *had* taken it then I would miss basketball practice. I can't do that when we almost beat our top competitor last year."

"You're such a tomboy, if you were more feminine then you'd have a boyfriend by now." Julie teased only to hold her hands up in surrender when Elaina rose an eyebrow. "I'm just saying that love can change a person."

"Obviously not." Elaina stated as she looked at the bruises around Julie's neck watching her flop hair to cover them.

"You're so cold you're practically icy." Julie snickered causing Elaina to roll her eyes.

"I'm a *realist*, but I'll be sure to write '*Elaina Scotts, so cold she froze the hearts of all around her*' on my tombstone." Elaina replied nonchalantly watching Julie cross her arms.

"Death isn't something to be laughed at Elaina."

"Ha." Elaina got out with a blank face making Julie howl with laughter.

"Good friends are so hard to find." Julie remarked as Elaina began to play again.

"Apparently, so is finding a good soloist." Elaina teased back when Julie missed the pitch for the third time only to get cracked in the back of the head. Elaina heard Julie's phone ring so she proceeded in playing a funeral song.

"That's not funny!" Julie yelled and hurried from the room so Elaina began to play a song by Mozart. "You really should consider competing." Julie smiled as she came back in as Elaina hit a wrong chord. "I have to go."

"You *just* got here." Elaina reminded Julie who only shrugged like it was nothing.

"Mark is just excited about the engagement, he wants to tell *everyone*." Julie said seeing Elaina looking skeptical. "Elaina?"

"Go then, but my window will be locked tonight." Elaina said so Julie left looking mad.

"Julie's leaving so soon?" Tricia asked after walking in making Elaina slam her fists onto the keys. "I'm guessing Mark called?"

"What gave that away?"

"Your temper, I know what's going on. Keep your window unlocked just in case." Tricia said so Elaina nodded as her aunt smiled warmly at her. "Oh and another thing while I remember, stop letting Daisy watch scary movies."

"*Underworld* is not a scary movie Aunt Tricia, it's an action movie. There just happens to be vampires and werewolves and a lot of killing in it." Elaina explained looking completely innocent in that discussion.

"Well then don't let her watch that *Boogeyman* movie. She's blocking her closet door with anything she can move." her aunt said so Elaina got an idea before going to the stairs and pulling herself into her lift. "What are you up to?"

"Nothing." Elaina went upstairs and got to work in Daisy's room. "DAISY!" she hollered forty-five minutes later watching Daisy appear with the others. Elaina watched Tricia shake her head to keep from laughing.

"What did you do? Attach every extra lock to the door?" Tricia inquired as Daisy looked excited before hugging Elaina who felt glad she could do something. "Nicely done Elaina."

"Now I won't have to block the door!" Daisy cheered and locked every one having no idea that all were useless except for the deadbolt.

"Elaina, why don't you show the guests to their rooms?" Tricia asked as Torrin and Talon peeked in to look at the closet door causing Elaina to grumble as she wheeled herself passed.

"This is Torrin's room and this one is *yours*. Welcome to America." she said seeing Talon frown at her sarcasm.

"Elaina can we watch another movie!?" Daisy asked as her little green eyes sparkled excitedly so Elaina got in the lift and sat Daisy on her lap. "I want to watch the v…" Daisy started but Elaina covered her mouth.

"Don't let your mom hear." Elaina snickered there a knock on the door. She wheeled over once downstairs and opened it, only see Mark standing causing her to frown as Talon and Torrin came down. "What the hell do *you* want?"

"I thought you'd want to congratulate me on my engagement." Mark smiled trying to make himself look as if he were important.

"You obviously did something wrong, you decided to *try* to think." she watched as he only smiled at her.

"Elaina don't be like that. We both know you're only mad because you wanted this." he said only to see her face go placid.

"Yeah, I definitely want a boyfriend who takes pleasure in beating a woman. Where do I sign up?" Elaina replied coolly watching him snarl but she wasn't scared of him either. "You think your God's gift to women Mark, I would've asked for an exchange *years* ago."

"Why you…"

"Awe, what are you going to do? Break my legs?" Elaina saw him go red with anger before grabbing her wrist painfully. "You have three seconds to let go and get out."

"And if I don't?"

Elaina punched him in the groin with her free hand causing him to lean over as he let go of her wrist right before she socked him so hard she made him fall backwards out of the house. "Now get out of here before I grab the shotgun."

"You wouldn't!" he snapped as he stood up.

"Wanna bet?" she asked only to see him hurry to his car and leave.

"That was a very impressive punch." Torrin voiced approvingly as she rubbed her knuckles seeing Talon looking a bit puzzled.

"Like my aunt told you, what I can't do I make up for." she replied before wheeling herself to the living room as the movie started. She sat in her chair and watched the movie with Daisy who rolled before making a punching movement.

"I did it!"

"I told you no more scary movies!" Tricia yelled seriously as she came in looking ticked as Talon and Torrin followed in only to stop and watch as a female vampire sank her teeth into a guy's neck.

"And now I'm hungry." Elaina joked seeing Tricia cross her arms and tap her foot impatiently. "What? Daisy show your mommy what you learned!"

"Look mommy!" Daisy cheered before rolling and punching.

"She learned *that* by watching *this*?" Tricia asked only to see Daisy jump excitedly. "Fine, limit the blood a gore. I don't need her having your personality."

"Awe, and what's wrong with my personality. I remembered you called me *unique*." Elaina laughed seeing Tricia smile warmly and nod.

"Unique you are but she's only four, I don't want her doing back flips or whatever before she's ten." Tricia replied before turning off the television.

"I thought you said…"

"Dinner is ready, or are you going to skip dinner again?"

"SKIP!" Daisy cheered and went to go turn back on the television so Elaina caught her by her waist but Daisy had been running.

Elaina was tugged out of her chair the floor hard making her glad it was carpeted. "ELAINA!" she heard Tricia called out before hurrying over right before she started laughing.

"I'm fine." Elaina causing Daisy to go from looking worried to smiling and laughing. Elaina flipped herself over before pulling herself back to the chair and then putting the breaks down before pulling herself in with only minor difficulty.

"Why didn't you…"

"She's a very proud person. Trying to help her in things she can do by herself only makes her mad at you. She's determined and stubborn so ask if she needs help before jumping in unless you want her to swat at you." Tricia explained as Elaina adjusted herself in her chair before unlocking the wheels.

"Come on Daisy let's go eat." Elaina said so Daisy hopped onto Elaina's lap before she pushed them both to the dining room.

"Let's see you do that when she's ten." Tricia snorted as Elaina pulled herself into the side that was missing chairs and parking herself there.

"Smells good." Elaina pointed out before poking at it experimentally with the fork only to see Tricia looking unamused. "Just kidding. Aren't they eating?"

"We've ate dinner before we got picked up by the cab." Torrin explained and wondered if Elaina had seen through the lie because she only glanced at him before going back to eating.

"Time for bed." Tricia said a couple hours later causing Daisy to groan and beg for another hour to finish the movie they were in the middle of. "Absolutely not! You go get in your jammies and brush your teeth."

"Okay." Daisy grumbled and hurried upstairs as Elaina yawned.

"You too Elaina, you will be in charge of making sure things go smoothly for Talon and Torrin at school. Introduce them to your friends and clubs, maybe they'll be interested in it." Tricia said so Elaina wheeled to the lift and parked the chair and pulled herself into the lift. "Thanks Elaina, for putting the locks on the closet door. I wouldn't have thought of it."

"It's no problem, I'm glad I thought of it." Elaina replied before hitting the button as the guys started up the stairs.

"So what's the school like?" Talon asked as Elaina sat there as if in her thoughts.

"You'll find out tomorrow."

Elaina pulled herself into the chair and went to her room where she closed her door before grabbing her nightclothes. She changed like always before going to the bathroom and opening the lower cupboard where her toothbrush was. She brushed her teeth and brushed her hair before sitting it back under the sink and heading out only to push her chair around the corner realizing Talon almost ran *her* over.

"Sorry." he apologized only to hear her grunt as Torrin came out of his room.

Elaina closed her door before climbing into bed and turned off her light before closing her eyes. She had dreams that turned swiftly into nightmares. She shot into a sitting position feeling sweat coating her forehead realizing her window was opened and something was cowering on her floor.

Elaina turned on the lamp seeing Julie curled on the floor bruised and bloodied. "Elaina." she threw herself off the bed and pulled herself to Julie who started crying in hysterics. "I…I can't do this anymore!"

"AUNT TRICIA!" Elaina called out hearing running before her door opened showing Tricia looking worried only to stare at Julie in horror.

"Let's get her to the kitchen." Tricia said before helping Julie up as Elaina pulled herself into the chair. "Elaina get the first aid kit."

Elaina flew to the bathroom where she got the first-aid and hurried to her lift. She pulled herself in as she murmured profanities left and right as Talon and Torrin came out of their rooms. She hit the button angrily only to feel her agitation rise because the lift was so slow.

"Damn it, this stupid thing…" she started before getting to the bottom and threw herself into her chair before racing to the kitchen seeing Tricia sitting with Julie as she drank some tea. "Here's the first aid, I'll get the shovel."

"Why do you need a shovel?" Julie asked as Talon and Torrin listened from the hall.

"I'm going to kill that stupid loser!" Elaina yelled seriously before fixing herself in the chair before leaving the kitchen and heading to the basement door.

"Elaina you aren't seriously think off scooting down all twenty steps to the basement and back up again are you?" Tricia asked seeing Elaina looking more determined then ever as a knock sounded on the door. "Torrin, sweetie, can you get the door please?"

"Sure." he said before Tricia went back to the kitchen.

"Is Julie in there!?" Elaina froze after hearing Mark's slurred speech causing her to turn her chair. "Julie get out here!"

Elaina rolled the chair down the hall not bothering with the wheels but with the motor. Elaina hit the brake two feet from Mark sending her flying at him and tackling him to the ground where she proceeded to try turning his face into hamburger.

"Don't. You. Ever. Hit. Her. Again!" Elaina yelled as she gave him a beating his parents should've given him. She felt him slap her but she only sank her teeth into his hand taking a good chunk from it making him yell in pain. She slammed her fist into his face making his nose gush blood.

"Get her away from him!" Tricia yelled before Elaina was pulled away not even caring her own lip was split open.

"You'll pay for this!" Mark snapped as Elaina narrowed her eyes.

"Go ahead and tell everyone how you got your ass kicked by a cripple!" she yelled and saw him snap his mouth shut knowing he'd make something up. He had to big of an ego to admit something like that and they both knew it. "Touch her again and watch what happens!"

"Is that a threat!?"

"No, it's a promise!" Elaina snapped back and struggled to get away from Torrin and Talon only to get lifted and sat in her chair. "Get your damn hands off me!"

She saw them jump away before she went over and slammed the door before locking it. She went to the bathroom before screaming in frustration feeling better. She washed her face and rolled back out seeing Julie come out after being patched up.

"How could you do that Elaina?" Julie asked only to see Elaina glower at her. "I love him Elaina."

"You *think* you love him, that's *not* love. A guy who puts his hands on you is wrong and you're just as much responsible for this as him. No one is stopping you from leaving, he probably has you believing no one else would want you." Elaina bit out seeing Julie go to slap her but she blocked. "*This* is what you're suppose to do. You're letting him get away with it so he thinks it's okay."

"That's not true!" Julie yelled but the tears were giving her away.

"Then open the front door and tell me if he's still there? He knows better then to mess with me Julie and that's exactly why you come here. You know I won't let him get away with it and when I pound his face in you criticize me for it." Elaina spoke the truth and even Tricia knew it but it only made Julie more angry.

"You don't know anything!"

"I know I'm done cleaning up your mess Julie. No one can help you until you *want* help. I'm *done*, don't come here anymore in the middle of the night. I'm not going to stay up listening to how you're going to *leave* only to run right back when he whistles. Have more pride in yourself!" Elaina said before pushing past Julie who had frozen over with shock.

"Elaina that was harsh!" Tricia yelled seeing Elaina continue to the stairs.

"She acts like she's the only one with problems." Elaina replied causing Julie to frown.

"Yeah, and it's just oh-so-hard being a paraplegic! Being a cripple is so freaking hard!" Julie yelled back only to see Elaina shrug her shoulders.

"At least the cripple doesn't let anyone use her as a punching bag! Ten bucks says the jerk isn't even in the driveway!" Elaina yelled so Julie marched over and opened the door seeing Mark nowhere in sight just like she knew he wouldn't be. "You owe me ten bucks."

"I'm going home."

"No you're not. You're going to come to my room and ask pillow and the gold fuzzy blanket and then you're going to fall asleep on the big living couch." Elaina said as she got to the top of the stairs before getting in the chair and going back to her room. She gathered the pillow and blanket before laying down with it seeing exactly ten minutes tick by before her door opened so she held them out causing Julie to freeze only to frown. She could see Torrin and Talon watching from the hall.

"I want the green one!" Julie yelled and went to the closet and grabbed the itchy green one. Julie yanked the pillow and marched out, only to march in and grab the gold one before throwing the green one in her face.

"Close the door!" Elaina yelled seeing Julie growl at her before slamming it. She laid back down and fell asleep.

She woke with a yawn when her alarm went off so she got dressed before grabbing an outfit from her clothes and getting in her chair. She pushed herself out seeing Torrin and Talon waiting in line for the bathroom. "You know she'll be in there for a while right?" Elaina asked seriously before the doorknob turned as Julie peeked out causing Elaina to hold out the clothes.

"Thanks." Julie grumbled and grabbed them before closing the door quickly.

"There's a bathroom downstairs." Elaina informed seeing them bolt down the stairs as she got there and went down to her other chair. Once in she went to the kitchen seeing the guys walk in as she made two pieces of toast with jam, half a grapefruit with a sprinkle of sugar, and a glass of apple juice.

"You must be a health nut." Torrin murmured only to get puzzled as Julie walked in looking irritated.

"Did you ever think that I might not want to eat that!?" Julie yelled seriously as Elaina poured cereal for herself.

"It's your comfort food, shut up and sit down. We both know you're going to eat it, you *always* eat it for breakfast." Elaina stated causing Julie to sit down and eat with a grumpy look on her face.

"Your lip is cut."

"It was worth breaking his nose." Elaina replied as if it explained everything. "That and taking a good chunk out of his hand with my teeth. Hope it gets infected and they have to cut it off."

"Thanks Elaina." Julie said and hugged her.

"Oh jeez, really? It's too early in the damn morning and I haven't had breakfast yet. You're gonna make me lose my appetite." Elaina said causing Julie to only hug her tighter. "So, you riding the bus or are you going to object that you aren't and still ride anyway?"

"Smartass." Julie snorted as Daisy came in only to pause.

"Mommy? What's a *smartass*?"

"An intelligent donkey." Elaina answered without hesitation causing Julie to choke on her apple juice while Tricia crossed her arms.

"No profanity in front of Daisy you guys."

"Mommy, Julie and Ellie are *girls*." Daisy corrected making Elaina laugh hysterically as Julie picked Daisy up.

"Yeah, Aunt Tricia. We're *girls* not guys." Elaina snorted seeing Tricia sigh and smile.

"Watch the profanity please?"

"You got it. Come on Jules, time to ride the short bus." Elaina said as Julie went to drink only to cough into her juice.

"Stop making Julie laugh while she's drinking. She's not going to be able to do anything." Tricia said seriously so Elaina murmured something to Daisy.

"That's what he said." Daisy repeated causing Julie to howl with laughter.

"ELAINA!"

"That's what he said!" Daisy said again as Torrin and Talon watched the girls laugh while Tricia look displeased.

"Oh no sweetie, that's not what *he* said."

"Bite me Jules." Elaina shot back causing Julie to shake her head.

"Sorry Elaina, you kind of aren't my type."

"Stop being disgusting." Elaina said after covering Daisy's ears. "Really? In front of a four year old?"

"Oops." Julie snorted before Elaina grabbed her backpack and headed to the door with the others behind her. "So are you going to homecoming?"

"Ha, no."

"Awe, why not?" Julie asked as they waited for the bus.

"I'm not going to the Homecoming dance Julie, I can't even stand…let alone dance. I'm not going to pop wheelies in my wheelchair either."

"I thought it was a really cool balancing trick too." Julie stated seriously seeing Elaina looking against going to the dance. "Just because you can't dance doesn't mean you can't go. You were even voted homecoming queen last year but since you weren't there it went to someone else."

"I don't care about some stupid plastic tiara, it's completely superficial, no offense to anyone who likes stuff like that. Since it did go to *you*." Elaina saw the bus pull up and stop before the driver got out and lowered the ramp as the others got on. She was pulled onto the bus before the door was closed.

"Oh come on! It's our last year! Our *senior* year may I remind you! What are you going to do about prom!?" Julie asked like it was a crime to skip school dances and yet she saw Elaina looking guilty. "You aren't going to go!? It's the most important dance of the year and it only happens for graduating classmen!"

"Sorry I can't be as enthusiastic as you Julie." Elaina said before going over her homework.

"Will you stop checking your answers, we know they're right and that you're using it as an excuse not to talk about the matter at hand." Julie said seriously seeing Elaina snap the book shut and look at her.

"I'm not going to get dressed up only to get there and sit in a corner. It only makes it worse going so please just drop it?" Elaina saw Julie start pouting but she shook her head. "I'm not going. If I want pity stares then I'll go shopping."

"That's so mean. You're suppose to go to *all* the dances your senior year." Julie pointed out seeing Elaina looking annoyed more and more. "Come on, at least go to homecoming. If you don't like it then don't go to anymore."

"If you stop pursuing then I will *consider* going." Elaina saw Julie smile looking as if she won before asking help with the homework. "Oh, you buy lunch today."

"Why me?" Julie asked as they pulled up in front of the school.

"You owe me ten bucks, that's why." Elaina reminded seeing Julie groan before nodding. Elaina was lowered in front of the school as the others waited. "See you in class Julie, you two follow me."

"Oh my gosh, who are the guys behind Elaina?" she heard a girl asked as she started up the ramp.

"I heard she beat up Mark so they're her bodyguards." another murmured and Elaina found it comical as she laughed.

Elaina opened the door seeing Talon go to grab it only to stop when she glared so he lowered his hand allowing her to go through just find. She went to the elevator and hit the up button.

"Elaina!"

She looked seeing Leon hurrying over to her. "Morning Leon, forget your notes again?" she asked seeing him nod quickly so she dug them out of her bag and handed them to her. "Just copy them and hand them back in class."

"Thanks, you're a lifesaver." Leon said and kissed her cheek before hurrying off.

"Is that your *boyfriend?*" Torrin asked as they got in the elevator causing her to laugh.

"No he's not my boyfriend. He's gay." the face they made was priceless.

"You mean he likes other men?" Talon asked seeing her nod slowly.

"He's one of my best friends, one of few guys who can kiss my cheek and get away with it." Elaina replied and they could tell she was messing with them as the elevator opened. "This way."

Elaina led them to the office where they got their schedules, they were all three in the same homeroom. "Good morning Ellie." she heard Joyce say before tossing her a lollipop so she caught it.

"Good morning Joyce, how's Buster?"

"Poor old thing tried to catch a rabbit this weekend and got his head stuck in the rabbit hole." Joyce chuckled so Elaina talked with the others until Torrin and Talon were ready so she waved to the secretaries and led the way to homeroom.

"You're late Elaina." the teacher said without looking up at her.

"New students." she replied and gestured to the guys causing the girls to straighten themselves up. She handed their slips to him before going to the only desk without a chair.

"Okay, I'll let you leave ten minutes early to show them to their classes. Now for announcements." the teacher said and went through some boring ones. "Don't forget the Homecoming Dance this Saturday, it's three dollars a ticket until Friday, if you buy at the door then it's five. It's from eight to eleven. There will been drinks and snacks provided and everyone will find out the Homecoming court. The dance itself is semiformal."

"That means all the fine little things in the school wear skirts or dresses!" one guy laughed before looking at Elaina. "That goes double for you Elaina!"

"Not even in your dreams Travis." she said seeing his friends bust up laughing as they patted him on the back for trying.

"So cruel, a guy can only take so much torture." Travis said before he pretended to fall out of his chair dead.

"Is he okay?" Talon asked causing everyone to laugh.

"It's just something he does every year." Elaina saw Travis get back in his seat when the teacher looked at him.

"Our new transfers are Talon Roberts and Torrin Cauldwell, they are cousins from Rome. Everyone answer questions should they have any. Ladies at least wait a couple hours before you bombard them *with* questions." the teacher said before moving on with the announcement. "The girl's basketball team has tryouts Wednesday. Everyone congratulate Elaina for getting us all the way to championships and getting MVP of the year."

"Way to go Elaina!" her teammate Scarlet cheered so Elaina smiled. "We are definitely winning this year!"

"Definitely!" Elaina said before they did their handshake. "Let me hear you hawks!"

Everyone cheered making the teacher sigh like it couldn't be helped.

"Elaina you are dismissed with the transfers, if not I won't get through the announcements." the teacher replied so she left the room with Torrin and Talon.

"Let me see your schedules." she said and looked over them. Torrin had to go to the third floor, and Talon on the second. Her first class was on the first. "Let's go, we have to hurry a bit."

Elaina gave them the run down that numbers in the one hundreds were on the first floor, twos on the second, threes on the third, and fours were in the trailers. "If you have trouble finding something just ask, someone will show your where to go. The smallest numbers on this end and get bigger going to the opposite end of the school. Just go back to the ramp outside after your fourth class, we usually eat in the auditorium, I'll introduce you both to my friends."

"It seems like the whole school is your friend." Torrin found himself saying seeing her shake her head.

"Mostly club heads, the jocks, the thespians, and singers. Avoid the football players, they are *all* friends of Mark. They'll be in a bad mood today so if really big burly looking guys ask if you know me then deny it. It'll save you a trip to the nurse's office." she replied before dropping them off at their classes and heading to her own as the bell dismissed for first class. That was record time.

"Damn Elaina, do you always have to shoot a guy so roughly?" Travis asked seriously as they got in class since they had first class together.

"Sorry Travis, I don't dance." Elaina replied seeing him actually sit next to her today. He usually avoided sitting near her, he *was* a football player. First string quarterback.

"It's not like I have a problem with it." Travis pointed out and gestured to the chair. "In fact, it might be perfect. I can sit in it and you can sit on me."

"Travis." she warned seeing him shrug. "Look, you're Mark's best friend and I *really* hate him. It wouldn't work out anyway."

"I saw what you did to him. He came by last night looking like he got jumped by a group of people. He even said he got jumped. He didn't did he?" Travis asked seeing her shake her head.

"Julie showed up in my room last night, he had beaten the hell out of her. When he showed up drunk I lost it." Elaina said seeing him look understandingly.

"Then he got what he deserved, but seriously? You *know* that despite being Mark's friend that I'm nothing like him. Go to the dance with me this weekend?" Travis asked as they sat there and she liked Travis but she never listened to anyone on the football team.

"Can't, I've already made plans for the weekend."

"Does it involve one of the guys who transferred here? I heard from Mark they're staying with you and your aunt."

He sounded really jealous and looked like he could care less that she knew he was.

"No, it involves me and a pint-sized four year old." Elaina replied seeing him look a bit relieved. "Now that you mention it maybe I'll just invite…"

"Elaina." he groaned and ran a hand through his sand colored hair. "Really? That's cruel."

"I was just kidding." Elaina snorted seeing him look at her and smile right before Mark and couple other football players walked in because they had the class as well.

"Travis why are you sitting next to *her*?" one asked like she might be diseased as others filed in for class.

"Just getting notes." they both said in unison seeing them all believe it.

Elaina knew the social ladder at the school, especially the athletic one. Footballers at the very top, cheerleading, then rugby, la cross, soccer, basketball, tennis, and then swimmers. She was at the bottom while Travis was near the top. Him and Mark were the most popular in the school while she was well known among everyone. People remembered her for scoring points on the court, being able to swim, her piano playing, and her singing. Her academics as well, she's what people stupidly called a *smock*. A *smart* jock. She also corrected them several times that a smock was worn to protect your clothes, that made them point out that she was practically a human encyclopedia.

Elaina was watching the film seeing everyone was practically asleep when something landed on her desk, a little paper football. She looked seeing Travis peek at her with one eye as the closed one faced his sleeping teammates. She opened it seeing a small message in his neat handwriting.

Lunch in the auditorium? Tap pencil twice for yes and once for no.

Elaina tapped her pencil twice casually before he closed his eyes completely as she took notes in class. Everyone like her notes because they were detailed and understandable. She made two dollars per person that copied them and when you had a class of thirty or so students you ended up with a good bit of pocket money. She didn't charge her close friends those.

Elaina went to her next class seeing Torrin there so she headed back to the place with no chairs. "Congratulations on making MVP Elaina." she saw Patrick say before he high-fived her. Elaina listened as she made herself and extra copy of notes, something she learned to do her freshman year before after so many people used it the paper somehow returned *ruined*.

She started the first project of the year, it was just a Rorschach card. She tapped the black ink on the paper in a random sequence before writing her name on the bottom right hand corner. They had to go around with paper and write what each one looked like. She saw Patrick stare at it before tilting his head sideways.

"It looks kind of like a rose." Patrick said before turning it a different way and she realized it did look like a rose. "Nice one."

"Okay, turn in your papers and cards." the teacher said so they turned everything in.

Elaina went to her third class only to see Talon already there sitting patiently in an empty chair looking perturbed. "Penny for your thoughts?" she asked seeing him look instantly perplexed. "Do you want to talk about what's bothering you?"

"Where's the bathroom?" he asked seeing her look close to laughing.

"Come on." she said before showing him to the bathroom and returning to class. Fourth went smoothly as well and soon it was time for lunch. She met Torrin and Talon out by the ramp before leading them to the auditorium. Julie, Travis, and Leon were already there waiting.

"Ah, just the one I was looking for." Leon said before handing her notes back so she put them in her bag.

Elaina saw the last of them come in before a delivery guy walked in so Julie paid for the food and gave Elaina hers. "Okay, everyone this is Torrin and Talon." Elaina said seeing everyone wave as they ate. "You know Julie and you saw Leon this morning as well as Travis. That's Rosa, Kelly, Rosa's twin Roberto, Josh, and Vince."

"Sup." Roberto said making them shrug. "How you liking the school?"

"It's good." Talon answered and Torrin nodded in agreement.

"Lets get the music playing." Leon stated before playing a song. "It's karaoke, if you know all the words then sing, it's a game we have going. The one who wins the most through the week gets a treat. It's usually either me or Elaina. It's girls versus guys, we each get a warm up song. Travis never sings though, he just sits there looking pretty."

"Play our song." Julie said before they went first and Talon was stunned to hear what an amazing singer Elaina was. "WOOT!"

"Guys turn, how about joining for once Travis?" Leon asked making him shake his head. They went through the game and soon it was Leon and Elaina.

"You have to sing the song perfectly to win. No back up singers, one mistake and you lose." Julie set the terms for sudden death.

"Is improvisation on solo allowed?" Leon asked making them shake their head before the song played. Leon could see Elaina smile, it meant she knew the song. He saw her start singing and knew he was definitely going to lose if he didn't get a perfect. Then he realized something. "Wait a minute! She sang this one last week!"

Everyone laughed.

"We were waiting to see how long it took you." Julie snorted making him frown.

"That's cruel, I want to pick the song."

"Then she picks the song for you." Roberto warned and Leon knew how mean Elaina could be. She once picked a Spanish song for Josh who had been taking French.

"Shall we call it a tie then?" Julie asked so Elaina and Leon shook on it. "Tie it is. Let's go back to eating already. I'm going to borrow Elaina for a minute."

"Girl talk." Leon said before following them to the corner.

"Okay, spill." Julie whispered as her and Leon sat down.

"What do you mean?" Elaina asked feeling confused about what she could be talking about.

"I heard from a very reliable source that Travis asked you to Homecoming this weekend and you made an excuse not to go. You said you had something planned with Daisy and that's so untrue. You said you were considering on whether you'd go." Julie whispered causing Leon to gawk before looking at Travis who was eating his lunch. "Why did you make up an excuse not to go?"

"Look, I just can't go okay...I mean he's *Mark's* best friend. I know he's not like Mark but how do I know he's asking me because he actually wants to go and not because Mark wants payback for last night?" Elaina asked quietly seeing them both look like she had a very good point. "Granted we became friends in like eighth grade but he never showed any interest. I believed he showed interest in every other girl *except* me. He just broke up with Rachel Brooks for crying out loud."

"It's four possible situations. He either is in it with Mark, you're the rebound girl because he doesn't have a date, he asked you because knew you didn't have a date making it a pity date situation, or he really wants to Homecoming dance with you." Leon whispered as he ticked them off on his fingers. "Why not just ask him why he asked you to the dance?"

"Then he would know that she really doesn't have anything planned for Saturday and that she blew him off because she's used to being *odd man out*." Julie grumbled like Elaina was completely hopeless.

"Maybe I'll just take Daisy to the movies, she's been wanting to see the one that came out." Elaina replied simply seeing them both shake their heads.

"Leon it's time for a reconnaissance mission. During sixth period we ask him why he asked her." Julie stated with determination only to see Elaina roll away. "Elaina get back here!"

"No way!" Elaina yelled back and wheeled herself back to the others who looked confused. She went back to her homework for the classes only to see Travis watching her. She looked at him seeing him look at his book quickly. Why did he keep looking at her!?

"Incoming jocks! Travis you better hide!" Roberto warned so Travis went behind the curtains on the stage and hid in them. A minute later Mark came in with some of his friends, even some of the cheerleaders were with them.

"Oh look, it's the nerd squad." Elaina saw Bethany say but Elaina knew Bethany's real character. She was a very nice person trying to get through high school. She helped look after her sick grandmother who had been in and out of hospitals for four years now. Elaina had been to do a silent fundraiser and donated the money to them personally to pay for in-home care so

Bethany's grandmother could be more comfortable. Bethany had burst into tears and hugged her so tight that day Elaina thought she might've cracked a couple ribs. Bethany called them *frenemies*. They acted like they hated each other but they were really good friends.

"We're looking for Travis." Mark asked causing them all to laugh.

"Why would you look here?" Leon saw Mark frown so he decided to ask. "What happened to your face, I heard you got jumped."

"Looks like someone really couldn't stand him." Elaina replied simply seeing him glare at her but she kept a placid face. "Wish I knew who it was so I could thank them for saving me the trouble."

"Mind your own business *cripple*."

"Nice comeback, I'll add it to the list of ones you've already been using for years you egotistical pigheaded jerk." she replied seeing Bethany calm to keep from laughing. No one in the school really liked Mark, they like him for two reasons and two reasons only. He was on the football team, and he had money. That was it.

People liked Elaina because she was funny, spirited, a little wild while still be classy, intelligent, talented, and some many more verbs they described her with. When it came to basketball she might not be able to dunk the ball but she could shoot a three pointer like no one's business. That's why people liked her.

"If any of you see him tell him we got practice after school today." Mark bit out and left with the others and Bethany waved to Elaina so she waved back.

"Since when have you and Bethany been friends?" Julie asked in shock so Elaina explained as Travis came out of hiding. "Oh, that's what that was about. So the annual bake sale thing goes to help with her grandmother?"

"Yeah, apparently her grandmother has actually been getting a lot better since the in-home care started." Elaina replied only to get hugged by Julie. "Why are you hugging me!?"

"You're so nice." Julie said and they all knew it, Elaina was as loyal as loyalty could be.

"Will you…let go…already?" Elaina got out before getting free. "Jeez, I'm never telling you about things like that again."

"I'm glad you did, can I help this year?" Julie asked so Elaina nodded before the others left leaving Torrin, Travis, and Talon.

"Do we go to class now?" Torrin asked making her give a small nod seeing them leave.

"Hey Elaina?" Travis asked seeing her stop.

"What?" Elaina saw him walk and stand in front of her only to kneel bringing them at eye level.

"Will you go to the Homecoming dance with me?" he asked again with a very serious expression and felt the question leaving her lips before she could stop it.

"Why?" It's like the word hung in the space between them seeing him sit his hands on the arms of her chair.

"It's cause I like you. Jeez, I've like you since eighth grade Elaina. Why you do think I dated so many girls?" he asked seeing her look like she'd rather not know the answer. He wasn't sure he wanted to know either. "It's because I didn't want to admit it."

"Why?"

"I don't know. I mean you're smart, you're just as good at your sports as I am at mine, you're pretty, and you are far from agreeing with anyone you know is wrong. You don't laugh at things that aren't funny either." Travis explained causing her to feel a bit speechless.

"I *can't* dance Travis, there's really no point in me going to things like this." she replied seriously seeing him looking even more determined.

"Then I'll give you a reason to go."

"There's absolutely no way you could get…" she started only to get cut off from there because he kissed her. Travis Brighton *kissed* her. Her! She saw him lean away before smiling and kissing her again. She found herself leaning away quickly seeing him look at the floor.

"I would really like you to accompany me to the dance. I'll wait until Thursday, let you think about it. If you decide not to then I guess I'll find someone else." Travis said before leaving her alone in the auditorium so she headed to class.

When school was over she went to the small little bus and got in seeing Julie get on with Leon along with Torrin and Talon. She saw Travis walk by with Mark and saw his eyes dart towards her so she looked at the floor.

"Penny for your thoughts?" Julie asked seeing Talon look at her so she rubbed her temples. "Oh my god, what happened?"

"I'll tell you later."

"You tell me right now." Julie said as her and Leon got in the seat in front of her.

"After everyone left the auditorium Travis asked me to Homecoming…again, right before he kissed me." Elaina murmured seeing Leon gawk in amazement.

"Seriously?! He kissed you!?" Leon exclaimed seeing both Talon and Torrin look at her. "Umm…you get kissed by one of the most gorgeous guys in the school and you aren't thrilled why?"

"She probably still thinks he's planning something with Mark. That's usually how it happened. She'd hit Mark and then they'd both do something to get back at her…until eighth grade when I started dating Mark." Julie explained seeing Elaina bite her lower lip. "Are you actually considering about going to the dance Saturday?"

"No, I'm not. He sure had a lot of reasons why he wanted to go with me though." she grumbled seeing Leon raise an eyebrow.

"He ticked off *real* reasons about why he asked you?" Leon asked causing her to nod. "Honey go to the dance with him! That's a guy who has been paying attention to you for a while. What did he say when you brought up the fact you wouldn't be dancing?"

"He said he'd give me a reason to go and then kissed me." she explained quietly seeing Julie look speechless. "Yeah, that's how I felt."

"He must *really* like you Ellie, Travis *never* makes the first move when it comes to a girl." Julie replied seriously seeing Elaina shrug like it didn't matter. "We have to find you a dress to wear for Homecoming, and get your nails done too."

"Definitely." Leon agreed as Elaina frowned.

"I never said I was going."

"We already got your ticket." Julie held it up making Elaina scowl at her. "You're going whether you like it or not."

Chapter 2

Elaina had dreaded Thursday approaching but when it did she seemed to find herself calming a little. Maybe he had forgot and just asked someone else? She couldn't stop waiting as if it was something set up by him and Mark.

She sat in homeroom with the others seeing Travis look at her so she look at her desk. If anyone had noticed they would've realized that her fingernails were now nicely manicured. Yesterday after tryouts Julie and Leon had taken her to find a dress and to get her nails done. She felt awkward as she looked at them. They were acrylic and felt foreign to her.

Elaina got flicked a note in first period from Travis and asked her if she knew or not, she couldn't even decide on whether she wanted to go. She went through the rest of the day but when lunch rolled around she was hesitant to go into the auditorium.

She went in seeing no one there except Travis so she continued in.

"Are you avoiding me?" Travis asked causing her nod slowly. "Why?"

"Don't know, thinking mostly." Elaina stated seeing him smile at that.

"You know you…" he started right before her friends and *the jocks* came in. Mark and half the football team came in with their girlfriends.

"Travis what the hell are you doing in here?" Mark asked seriously and looked at Julie who stayed completely away from him.

"He's probably just getting notes from her, right?" she saw Frankie asked and she expected Travis to agree with that as she started towards her friends.

"Actually I'm waiting for her answer." Travis replied causing her to freeze as Mark got confused.

"Answer to what exactly?"

"On whether or not she'll go to Homecoming with me." Travis saw Mark looking furious as the others just stared with dumbfounded looks.

"You asked her to Homecoming!?" Mark roared like Travis had broken some kind of sacred code or something. "Are you trying to commit social suicide?!"

"Who I go to the dance with doesn't concern you Mark." Travis stated warningly as Julie crossed her arms.

"Yeah besides, she's already going with him." Julie replied and Elaina wanted to run her over because Elaina hadn't actually told Travis yet.

"She is?" Travis asked so Julie held up Elaina's hands.

"She didn't get her nails done for nothing, she was even complaining the whole time." Julie watched Travis walk over so he moved away as Elaina felt her face starting to burn. "Did you not tell him yet Elaina?"

"No, I hadn't." Elaina replied through gritted teeth only to see Travis smile and it caused her to relax.

"This won't happen." Mark growled before leaving with the others who gave a thumbs up. He wouldn't let it happen even if it killed him.

"What time should I pick you up?" Travis asked so Julie gave him a time as she just sat there.

Elaina got home and was doing her homework when the doorbell rang so she headed towards it. Her aunt and Daisy had taken Torrin and Talon to pick out clothes for the dance. She opened the door seeing Travis standing there pacing back and forth.

"Travis what are you doing here?" she asked and saw him smile.

"Julie said you had something to tell me." Travis stated making Elaina know exactly what Julie was up to.

"Julie *lied*."

"Oh, she sounds pretty convincing on the phone." Travis supplied so she opened the door to let him in. "Wow, I never seen the inside of this house. It looks great."

"Are you trying to start a conversation?" she asked after closing the door seeing him nod slowly. "Maybe a different topic then."

"So it's really nice outside." Elaina couldn't help but laugh. "What?"

"You're talking about the weather?" Elaina led the way to the kitchen seeing him sit next to her after she grabbed a couple sodas. "Here." she handed him one seeing his hand brush hers.

She saw him look at it and then look at the table. How could he be shy all of a sudden? That's when she remembered Leon saying how he never made the first move. Would this be considered the second move? Was it her turn to initiate some kind of affection?

Elaina sat the sodas on the table before taking his hand into hers. She saw him look at her but she was focusing on writing with her left hand. "I didn't know you were ambidextrous." she heard him say as if it were genuinely interesting.

"Only my aunt, Daisy, and Julie knows." Elaina supplied as he twined his fingers with hers. She felt him tighten his hand slightly so she turned to look at him only to see his face a couple inches from hers. Next thing she knew he was kissing her. She didn't know much about it since she never had a relationship.

"I'm sorry Elaina." she heard him say as he moved to her neck.

"What for?" Elaina felt his breath against her neck as he stilled and nuzzled it.

"I'm really hungry."

Elaina couldn't grip what he had meant. She felt a pain in her neck and it got worse so she did the only thing she could. She socked him in the gut making him hiss and she watched blood run down his chin. She went to scream but he covered her mouth so she sank her teeth into his hand tasting blood.

"It won't hurt for long Elaina." Travis said right before he pinned her hands and bit her throat again but not before she let out a piercing scream. He hit her in the head seeing her go unconscious. Now he needed a place to hide the body.

Travis carried her to the car and sat her in the back seat. He drove to the forests as the sun started setting and tossed her body in a pile of grass. "Sorry Elaina, you were a good friend though." he said and saw a huge wolf come out followed by four more. He hurried to the car since he didn't mess with werewolves, humans were fair game but not Weres.

Elaina could barely make out a rough yet gentle hand rolling her over while her heart beat frantically in her chest. That's when something bit her hand causing her to cry out in pain. She couldn't move though, so when she was picked up she could head to the fate awaiting her.

She would occasionally come around to whispers and growls. She even felt her own eyes connected with a beautiful pair of caramel eyes that caused her heart to do a little flutter before she passed out completely. She was aware of different hands adjusting her every which way.

Elaina started coming around letting her eyes open slowly and looked around not recognizing anything she looked at. She noticed she was also alone in the room as her hand throbbed so she looked seeing a bite mark, it looked like she'd been bitten by a dog. She suddenly remembered what had happened with Travis and wondered if he was holding her hostage.

"Oh, you're up." Elaina looked seeing a guy about twenty-seven standing there so she got on guard seeing him hold up his hands in surrender. "Just here to check on you."

Elaina was aware of him heading towards her slowly as she tried to figure out why she had sharper vision, she could smell the recent rain in the air, and it felt like she could taste the oak the house seemed to be made of on her tongue. She felt the guy go for her neck making her hear a feral growling only to realize it was her after the guy jump away from her.

"I need to make sure your neck is healed."

"Stay the hell away." she warned but he managed to get near her so she aimed a punch. She felt him catch her arms so the logical thing was to try to kick him. Her leg retracted and kicked him sending him into the wall so only to feel speechless.

"Ow." the guy grumbled so she ran towards the door in a stumble so he blocked it.

Elaina jumped out the window and rolled before getting to her feet. That's when she realized there were three others outside looking at her. "Don't let her leave!" the guy inside yelled so they started towards her making her take off running, feeling herself stumbling as the others chased after her.

"Gotcha!" one called as he lunged at her feet making her jump and catch a branch. Before swinging across a creek.

It felt like someone else was controlling her body and she couldn't help but realize it felt absolutely wonderful. She had never thought she'd ever run again. She kicked off her shoes and hopped taking off her socks before running with her arms pumping at her sides.

Elaina felt herself get tired so she stood in a small clearing breathing deep before looking at her legs. They didn't look brittle or unused, they looked strong and toned. She dug her toes into the ground with a sigh as she closed her eyes. She heard a stick branch snap to the left before hearing a growl so she looked seeing a black wolf with amazing caramel colored eyes.

Why did those eyes look familiar?

Why did she feel like it was deciding on whether to kill her or approach her?

It started towards her making her stumble back landing in front of a tree. "Back off wolf, I got two legs and know how to kick a face in." she said seeing it stop as if it understood her. She found herself looking at her foot and flex it as a test. "This is completely impossible. This really can't be happening to me."

"Did you find her yet!?" she heard one yell yet causing her to judge about fifty yards of distance. She sat perfectly still in the little clearing surrounded by high bushes.

Elaina sat there hugging her legs feeling close to crying. She didn't know who to be around, where she was, how long she'd been unconscious, or where to find a phone. She heard them moving away so she sat her head on her knees looking at the wolf sitting there watching her. She couldn't help the tears that started rolling down her cheeks.

"This is all wrong." She heard the wolf whine before walking towards her and sitting it's head against her knee. "Thanks but I think I'm far from being cheered up. It doesn't offer must assurance when your Homecoming date tries to rip your throat open…or I guess that's what he intended to do anyway."

Elaina stood up slowly and shakily and rubbed the side of her neck. It still felt as if his teeth were still buried there. She shuddered at the thought of running into Travis again but then again they went to the same high school. Anger suddenly went through her.

"I guess I'm going to have to go back to that damn house." she grumbled hearing the wolf bark as if agreeing with her. "Who asked you anyway? Damn, I'm really losing it. Talking to freaking animals."

Elaina saw the sky start darkening right before it started raining. She was aware of the wolf walking next to her making her a bit relieved. She didn't even know how she got back, she never had a sense of direction. She saw a dog in the yard causing her to move away. It was unleashed and standing in the yard.

She suddenly felt the need to run, she didn't need to go back to the house. She needed to get home. Home. That word echoed through her head making her chest hurt. "Need to get home." she said seeing the wolf get in front of her and growl. "Don't act like that, they're the only family I have left. It was never a lot…but they always took care of me. Oh god, Travis could go back after them."

Elaina felt panic go through her so fast she started hyperventilating. "He could go after Julie and the others too." she choked out because they would look for her and when they didn't find her they'd ask Travis. "Damn it to hell, Julie was the one who told him to come over…she knows he's the last person around me."

Elaina threw risk out the window and bolted through the yard seeing a trap spring and without meaning to she ended up somehow doing a backhand spring landing in a crouch.

"Wow, she has really good reflexes for only waking up. Not even Ravyn is that good." she heard a guy say right before she felt something lodge into her shoulder seeing a dart making her rip it out instantly. "Hey Connor, I don't think the knock out darts are working. They're only ticking her off."

Elaina heard the same feral growl causing her to choke off before looking at her hands seeing her nails sharpening. "What…What the hell is happening to me!?" she yelled after standing up and took deep breaths to calm down seeing her nails return to looking normal. She noted the acrylic missing and her nails were definitely longer.

"Putting it simple: you're a newly turned werewolf." the guy with the gun said simply and figured he was Connor. "You're too dangerous to go home right now."

"I have to! That stupid little slime ball can be after my family!"

"Unfortunately *we* are your family now. A werewolf has no human ties because it's easy to kill them." Connor said only to see her eyes give a luminescent glow as she glared.

"Like hell you say! They're the only family I have and know so I'm going back!" she bit out and turned only to get hit with the dart so she ripped it out. "You are *seriously* pissing me off! How about I come over there and shoot one down you throat!"

"She's gutsy, I can see why you like her Ravyn." the shortest said causing her to see the black wolf walk forward and change into a guy.

A very *gorgeous* guy.

"I told you she'd be difficult to control." Connor and before any could blink she had him pinned to the house by his neck.

"I'm not a freaking robot." she replied icily seeing him look at her like she wasn't normal. "There's no such thing as normal."

Elaina dropped him and moved around feeling light headed so she shook it a little seeing them looking at her. She saw *Ravyn* walk towards her so she moved away instinctively. That guy was way to overwhelming to be near.

"It's too dangerous for you to go home before the first turning." he said and she could tell he wasn't lying but she couldn't leave her family unprotected.

"It's cause Ravyn's the one who bit you. You see, he isn't a normal *lycan*." Connor explained as she felt the rain continuing to patter against her skin.

"From how you looked at me I'm guessing I'm not either." she grumbled seeing them look like it couldn't be helped. "I didn't ask for this. I won't stay just cause it happened. I need to protect my family."

"Your family can fend for themselves." Connor bit out and she saw red.

"Daisy is four years old! She can't do anything to save herself! For crying out loud I hooked ten different locks to her closet cause she thought there's a boogeyman living in her closet!" Elaina yelled seriously seeing them look at Ravyn as if he had any say in the matter. "To hell with staying here while they have a chance of dying."

Elaina ran, she could hear them chasing after her but she didn't care. "You can't go back until they know there's nothing different about you!" Elaina stopped instantly hearing them stop behind her.

"What if they know there is something different?!"

"You would have to leave!" Connor yelled seriously causing her to look at her legs.

Elaina felt as if someone had punched a hole in her chest because she couldn't even explain how she could walk again. "I'll never be able to go back." she cried and covered her face with her hands.

"You'll be able to go back, not until the first turning though." Ravyn reassured as he put a hand on her shoulder making it shrug it off and turning around.

"No I can't."

"Why not?" Connor asked making her wrap her arms around herself.

"Before all of this happened I was paralyzed." she said and then everything went dark feeling arms catching her.

"What do we do Ravyn?" Connor asked after Ravyn picked her up. "How would she even be able to explain that she can miraculously walk again? The doctors would want to blood work and it'll expose us."

"Let's take it one step at a time." Ravyn replied before heading to the truck parked in front of the house.

"You can't be serious?!" Connor yelled as if Ravyn was risking everything.

"Looks like we're moving, Connor I want you to find a house as close to hers as possible." Ravyn said seeing them nod before he sat her in the truck and got in next to her. He drove towards the town seeing her fall against his shoulder. He had never seen such a more adorable and domineering creature. He couldn't believe she'd been completely paralyzed either, not when it came to how she ran.

Ravyn saw her stir slightly as he parked a good twenty feet from the house that must've been hers. He carried her and sat her in front of the door before knocking and going back to his truck. He saw a woman answer the door only to call for help from in the house. He saw them carry her in wondering why he felt so jealous.

Elaina woke up slowly only to see she was in her room and wondered if everything had been a weird dream. She had been changed into her night clothes. She sat up and rubbed her head only to hear horns honking. She looked at her legs seeing they still looked strong and toned.

She stood up slowly feeling how amazingly soft the carpet was. She walked around her room just before the door opened and the tray with breakfast crashed to the floor. She looked seeing her aunt standing there in shock.

"Elaina...you're...walking!" her aunt exclaimed before pulling her into a tight hug and crying. "How is this possible!? I mean the doctors said it was *impossible*."

"I think maybe I just had a pinched spinal cord." Elaina replied seeing her aunt look as if it were possible.

"We should take you to the hospital. You've been missing for almost a week and now you're suddenly back and can walk. Something must've happened." Tricia said and Elaina knew she couldn't go to the hospital.

"Please Aunt Tricia, no more hospitals. I don't want to go." Elaina begged softly because she truly had been poked and prodded with every needle known to man. They thought it was fine because she couldn't feel anything.

"Okay, let's go to the kitchen. Torrin and Talon were glad to see you back. So was Daisy and Julie." Tricia replied so Elaina *walked* down the stairs and into the kitchen seeing Julie go to eat only to drop her fork in complete shock.

Elaina caught the scent of something foul and making her breath deep before looking directly at Torrin and Talon. She saw them jump instantly as the hairs on the back of her neck rose.

"You're walking!" Julie cried before pulling her into a tight hug but she never took her eyes from the guys.

Elaina couldn't hear a single heartbeat coming from either of them. She bared her teeth seeing Torrin step in front of Talon causing her to narrow her eyes since no one could see.

"Could we talk to Elaina really quick, it's urgent." Torrin said so Tricia nodded before Elaina followed them to the backyard.

"Get away from my family." she warned seriously seeing them hold up their hands.

"We are only here to be in hiding I assure you. We have no intention in harming your family we swear." Talon said and she could see the honesty in his eyes. "I am simply hiding so that my own family will not be harmed."

"You're a werewolf and yet you move like a vampire." Torrin described and she remembered what happened causing her to touch her neck. "You've been attacked by a vampire? Who is it, they might be rogue."

"Travis did it, attacked me and then dumped my body in the middle of nowhere. That's how I got bit and obviously became a werewolf." Elaina explained seeing Talon look at Torrin who nodded before hurrying off.

"I'm very sorry that you seemed to have suffered because of one of my kind but it doesn't explain how you can be walking. Becoming a werewolf makes you strong but it doesn't cure paralysis. Did you drink blood from Travis?" Talon asked seriously and realized she had when she paled.

"He went to grab me so I bit him. I didn't even think that would do anything." Elaina said and rubbed her head seeing him step towards her only to stop when a growl sounded.

It wasn't her this time.

"Get away from her *leech*." Elaina turned seeing Ravyn standing there causing her to feel a bit flustered.

"Back off *wolf*." Talon bit back and they went towards each other causing Elaina to get between them.

"No fighting." she warned seeing Ravyn look like she was insane.

"One of them could've been the one who threw you in the woods." Ravyn bit out seriously seeing her look at him and shake her head.

"I *know* who it was." she said seeing him relax after she touched his shoulder seeing him continue to glare at Talon. "They've been staying here since school started, they're live-in students."

"You've been letting *leeches* stay in your home?" Ravyn asked like it was sickening.

"I didn't know, I was *human* mind you. It's not like I went around checking for a pulse." she saw him look amused by the idea as his fingers brushed against the inside of her wrist. "They haven't done anything wrong."

"Fine, I'll allow it, for now." Ravyn said seeing Talon bare his teeth at him.

"WOW!" Daisy exclaimed from her hiding spot in the garden. She ran over and latched to Elaina's leg. "You're like the doggies from *Underworld*?"

"This is bad." Talon got out as Elaina got an idea.

"I'll handle it." she said before picking up Daisy and taking her to the swing.

"Daisy this has to be a secret okay? You can't tell your mommy or anyone else that I'm a doggie from Underworld." Elaina said while sitting her on the swing and swaying her back and forth.

"How come?" Daisy asked so Elaina felt bad about this.

"Remember in the movie that people weren't allowed to know about the doggies?" she asked seeing Daisy nod slowly. "Well that's exactly how it is. No one can know doggies are real because then they'll try to hurt the doggies."

"Does that mean they'll try to hurt you Ellie?" Daisy asked making Elaina nod slowly seeing Daisy close to crying before throwing her little arms around Elaina's neck. "I won't tell, I don't want Ellie to get hurt by bad people. No one will know you're a doggie. I'll even pinky promise!"

"Okay, pinky promise it is." Elaina said and pinky promised with Elaina. "That's it Daisy. No one can know doggies exist."

"Okay." Daisy said looking determined so Elaina kissed her forehead.

"Good girl, I'll make you chocolate chip cookies as a present." Elaina saw Daisy light up like the fourth of July and hurry into the house asking Tricia to buy stuff to make cookies.

"I don't think that'll work." Talon said causing Elaina to stand up and dust herself off.

"You don't know Daisy." Elaina murmured knowing they heard her before she looked at Ravyn. "We need to talk."

"Follow me." he said causing her to cross her arms. "Please?"

"That's better."

Elaina followed him across the road seeing the others moving stuff into the empty house. She saw the others except Connor grin. "You all moved here?" she asked seriously like it couldn't be possible.

"Elaina!" Julie yelled making her turn only to get plowed into and pulled into a huge hug. "I'm so glad you're back! I'm bummed you disappeared before Homecoming though!"

"Julie too early in the morning." Elaina grunted so Julie let go before looking at the guys only to smile brightly.

"So this is why you came over? I completely support you a hundred percent." Julie replied with a sly smile and Elaina swatted her.

"That's not what it is at all." Elaina said only to be completely ignored by Julie who smiled at the others.

"Hi, I'm Julie. I'm Elaina's best friend. Welcome to the neighborhood." Julie said causing them to give friendly waves. "Elaina you won't believe what happened at Homecoming."

"What?"

"You got voted Homecoming queen again. Is it me or are you only voted for such an honor when you *aren't* there, not that I'm complaining since I was runner up again." Julie replied only to see Elaina give her a droll look saying she should stop talking. "Awe, I saved the tiara. It's sitting on *your* dresser."

"Yippee." Elaina got out sarcastically only to get cracked upside the head.

"So who are they anyway?"

"I'm Ravyn and these are my brothers." Ravyn said seeing Julie nod slowly before nudging Elaina in the ribs only to get glared at.

"I'm Connor." Elaina noticed Connor seemed interested in Julie, "This is Seth, Blade, and Larkin."

"Nice to meet you, Elaina can I ask you something?"

"Absolutely not." Elaina replied without looking at her seeing her practically bouncing up and down.

"But I need help with the solo!" Julie begged so Elaina gave up. "Great I'll go get everything ready."

"You have an…interesting friend." Larkin snorted as Elaina pinched the bridge of her nose.

"She has a one track mind sometimes."

"So what did you need to talk about?" Ravyn asked as Elaina thought for a moment trying to remember.

"Oh right, the day I was dumped in the woods I might've *bit* the vampire who put me there." Elaina replied seeing them look at each other and looked at her. "It's probably why I can, um, walk."

"The vampire blood healed your spinal cord and when you were bitten it reinforced it. This is very interesting." Connor murmured and looked at her only to watch her shake her head.

"I know that look anywhere, I am so not being a freaking science experiment." she replied seriously seeing Connor look at Ravyn. "Why the hell are you looking at him for permission!? It's my body you moron!"

"She *does* have a point." Seth pointed out as she looked serious.

"I had enough needles stuck into when I *couldn't* feel them, I'm sure as hell not letting you when I can." Elaina got out because doctors freaked her out now. She saw Ravyn look at her and sigh.

"I can't make you do anything you're against, it would help to explain why you seem to have better reflexes and senses then me though." he said causing her to cross her arms.

"Reverse psychology isn't going to work."

"Just *one* vial of blood, that's it." Connor stated and saw her look at the ground.

"One vial? No more then that?"

"She's curious about how's she changed." Blade snickered, Elaina sighed before nodding.

"Great, we can compare samples from both Ravyn and Blade." Connor looked ecstatic about doing some research so she sat in a chair along with Ravyn and Blade.

Elaina watched him take samples from Blade and then Ravyn before getting in front of her. She saw him pull out the needle making her move away from it without realizing she was doing it. "Maybe I should've mentioned that I was usually restrained for stuff like this." she choked out since she couldn't help it. She saw four hold her arms down.

"Elaina, look at me." Ravyn said so she looked feeling as if she were being pulled into those brilliant caramel eyes.

"Done." Connor stated and got to work before she heard cars heading to her house.

"Where is she!?" Elaina stood up after hearing Leon ask excitedly so she ran from the house.

"LEON!" she laughed before bolting over and pulled him into a huge hug making him laugh.

"Glad to see you're okay." Leon said and hugged her tightly. "What happened and why they hell are you standing?!"

"I'll explain everything later." Elaina felt so relieved to see her friends as they all pulled in. She hugged every single one of them as if she hadn't seen them in years.

"I want to see you dunk a ball. Now that you can run and stuff our basketball will be undefeatable Ms. MVP." Georgia cheered before they did the secret handshake. "I'm glad you're okay Ellie."

"I think we all are, everything seemed so *boring* without you in the school. Even the teachers didn't even want to do anything." Leon said as they all group hugged on her causing her to laugh.

She felt normal even though she knew she wasn't.

"Looks like she was missed more then we thought she'd be. She has practically the whole school there." Blade said as the others nodded dumbly. "Let's go over."

"We shouldn't." Connor said but Ravyn was already out of the house heading over as music started. "Let's go."

Elaina saw Leon start music causing her to laugh getting everyone dancing. She didn't even see the others in the crowd as she started singing. She loved this song and even saw the other choir girls and start dancing so she followed the steps. She finally felt her eyes connect with caramel eyes as she continued to sing while the others did backup with Leon. She was more aware of how her body moved for some reason as her skin seemed to feel sensitive all of a sudden.

After they finished the applause caused her to snap out of whatever she was in seeing him talking with the others. "We should go, we don't need to be here." Elaina heard him say causing her to see them leave not even realizing she's been watching him the entire time. She saw him glance back only to look surprised that she was looking at him.

"Earth to Elaina?" Leon asked and waved a hand in front of her face so she looked at him. "Something wrong?"

"No, why would there be?" she asked seeing him look over at Ravyn before looking back at her.

"Good luck." Leon snickered before he jumped into the crowd which carried him to his car. "Okay, we can see her at school. Let's give her a night to recuperate from us bombarding her!"

Elaina say her goodbyes before going to her music room not even knowing that Blade had snuck over causing Ravyn to hurry after him. She began playing as Julie came in and smiled. "Hey." Elaina said as she played not seeing them both peeking in the room.

"Elaina what's going on? None of this make sense. Don't get me wrong, I only pass my classes because you tutor which I'm completely grateful but even I know that after fourteen *years* of being paralyzed you can't just get up and walk." Julie stated seriously but Elaina acted like she hadn't heard. "You're hiding something and I don't know what to make of it. You look and act like yourself but there's something really different about it."

"I think you might've hit your head." Elaina snorted as Julie sat next to her on the bench.

"You even sound *guilty*. We've been friends ever since you moved to live here when you were five. We've never kept secrets from each other. Granted that you've always had my back more then I've had yours but I'm concerned." Julie explained and Elaina could tell but she didn't want to endanger Julie.

"Nothing's wrong, I promise." Elaina said with a warm smile seeing Julie look even more sullen.

"I really, *really* want to believe you but you smell really weird." Julie grumbled and smelled her. "You smell almost like a…a *dog*."

Elaina knew she didn't smell like a dog and it caused her to stand and look at Julie who just sat there. "I don't smell like a dog!" Elaina yelled seriously because there was no way Julie could even pick up that scent.

"What happened when Travis came over last Thursday Elaina." Julie asked seriously and stood up causing Elaina to be wary.

Elaina saw Julie looking a bit sick and Elaine was really confused. "Julie I think you should sit down." Elaina murmured seeing Julie give her a deep frown.

"I don't think you're quite grasping the situation." Julie replied before her eyes got a deep burgundy color.

Chapter 3

Elaina woke up feeling completely exhausted in her room because last night had been a complete wreck. Julie had tried to kill her, Ravyn had come through the window and restrained her, and then Elaina found out her best friend was being controlled by a vampire who was likely to be Travis.

She got dressed, put her hair into a messy bun, she went downstairs for a quick breakfast, and headed for the door. "Elaina can you take with Daisy with you, I have to go grocery shopping!?" she heard Tricia asked as Daisy ran out and latched to her leg.

"Yeah, see you when you get back!" Elaina said before walking across the road quickly despite Daisy sitting on her foot. She knocked on the door only to see Larkin answer the door with a yawn…and with no shirt on. "Morning Sunshine."

"Morning." he said with a grin and slightly flexing his muscle.

"How's Julie?" Elaina asked only to follow him in as Daisy continued to sit on her foot.

"Ellie is he a doggie too?" Daisy asked shyly causing Larkin to look at her.

"Yep, I'm a doggie too." he said only to see Daisy bury her face into Elaina's leg with a giggle. "She's cute. How old is she?"

"Four." Elaina said before Connor and Ravyn came out, also shirtless. "Does every person who lives here walk around half naked?"

"I don't." Blade volunteered after walking out in cargo shorts and a tank.

"Liar. He threw it on after hearing you at the door." Connor replied before looking at Daisy. "I don't think she should be here."

"DOGGIES!" Daisy cheered before running around them. "Ellie can I play with the doggies!? Please, please, please!?"

"She knows?" Connor choked out seeing Ravyn and Elaina nod slowly. "Isn't she scared?"

"Why would I be scared of Ellie?" Daisy asked after looking up at him. "Ellie keeps away the boogeyman and boogey lady."

"Eh?"

"Simply put it, she's a huge fan of *Underworld*." Elaina stated seeing them looking puzzled. "Really? Vampires versus werewolves."

"I like Michael, he's a vampire *and* a doggie!" Daisy piped before dancing around the room.

"She wasn't really supposed to watch those movies but I might've *forgotten.*"

"You let a *kid* watch movies about vampires warring against werewolves?" Connor asked looking completely aghast.

"It's okay, the vampire lady and the doggie end up together!" Daisy cheered as she bounced up and down.

"How was I to know she'd be so observant?" Elaina laughed with a shrug. "Show them what you learned from the movie Daisy."

Daisy jumped before rolling and punching. "She learned that from the movie?" Blade asked seeing Daisy nod quickly. "I gotta watch that movie."

"There are three." Daisy admitted as if it took forever to watch them.

Elaina heard a cry from upstairs and recognized Julie so she hurried up without thinking and opened the door seeing Julie sitting in the room tied down to a chair. She saw Julie glare before struggling so Elaina went over and grabbed her face.

"Julie, it's just me." Elaina said seeing Julie look awake and look pleadingly before going back into the daze looking completely demented. "Who did this?"

"Ellie…" Julie got out in pain before trying to bite her making her jump away. "Tra… he…"

"Was it Travis?" Elaina asked seeing Julie trying to say something. "If it was Travis blink twice."

Elaina saw her blink twice after looking coherent before going in a daze and crying out as if she was in pain. She could feel rage go over her causing her to feel her teeth lengthening as she nails sharpened into deadly points. She turned only to see Ravyn there.

"You shouldn't go after him by yourself." Ravyn murmured after sitting a hand on her shoulder. "Not so close to the first turning, your anger will likely make you do something you'll regret."

Elaina didn't seemed bothered by it but she wouldn't let Travis get away with it. "I didn't let Mark get away with anything so Travis is no different." Elaina murmured feeling him take her hand and rub the inside of her wrist. She couldn't imagine why it was so comforting to her either.

"Then let me or one of the others go with you." Ravyn suggested, she could only shake her head slowly. "Why not?"

"This isn't your fight. I'll take care of Travis." Elaina said watching him go to protest but she only shook her head.

"Your choice is your own." Ravyn murmured as she went down the stairs to find Daisy on the back of a sandy brown wolf and since Seth, Larkin, and Blade were howling with laughter it meant that the wolf was Connor.

"Hey Ravyn, look at Connor." Blade laughed seeing Ravyn look only to shake his head.

Elaina hung out there until her aunt came back so she hurried over with Daisy before helping put groceries away. She explained to Tricia that she'd be going out tonight.

Elaina slipped on black pants, black thick heeled leather boots, and a black tank. She put her hair in a braid before heading passed Daisy's room seeing her locking the closet door. "Lock your door Daisy, don't let the boogeyman in through the window either okay?" she asked quietly seeing Daisy nod before looking seeing Talon and Torrin standing there.

"You're going after Travis aren't you?" Talon asked seeing her frown.

"So what if I am?"

"Put this in your boot." Torrin said and tossed her a good sized dagger. "Happy hunting."

"Gracias."

"De nada." he replied casually so she left the house when her aunt wasn't paying attention seeing the lights on in the pack's house.

Elaina smelled around the house only to see Blade run over looking panicked and she could tell something was wrong. "Your friend is *gone*, it's like she vanished." she watched him say so she hurried over with him only to catch the scent of Julie causing her to change directions. "What are you doing?!"

"Going to get her." Elaina bit out seriously and ran full speed jumping over fences and across roads. She looked in the sky seeing the moon would be full in a couple days. She felt powerful though so why knock it?

She followed the scent all the way through campus and down to the river where she saw Julie in Travis' arm while he fed from her neck. Elaina walked out with a snarl seeing Travis look at her causing Julie to hit the ground. Elaina could hear her faint pulse. She'd be fine if Travis didn't finish her off later.

No, there wasn't going to be a later because she was gonna stake the little piece of crap.

"Hi Elaina, I heard you were alive." Travis said and gestured to Julie as Elaina stalked towards him feeling like the ultimate predator noting he looked worried. "You look lovelier then ever."

"Cut the mushy crap. You ready to die?"

"Are *you*?" Travis asked with a sadistic smile before lunging only to get taken by surprise when she lunged back. "I should've snapped that pretty little neck of yours."

"Too bad, you'll get over it." Elaina growled only to get thrown into a lamppost, that's when ripples shocked her body causing her to groan.

"Isn't it early for a changing?" Travis snickered only to kick her in the gut causing her breath to hitch making her cough before he did it again.

Elaina raked him with her claws causing him to snarl before slamming her head into the concrete slab next to her. She felt something warm running down the side of her head. She knew she was bleeding.

"You healed way too fast for werewolf unless…" Travis started before smiling showing fangs. He sank them into her arm after grabbing it so she kicked him in the face. "You are an interesting *creature*."

Elaina lunged changing midair into something that was far from being normal. She was a werewolf but she was slightly larger then the guys. She sank her teeth into Travis' throat causing him to gurgle before she snapped his neck knowing he'd heal slowly from it. She looked at herself seeing her fur was a white with an almost silver shimmer.

Elaina saw her clothes on the ground so she pulled out the knife before jerking her head allowing it to slam into his chest seeing his eyes bug out before turning to ash. Elaina padded over and nudged Julie seeing her eyes open barely.

"What a beautiful wolf."

Elaina started crying hearing it come out in whines. She put Julie on her back before hurrying back to the pack's house. She went up the stairs carefully before scratching the door with both paws and a whine.

"It's probably another dog." Larkin groaned and opened the door only to stare at her. "RAVYN!"

Elaina stood there with her clothes wrapped around the dagger which where tucked in her boots that she carried in her mouth. She saw Ravyn hurry out with the others only to freeze causing Elaina to start crying because her head hurt like hell and Julie was starting to wake up.

"It's not a full moon yet." Connor murmured like it couldn't be possible so she padded in quickly and went straight to the living room and laid Julie on the couch.

Elaina hurried from the house to hers and gave a bark seeing Daisy look out her window. "Ellie?" Elaina hopped up and down before pretending to act like Julie and then pretending to be asleep. "The comfort blanket and pillow?"

Elaina bounced up and down again seeing the others watching from their own windows. Elaina saw Daisy leave before throwing out the blanket and pillow. Elaina grabbed the pillow in her teeth after crawling under the blanket before darting across the road and into the house after Blade opened the door.

Elaina bounded into the living room seeing Julie looking freaked out at Connor and the others. "The dog that saved me." she saw Julie say only to look at the blanket and pillow. "Elaina!?"

Elaina saw Julie look like it was impossible before cuddling the pillow and wrapping the blanket around her. Elaina started crying hearing the dog like whines as her put her front paws on Julie's legs.

Julie burst into hysterical tears before pulling Elaina into a tight hug and Elaina didn't mind the overly tight grip either. "I'm so sorry!" Julie apologized over and over as she cried and eventually calmed down.

"Now what do we do?" Connor asked so Elaina went to the phone and dialed Torrin's cell number carefully. "How is it possible she can hit the buttons like that?!"

"Hello?" Torrin asked tiredly so she started barking into the receiver only to growl impatiently. "Is this some joke?"

Elaina started barking again hearing a thump.

"Is this *Elaina*?" he asked in shock making her bark again. "Bark twice for yes."

Elaina barked twice.

"Did you find Julie?"

Elaina barked twice.

"Where are you?" he asked causing her to growl because it wasn't like she could tell him. "Are you across the road in that freaking werewolf house?"

Elaina barked twice.

"I'll be over in a couple minutes." the line went dead so she bounced up and down in triumph.

"Okay, she's really smart." Seth pointed out before the doorbell rang. He opened the door only to see a vampire there. "Or not."

"What the hell happened to you Elaina?" Torrin asked causing her to growl making him get the picture. He followed her into the living room showing Julie sitting there drinking hot chocolate. "You look a bit…ill."

Elaina felt her insides start popping causing her to collapse to the floor with a groan. She felt a blanket get thrown on her right before changing back. She felt herself shaking like crazy because she was freezing. Her teeth were chattering and yet she was covered in sweat.

"Elaina?" Julie asked as they heard her breathing heavily.

"Her body might be in shock. She changed two days before she's suppose to and was in the body for probably over two hours." Connor murmured to Ravyn who made sure she was completely covered before picking her up. "She needs to rest, she could shock herself back into being a wolf if we aren't careful."

"What do you want to do?" Torrin asked seeing Julie sit her cup looking determined.

"I'll stay with Elaina, she's my best friend…and she's in a house full of guys who'll probably try to take advantage of her." Julie said seeing them look offended.

"Shall we remind you who just carried her upstairs wearing nothing but a blanket?" Seth asked seeing her stumble a bit but bolt up the stairs.

Elaina had felt strong arms laying her on an incredibly soft bed so she opened her eyes seeing Ravyn looking down at her. "You did okay for someone who had no idea what they were going to do in wolf form." she heard him say and she couldn't help but smile at that.

"I really did huh?" she asked seeing the corners of his mouth turn up and nod. "Thank you."

"For what?"

"Letting me handle it by myself. It must've been difficult to decide that with all this being so new to me. It meant a lot to me though, so thanks." Elaina said as he pulled the blankets up to her chin.

"Get some rest, see you in the morning." he replied and brushed the hair from her face.

"Alright *wolf boy*, paws off the best friend." Julie warned causing Ravyn to feel stunned as how protective she was being towards one of his kind when she was human. "This is when the best friend must fulfill her duties to make sure she's not taken advantage of...not that I'm saying you'd even have a chance though. She's pretty tepid towards the opposite gender."

"Julie stop instigating." Elaina groaned because she was tired so Julie went over and laid next to her. "Really tired."

"You always got my back don't you?" Julie asked causing Elaina to laugh at that. "She's not insane is she *wolf boy?*"

"Julie, his name is Ravyn." Elaina pointed out with a yawn before falling asleep missing Ravyn looking a bit speechless.

"Is she going be okay?" Julie asked causing Ravyn to nod dumbly.

"There are shorts and shirts in the dresser she can...use." Ravyn left quickly because he was feeling a bit *uncontrollable*. He had nearly managed enough self-control to carry her up the stairs. When she had smiled it nearly undid him. He couldn't do that to her though. He'd seen her kissing a human male meaning she had romantic feelings for him and Ravyn already felt guilty about biting her.

"How is she?" Seth asked only to watch as Ravyn left the house.

"Looks like someone needs a run desperately." Blade murmured seeing Connor shake his head slowly not understanding why Ravyn didn't just lay claim on her.

Elaina woke feeling achy as ever as light flitted through the blinds on the window. She saw Julie sleeping next to her and she also realized she was wearing shorts and a shirt. Julie probably put clothes on her causing her to snort. Elaina got up wondering whose room she was in. She tiptoed down the stairs before catching a whiff of something pleasant. It smelled like a mixture evergreen pine trees but a more smokier version, mud, and rain.

She followed the smell to the kitchen only to see Ravyn there with his back to her making breakfast. She saw him smell the air before looking directly at her so she smiled sheepishly. "Morning." Elaina couldn't fathom why she felt awkward with him looking at her. It's like it made her want to flirt and shy away at the same time.

"Have a seat, the others will be down in a couple seconds." Ravyn got out right before the others ran in only to laugh at what she was wearing.

"Julie not eating?" Connor asked nonchalantly as he poured everyone juice.

"She sleeps like the dead and you don't want to be the one waking her up. She's practically demonic if you wake her before she's ready to get up." Elaina replied only to gawk as Julie walked in wide eyed and smiling. "No way! It's before noon! You try to kick my ass every time I wake you up for school!"

"I wasn't restless." Julie murmured before the front door flung open showing Daisy and…Leon. "Leon what are you doing here."

"Daisy told me you all…holy hell! Why is Julie up so early!?" Leon yelled after walking in causing Ravyn to growl softly only to stop when Elaina looked at him. "Brought the work you missed when you went MIA. It's not like you won't get done quickly, you're a freaking whiz kid."

"Leon talk for, you guessed it, smart ass." Julie said caused Daisy to stop and paused before looking at Leon.

"Oh! You call Elli an intelligent donkey too!?" Daisy asked and the look on Leon's face was priceless causing Elaina to howl with laughter before she could help it.

"Okay, I can deal with that. She's a kid after all." Leon said only to look at Elaina for a moment. "Hey Ellie, whose clothes are those?"

"Hmm?"

"Those aren't yours, I've been through your closet well enough to know you don't wear anything like *that*." Leon stated seriously only to see her look elsewhere. He marched over and yanked the front of her shirt out and looked down it. "Jeez, what happened?"

"You perverted little *flamer*!" Elaina yelled causing Leon to jump away with a shrug. "Where you aware that there is a kid and other people in the kitchen!?"

"I give him points, I would've *never* had the guts to do that." Larkin snorted and held out a hand to Leon who rose an eyebrow.

"Please tell me those aren't your clothes she's wearing?" Leon asked seriously after crossing his arms looking a little tick.

"No, they're mine." Ravyn stepped forward seeing Leon look at him and then Elaina.

"Hey Ellie it's about time…"

"Get your head out of the gutter Leon." Elaina warned because she knew exactly what he thought.

"You should have more respect for women…especially your girlfriend." Ravyn replied only to watch Leon, Julie, and Elaina start laughing as Daisy sat on the stool near Elaina with her backpack.

"Leon's not my boyfriend!" Elaina laughed seeing Ravyn looked confused.

"But he kisses you."

"He's the only guy who does and it's cause he's gay!" Julie replied causing the guys to look at Leon.

"Sorry, if I were into girls maybe I'd consider Elaina but I like guys." Leon admitted so Ravyn just went back to making breakfast feeling like an idiot. "Don't feel bad, most people say we look like a good couple."

"It's cause you were the only guy who'd come within ten feet of me while I was in a wheelchair without needing help with homework." Elaina grumbled before going back to her juice.

"Well you aren't anymore. I have to say I am going to miss you flying down the hallway and hitting your brakes before tackling Mark to the ground and beating the hell out of him." Julie got out thoughtfully so Elaina rolled her eyes as Leon looked at the guys as if trying to decide.

"Leon, I seriously doubt any of them are gay." Elaina answered his thoughts seeing him look a little disappointed.

"Well I'm off, see you Monday." Leon said with a wave so her and Julie waved back as Daisy started jumping.

"I brought the movies to watch today."

"Awesome." Blade replied excitedly watching as Daisy took the three movies out of her little backpack and held them up.

"Ellie, you're a pretty doggie." Daisy giggled causing Elaina to feel her face heat slightly.

"That's what we need to talk about." Connor stated suddenly and Elaina felt sick to her stomach because it felt like bad news.

"Jeez, don't say it like that, she looks queasy now." Julie grunted so Connor looked apologetic causing them both to relax slightly.

"So, your cells are only slightly different then Ravyn's. You're cells multiple at a very quick rate which would explain why you changed two days before the actual turning night. Your body is going through the preparations of changing then ours did. Your senses are more powerful then ours, you could probably run faster and jump higher as well, and as we saw… your wolf form is larger then all of ours except Ravyn's." Connor explained as Elaina rubbed her head.

"So you're telling me that I'm sort of *mutated*?" Elaina asked as her mouth went dry so Connor nodded.

"It can't be…"

"Julie don't jinx me." Elaina groaned because this was making her feel even worse.

"It's not a bad thing, it just means you'd be physiologically advanced. You could probably change anytime you wanted." Connor explained further so Julie elbowed her.

"See, not bad at all."

"The others are going to be excited." Seth saw Elaina go from looking at Julie to looking at him.

"Others?" she got out seeing them nod.

"The rest of the pack, they live about two hours away. We'll be leaving tomorrow at four to make it there before sundown. It'll give you time to get acquainted with everyone before we change." Larkin said causing her to feel overwhelmed.

"More doggies!? Can I go to?!" Daisy asked causing Elaina to see them look worried about that.

"No Daisy, you can't go. You have school the next day."

"So do you!"

"Yeah, but I'm a grownup." Elaina replied seeing Daisy looking disappointed.

"We'll also be there for three days." Connor answered causing Julie to look at Elaina who was looking disappointed.

"Wow, your school attendance has been shot to hell." Julie said what she was thinking as they ate seeing her stab her egg.

"She okay?"

"She doesn't like to miss class, she's a nerd." Julie snorted as Elaina grumbled something about Julie not complaining about that. "Looks like you have more days to mark on your calendar. Don't worry, you know that me or any of the others will grab the notes for you."

"Aunt Tricia is not going to buy any reason for me leaving for three days. She's going to know something is wrong. She won't believe the hospital excuse either, she knows I *hate* them." Elaina pointed out as Julie tapped her chin.

"Too bad we can't hypnotize her or something." Julie replied making Elaina get an idea so she grabbed Julie's phone and texted Torrin. "What are you doing?"

"Here, just tell me if they say they're up for it or not." She saw her nails sharpen so she took a deep breath and let it out slowly to calm herself seeing her nails shorten.

"You'll still need to pack to leave tomorrow…unless you want guys going through your dresser." Julie snickered only to get *the look* from Elaina as the guys got a perplexed expression on their faces. "Is she going to be able to go to school tomorrow?"

"She shouldn't but she could if she needed to." Connor shrugged like it didn't matter what.

"Just go half a day then. You're eighteen so you can sign yourself out of school…never mind, you're mentally incapable of lying." Julie saw Elaina look at her like she was a horrible person for disclosing that information. "What!? It's true."

"I'll deal with it, you just…go do something." Elaina grumbled and she couldn't help but be flustered. "I need to go do my homework."

"Look, I say you just tell your aunt, what's the worse that could happen?" Julie asked only to get looked at like she was insane. "It'd be better if her aunt knew, we'd have her only family on her side to help make excuses for her."

"What car just pulled in front of the house?" Elaina asked seriously before hurrying to the living room and looked seeing a sleek black van pull up in front of Tricia's house. "Daisy come on sweetie, we need to get over there."

"Why!?" Daisy whined like she didn't want to go.

"Daisy come on!" Elaina got out and picked up Daisy before running over completely barefoot without a care. Elaina saw her aunt come out only to burst into tears so she hurried to her only to catch her aunt who started crumpling to the ground.

"We're terribly sorry for your loss." the soldiers said before saluting and going back to the car.

Elaina hugged her aunt as Daisy tried to figure out what had happened. "It'll be okay Aunt Tricia. It'll be okay." Elaina said as her own tears mixed with the stone steps. Elaina saw her aunt pass out completely as Julie hurried over with the others.

"What's wrong?" Julie asked as Elaina opened the letter which delivered the news. Her uncle was missing, it either meant he was dead or being tortured to death. The military was going to wait for the body to turn up.

"Not in front of Daisy." Elaina said before picking her aunt up wondering why she felt like a feather and carried her inside to lay her on the couch. She paced back and forth, her movements were fluid…nothing like a werewolf at all but more like a vampire.

"Elaina you need to decide what you're going to do." Julie stated causing Elaina to feel angry as she balled her hands into tight fists causing the nails to bite into her hands.

"Ellie what's wrong?" Daisy asked as Tricia groaned so Elaina looked at her.

"You're going to tell her aren't you?" Connor asked and Elaina felt like pulling her hair out.

"I don't know, okay!?" Elaina snapped before running up the stairs and locking herself in the room. She closed the heavy curtains before throwing the blanket over her head. She didn't know what to day.

"Elaina?" Julie was knocking on the door. "Elaina open the door. Please?"

"Julie please go away?" Elaina was having a really tough time right now. She heard them leave and she found herself falling asleep. She woke to a soft knock on the door so she shuffled over and opened it seeing Tricia there.

"Your friends, the boys across the road, asked me to tell you to come over really quick after you woke up." Tricia looked worse then Elaina felt.

"Aunt Tricia can we talk?" Elaina asked so Tricia walked in allowing Elaina to close the door. "I need to tell you something very important and you have to believe me."

"What's wrong Elaina?"

"Well, I wouldn't say it's something *wrong* but I don't want to hide it from you so I'm hoping you'll accept it." Elaina started only to watch Tricia's eyes widen.

"Elaina are you pregnant?!"

"No!" Elaina yelled seriously seeing her aunt relax. "I'm a werewolf."

"Come again?" Tricia asked so Elaina nodded slowly, she couldn't help but laughing. "No really Ellie, what's the news."

"Aunt Tricia look at me. You knew deep down something was off when I came back. My legs look like I've never sat in a wheelchair a day in my life. There's no way someone can walk in a week after being paralyzed for fourteen years. I'm a *werewolf*, even Julie and Daisy know." Elaina saw her aunt look at the floor and rub her temples.

"Elaina we're going to get you some help okay?" Tricia stood up only to see Elaina hold up her hand and she saw the nails lengthen into claws.

"I'm not imagining it and neither are you. It happened because of Travis." Elaina explained seeing Tricia look confused. "Travis was a vampire and tried to kill me. He dumped me in the woods to die and I got bit by a werewolf."

"Now vampires exist!? Elaina you're losing your mind!" Tricia opened the door showing Torrin and Talon standing there. "Please don't tell me that you two…"

"We are though, Elaina isn't lying to you. She's telling you because she doesn't want to lie to you." Talon saw Tricia shake her head so he captured her eyes. "Tricia, you will forget everything you heard from Elaina and myself. Elaina is going away for three days, it's a camping trip with some very important people."

"Okay." Tricia said before heading to the kitchen.

"I can't believe you hypnotized my aunt." Elaina grumbled seeing them look at her. She'd changed out of Ravyn's clothes for her favorite *Happy Bunny* pajamas and they both looked close to laughing hysterically.

"We'll take your homework to school for you. Is it finished?" Talon saw her pull out the papers and hand them over before packing a bag with clothes for three days and a couple pairs of nightclothes just in case. "Have fun on the run."

"Whatever." she grumbled and going to the laundry room since she'd taken them down to wash and dry. She folded them before slipping on her sandals. She left her bag in her living room before going across the room and knocking on the door.

"What are you wearing!?" Larkin howled as he moved out of the way to let her in. "You're just in time too, we're starting the first *Underworld* movie."

"My aunt said you wanted me to come over when I woke up." Elaina saw them nod before pointing to the television as they started the movie. "Prepare to see a lot of werewolves die."

"EH!?" they all yelled but she only sat on a reclining chair.

"Just watch the movie, I'm not explaining it."

Elaina watched them look ill every time a werewolf was killed. She saw Ravyn pause the movie as Seth went to go make popcorn. "So how did it go when you told your aunt?" she heard him ask so she looked at her hands.

"She thought I was insane at first and then she saw my arm start changing. She *almost* accepted it until she opened the bedroom seeing Torrin and Talon there. She realized they were vampires before flipping the hell out so they erased her memory and told her I was going on a camping trip for three days." she saw them raise their eyebrows. "What?"

"You really are incapable of lying aren't you?" Connor asked seeing her cross her arms at that.

"I figured it was something that shouldn't be lied about if you must know." she replied defensively and knew she was right because she was part of the pack now, whether some of them liked it or not. "So what should I expect tomorrow?"

"A huge party, you're the first person Ravyn's ever bit." Blade replied excitedly so when she looked at Ravyn he seemed a bit uncomfortable.

"I remember you saying I was different because he bit me, why is that?"

"He's the pack leader." they all said in unison except Ravyn who looked as if they shouldn't have opened their mouths.

"And that means?"

"You'll be included in the dance of the females." Blade said it like it would be an honor and yet she didn't miss Larkin elbow him.

"What's that?"

"Ignore them, you don't have to participate." Ravyn replied like it would be better if she didn't so she looked back as she smelled the evergreen pine circling around her. He found his eyes going towards her seeing Blade raise an eyebrow towards him so he focused his eyes back to the movie in time to see a werewolf get killed. He didn't like this movie but she didn't seemed to mind it, why would she? She had been human to begin with. He doubted she'd even get along with any of the others.

They watched the first movie and the second making her notice that the guys didn't seem to enjoy them that much. She put in the third one. "What's this one?" Larkin asked as she sat back in the chair.

"*Underworld: Rise of the Lycans*. It's a prequel to the first one, it's what started everything." Elaina saw the movie start seeing the others looking interested.

"Go! Go! Go!" Larkin cheered near the end of the movie as the Lycans took over the castle and started to maul the vampires. "This one isn't so bad."

"Sucks for that Sonya chick though." Seth pointed out as they kept watching until it was over. "Okay, I like that Selene character from the first one. She killed the jerk who started that whole damn thing."

"Damn straight." Blade said before going to ask Elaina question seeing she was probably already asleep. "She sleeps like the dead too."

"I heard that." Elaina grumbled before sitting up with yawn. "What time is it?"

"Three in the morning." Connor took the movie out and put it back in the case.

"I need to head back over." Elaina grumbled as she stood up and headed to the door with a yawn only to smack into a wall.

"You shouldn't walk with your eyes closed." Larkin was holding in a laugh, they all were. "Maybe you should just sleep here, at least this time you're already wearing your own clothes."

"That reminds me." Elaina said and held the plastic bag she'd brought with her to Ravyn. "Your clothes. See you tomorrow."

"See you later." they said hearing her leave.

"Hey, what's that?" Larkin asked before picking up a key and tossing it to Ravyn. "Must be hers."

Elaina had gotten to the door only to search her pockets. She could've sworn she'd put her key in her pocket. She breathed in the air tasting the pine on her tongue before turning around seeing Ravyn three feet from her. "What…"

"Key." he asked and held it out. He saw her take the key so he let his thumb brush across her wrist feeling her shiver. From what though? He found himself hesitating completely.

"G'night." Elaina murmured since she didn't know what else to do. She saw him nod before heading across the road back to the house. She noted that the others had been staring out the window watching in anticipation.

Elaina went in and locked the door before going to her room where she laid down staring at her ceiling. She rubbed her wrist, it felt like his thumb was still there. Elaina fell asleep remembering those beautiful caramel eyes.

When it was time to leave the next day Elaina ate her late lunch quickly before grabbing her bag as the horn honked outside. She went out seeing the guys waiting in a big white van. She went over and got in seeing them laugh at what she was wearing again.

"At least it's not *Happy Bunny*." Larkin snorted since she wore short jean shorts and a form fitted shirt reading: *Caution: May Geek Out Without Warning*. "We got a good two hour drive."

Elaina noticed that Ravyn was sitting next to her so she glanced over seeing him glancing at the same time. She felt heat start up her neck so she pulled her book out of her bag and started reading. Without realizing it she soon fell asleep.

"Hey Elaina, time to wake up." Was that Larkin snickering?

Someone shook her shoulder but she liked where she was. She was against something solid yet comfortable and it smelled wonderful. She opened her eyes slowly realizing she was leaning against someone. She followed the deliciously toned tanned arm up a strong corded neck seeing Ravyn looking like he was being tortured.

"My head." she murmured and rubbed the little knot seeing them point to the window.

"You feel against the window and smacked your head off it when we hit a bump." Blade said so she sat up only to look out her window seeing a bunch of people heading to a lake.

"Wow." she murmured as she stared so they all got out only to realize all the guys were walking around without shirts out. The girls wore skimpy outfits. She had more respect in herself besides, she thought clothes like that were degrading.

"Who's the pup?" a guy asked with a laugh only to look taken aback when she looked at him. "I apologize, it seems you are *far* from being a child."

"I really hope that's not your pickup line." she said before going back near the others causing the guy to look rebuffed as Blade, Seth, and Larkin rolled on the ground laughing. "Sorry if I don't wear clothes like everyone else."

"You have to understand Elaina, we're either born werewolves or we've been werewolves long enough to get use to the way of life. We are comfortable in our sensuality." Connor said only to cause her to feel a bit uncomfortable about that. "You'll get used to it in time."

"I highly doubt it." Elaina whispered because she was as far from sensuality as a nun. She'd been in a wheelchair all her life and her first kiss had been with Travis. She found herself rubbing the side of her neck.

"We'll let you in on something. You're a *single* werewolf and there are a lot of single *males*. They'll be coming around you since you aren't claimed. If you get overwhelmed just excuse yourself, they'll get the picture." Larkin said seeing the others nod so she followed behind them slowly seeing people look at her oddly.

"Why are they looking at me like that?" she asked quietly but none of them said anything.

"Welcome Ravyn and brothers. Who is that?" an older man asked before pointing to her causing her to feel a bit outnumbered for some reason.

"She's new, I bit her." Ravyn said and she heard murmurs noticing the women looked ticked off.

"Her name?"

"Elaina Scotts." Ravyn could see interest peak in every male's eye as they looked at her. He ushered her forward to stand in front of him seeing her looking hesitant.

"Welcome Elaina Scotts!" the man boomed causing the others to cheer but just caused they looked happy didn't mean they really were.

Elaina wanted to get away from everyone. The guys looked too friendly and the women looked like they'd sooner rip her head off before welcoming her near them. She could feel the small bead of panic starting to grow bigger.

"So this is your candidate Ravyn?" Elaina looked when a girl asked seeing the girl was probably a little older then her. Elaina saw her slash at her so Elaina blocked watching her eyes narrow before smiling. "An opponent then."

"Opponent?" Elaina asked only to see Ravyn throw the girl's arm away from her.

"It's her choice Crystal." Ravyn bit out loud enough for them to hear. "She's new to our ways."

"Like that's an excuse!" Crystal snapped and shoved him out of the way. "When the moon rises, you had better watch your tail."

"What the hells up her ass?" Elaina asked as Crystal walked away only to freeze.

"What did you say!?"

"Huh?" Elaina felt puzzled wondering if she'd said her thoughts out loud. She saw Crystal glare before marching off with a group of others with her. "Is she on permanent PMS or something?"

"Avoid going around her and watch your back. She'll start a fight with you if you don't." Connor voiced seriously so the pack dispersed to talk to old friends and when they did other guys started flooding around her.

Elaina could barely comprehend the questions they were all asking at one time so she excused herself and hurried off. She went right back to the van and laid flat on the back seat. She heard the door open before it closed.

"Why the attitude Ravyn?" she heard Connor grumble so she stayed still.

"Crystal is going to initiate the attack. Get the others to make sure she doesn't start with Elaina. She doesn't need dragged into our traditions when she has her own." Elaina kept herself calm as she laid there listening to them talking.

"Did you think she might be able to accept our traditions? If the fight between the males start and you win, you'll become the new pack leader. There will be a lot of females participating to win the right to call themselves your mate. If Crystal initiates an attack on Elaina we can't get involved. Elaina will either have to fight back or surrender. If you're so worried then just explain what will be happening tonight." Connor growled seriously seeing Ravyn looking defeated. "Oh hell, you like her!"

"Will you shut it, someone will hear you. Why do you think I was having second thoughts about bringing her here?" Elaina felt stunned, did he really like her?

"Then either tell her how you feel or take another for a mate." Connor bit out before leaving the car with Ravyn sitting there feeling confused.

"It's not that easy." Ravyn bit out and raked the seat before leaving and slamming the door shut.

Elaina laid there until the sun started setting wondering about what Connor and Ravyn had been talking about. Just the thought of being able to see those beautiful caramel eyes everyday caused her to shiver. She liked him to but did she want to be his girlfriend?

She left the car and headed back to the group as the moon started rising. It felt hypnotic to her as she looked at it. She saw a hand wave in front of her eyes so she looked seeing Ravyn standing there.

"You shouldn't stare at it for too long. This is your first turning, it'll be a little painful." Ravyn informed as she felt her stomach fluttering as if a million butterflies were trying to escape.

"I've already…"

"You and I have two forms. That of a wolf and then you have the form we take with the full moon. They aren't the same. You might've changed into a wolf but you've yet to assume your *werewolf* form. That will happen in front of all of us. Ours will be faster then yours."

Ravyn explained before leading her to the platform to sit. "Whatever you do, don't fight the process. It'll become even slower and will hurt a lot more. Just go with it."

"Okay, I can do that…I think." she said before he went down to the others before they started changing before her very eyes. It looked like it had only taken seconds. She found her own bones start popping as they looked at her, her head spun dangerously. She hunched over feeling like it only took a snap of her fingers. She didn't just go with the change, she embrace it.

Cheerful howls erupted around her and yet she found herself looking at the others seeing Blade, Larkin, and Seth jumping up and down like idiots. She *walked* down right before the older man rose his hands.

"The fight for leader begins when all eligible males step onto the circle. Those who get thrown out must back away, once out you can not enter again." the man said and Elaina swore Ravyn brushed her wrist on the way forward. "Everyone accounted for?"

She watched them howl.

"Begin!" he yelled and she watched in awe as one ran straight for Ravyn only to get thrown like he weighed nothing.

One by one wolves were eliminated by being thrown from the circle, even Connor had been thrown out like a sack of potatoes. It was just Ravyn and a gray wolf.

She saw them cheering and with one quick move Ravyn had thrown the wolf out of the circle. She felt happy for him and no sooner had that thought left her mind something plowed right into her. She felt as if she'd been hit by a bulldozer.

Elaina looked seeing a timber snarling at her and figured it was Crystal. Elaina saw Ravyn go to intervene only to be held back by others. She saw Crystal growl before clamping her jaws around Elaina's neck. She yelled in pain hearing it sounding all the same. That caused Crystal to bite harder.

Elaina found her vision dimming and wondered if she wanted to fight. Truth was that she did. Without another thought she forced herself to stand and twisted her body hard slamming Crystal into a tree enough to make it splinter. She grabbed Crystal's jaws and forced them off her neck before Crystal bit into her arm.

Elaina snarled before ripping Crystal off her and slamming her into the ground. She looked at her bleeding arm only to watch it heal instantly. Her neck had healed as well. She watched Elaina breathing hard on the ground before getting into a crouch and lunging. Elaina moved seeing her run right into a tree. That only caused Crystal to get angrier.

Elaina was raked multiple times only to see them heal faster then they could bleed. Elaina clamped her jaws around Crystal's throat and bit down. She listened to Crystal yipping trying to pull away. She felt Crystal starting to go limp so she dropped her to the ground seeing her gasp for air only to continue laying there.

She watched the others howl causing her to think she'd done something wrong causing her to panic as the man straightened up looking at her proudly. "Our new queen!" he called causing her to be absolutely stunned as the others laid on their backs. She didn't understand what that was about.

Elaina saw Ravyn step forward and growl and she could see the others look at him. She moved away because she felt overwhelmed only to see him stalk towards her. She almost yelped when he grabbed her arm and dragged her away from the others. She saw him grab one of the many blankets littering the ground and hold it around his waist before changing back.

"Do you have any idea what you've just done!?" he roared at her so she grabbed one of the blankets and wrapped it around her before changing back.

"Why the hell are you yelling at me for!? That moron was the one who practically tried to kill me!" she yelled seriously hearing it come out a bit hoarse seeing his face soften. She saw him reach for her but she moved away feeling really angry with Ravyn who was obviously a moron.

"These aren't your people."

"Should've thought about that before you bit me." Elaina growled and she could tell he was guilty about it. "Whatever, I'm going home."

"You're too far."

"Not a normal wolf remember?" she pointed out and flashed into a normal wolf before heading home. She wasn't that far and would be home before the sun rose. She ran making sure to stay in the woods.

As the sun rose high in the sky she made it home only to see the van already back at the house. She ignored it as Ravyn came out of the house but she only went to hers and rang the doorbell with her nose.

"ELLIE!" Daisy cheered so Elaina went inside the house as Ravyn hurried over.

Elaina was tired, sore, and her paws were bleeding a little bit. When Ravyn started into the house she started snarling and snapping her jaws at him so angrily he stumbled away. Unfortunately it made Tricia and Julie to hurry out of the kitchen.

"Uh-oh."

"Why is there a wolf in the house!?" Tricia yelled as Elaina kicked the door shut in Ravyn's face before she started changing back. "Elaina!?"

"Aunt Tricia…" she got out before hitting the floor unable to move an inch. She could hear Daisy crying before something fuzzy covered her so she looked over seeing Julie looking at her with worry.

"Impossible." Tricia said seeing Daisy crying.

"Mommy, Ellie's a doggie. Is she going to be okay?" Daisy asked and Tricia nodded solemnly.

"Yeah, let's get her to her room." Tricia said before they sat her in the lift since she was heavy. They got her to her room and laid her down so she could rest.

"Aunt Tricia?"

"Shh, it's okay sweetie. Get some rest, you look terrible." Tricia could see her hands were cut up but healing slowly but she was covered in dirt. "Just rest."

"Please…don't tell anyone?" Elaina cried because she didn't want to have to leave her home. She didn't want to leave the only home she had.

"Not a soul."

Elaina could read the honesty in her eyes before she was hugged tightly so Elaina fell into a deep sleep. She had dreams of running as far as possible only to wake up in a sweat. For the next two days she stayed in her room because she would get irritated so suddenly it made her change.

Chapter 4

Elaina had started going back to school putting the pack life behind her. Ravyn had been right, those weren't her people. That meant they didn't want her there and even as her mind told her that she wanted to be around them and run through the woods every chance she got she kept herself busy so she'd forget about it.

She noticed guys acted differently around her too. They seem to flock around her which seemed to make Julie think it hilarious. The down side was that Seth, Larkin, and Blade had started in the high school and they looked at the guys like they were disgusting. They also had no problem glaring at the guys and scaring them off.

"Elaina, Connor needs to talk to you after school today." Blade said only to see her frown at him.

"No thanks, I have plans already."

"Elaina…" Larkin started seeing her turn looking serious.

"It's like Ravyn said, you all aren't my people. I'm pretty sure that's a more subtle way of saying '*bug off*' so I have nothing to say to anyone. Not a single word so please, just leave me to my somewhat *human* life." Elaina said and hurried off to class without another thought towards the matter. She heard the bell ring wondering what the Halloween dance was going to be like. She was going stag because so many guys had asked her. She saw the three waiting for her and talking to Julie.

"Hey, ready to go costume shopping?" Julie asked exactly so Elaina gave a nod leading Julie to the car her aunt had loaned her to go shopping. "We have to wait for the others."

"Who?"

Elaina saw Julie gesture towards Larkin, Seth, and Blade who smiled sheepishly so she grunted before getting behind the wheel. She drove to the mall and stuck her debit card in her front pocket.

They went into the Halloween store seeing costumes galore so Elaina hurried off with Julie to the girl's costumes. "You should definitely go as Little Red Riding Hood." Julie laughed causing Elaina to look at her.

"I can only imagine the irony. Next thing I know it, you'll want me to dress as a sheep." Elaina said only to turn and recognize one of the guys from the so-called *camping trip*. He was a werewolf too.

"A wolf in sheep's clothing, very good idea." he grinned but she didn't like him one bit. He then looked at Julie and realized she wasn't a werewolf.

"Keep your snout away from my best friend." Elaina warned seriously when his eyes narrowed causing Julie to look at him.

"Are all the guys, like, amazingly gorgeous or what?" Julie murmured and it caused the guy to chuckle before nodding.

"Julie let's go." Elaina said and dragged Julie to the costumes away from the guy. Elaina saw a costume that seemed to be her taste so she grabbed it before going into the changing rooms. She slipped the costume on.

"Elaina come out, I want to see you in it." Julie said so Elaina came out causing her jaw to drop. "And you said I wore clothes that fit me too well?"

"Holy mother of god." Elaina heard Ravyn say making her turn in the costume seeing him standing there with Connor.

"Actually, it's holy *Mother Nature*." Julie corrected after looking at the tag. "I like, very natural and it fits you perfectly."

"I think I'm getting this one." Elaina voiced before going and changing into her regular clothes. She didn't wear jeans anymore to hide her thin frail legs. She wore a blue jean miniskirt and a navy blue halter shirt and blue flip-flops. She walked out and saw something spark in Ravyn's eyes but she only headed straight for Julie. "Let's find you a costume and head out."

"Okay." Julie was trying to figure out why Ravyn was staring at Elaina in shock and why Elaina was easily ignoring him. "Umm, I think he needs to talk to you."

"Oh believe me, I think he's said everything he's needed to." Elaina replied seriously seeing Connor sigh only cause she was being difficult. "It's really that easy."

"What?" Ravyn asked only to see her look knowingly before ushering Julie away from them.

"You don't think she'd heard our conversation do you?" Connor seeing Ravyn looking unsure as Julie picked out a costume before hurrying into the changing rooms.

"Elaina!" Julie called so Elaina came back over ignoring them completely as Julie came out. "What do you think?"

"You look great." Elaina said with a bright smile so Julie went back in and changed. "Ready?"

"Elaina?" Ravyn asked and saw Julie look at him and then her.

"Right, let's go." Elaina pretended to not even see him so when he grabbed her wrist and yanked her into one of the changing rooms she growled at him. "Get your damn hands off me."

"I think you've ignored us long enough." Ravyn bit out only to watch her narrow her eyes.

"Coming from the one who said you all weren't my people but it was fine and freaking dandy when you needed to experiment on me." she said icily seeing him look at the floor. "Just stay away from me."

"Whether you want me away from you or not I'm not allowed to leave your side."

"I don't care. Stay out of my life." Elaina said and left hearing him sigh but she didn't care. She'd been angry ever since that night so she paid for her costume and waited in the car. She could feel tears coursing down her cheeks as she sat there. When the door opened she looked seeing Julie sitting there only to pull her into a huge hug.

"What happened that night Elaina?" Julie asked and listened to her explain everything on the way back to the house. "That big stupid jerk, and here I was feeling sorry for him! Let's have a girls night, we'll watch sappy movies and eat ice cream."

"I'm fine, you go home okay?" Elaina asked seeing Julie nod and drive off before going inside and hanging up her costume. She saw that her aunt and Daisy had gone grocery shopping taking Torrin and Talon with them. She heard a knock on the door so she opened it seeing Seth. "What?"

"Connor needs to talk to you, he says it's extremely important." Seth murmured seeing she followed over angrily seeing Blade and Larkin looking like something had happened.

"Okay, what's the four-one-one?" she asked after seeing Connor and Ravyn in the small little lab.

"I'm afraid I need to do another test." Connor asked seriously causing her to shake her head. "Look, you had already ingested vampire blood when Ravyn had bit you. When he bit you it altered you both. Ravyn has completely stopped aging and we believe you might've as well."

"So, what's so bad with me not aging?" she asked only to realize what had been said about the leader of the wolf pack and his queen. "I'm going to be stuck with him forever!?"

"How did you even get that?"

"You should check to make sure whoever you're talking about isn't within earshot." it was all she said causing Connor and Ravyn to look like she had to be joking while the other three looked confused.

"You were near the car?" Ravyn asked only to watch her shake her head.

"I was in the backseat *of* the car." she corrected only to see him start towards her so she moved you away. "I could stand you then, I hate you now."

"I was trying to keep you out of it."

"First of all it's *my* choice on what I do or not so don't even try to pull that crap, second is that you should've just did what Connor suggested because it really is that easy to tell someone that you like them, and three is that you aren't my parent so don't even try bossing me around." Elaina saw Connor actually smiling behind him trying not to laugh.

"If you knew before Crystal attacked then why did you hesitate to fight her?" Connor asked seeing her roll her eyes.

"Why does anyone hesitate? I was trying to figure out if it was even worth fighting over, obviously I was hugely mistaken. Now if me not aging is the only thing you had to tell me I'm going back to my aunts." Elaina spun on her heel and walked right towards her house seeing a car pull out before seeing a man getting out. "Uncle David?"

Elaina saw him turn and look at her causing her to beam. "Uncle David!" she cheered before running over and hugged him tightly. "We heard you were missing!?"

"Actually we were climbing a hill and when a bomb went off the ground gave way and I fell into a hole." he said only to stare at her legs. "Elaina you're walking!"

"Uh-huh." she said before Tricia pulled in so she stepped back before watching her aunt launch herself into her uncle crying with relief.

"Daddy!" Daisy giggled before running and latching to his leg. "You're home!"

Elaina made a huge dinner that night so that her aunt could have some alone time with her uncle. She ate with them and laughed and talked until Daisy was falling asleep in her chair.

"I'll get her." Elaina said when Tricia went to stand seeing her smile warmly. Elaina carried Daisy to her room and laid her down before locking the closet. She went to her own room after showering making sure to lock the door. She ran the towel through her hair only to hear something scratching her window.

Elaina went over and opened them only to see Ravyn sitting in the tree. She frowned before closing the drapes and laying down only to remember her window was unlocked. By the time she got on her feet he was already in her room so she stayed on her guard.

"Can we talk?"

"No, I believe you've said more then you should've."

A light breeze blew into the window sending his scent around her room and it made her giddy but she kept the anger wrapped around her. The breeze continued into the room as he walked towards her.

She soon found herself trapped in a corner seeing him brace a hand on either side of her. She glowered at him but he looked calm and solemn as he stood there in front of her.

"I'm sorry if what I said hurt you Elaina, you gave no knowledge of knowing what you were doing so I panicked. I shouldn't have said something like that to you, if I had known you knew I would've done something entirely different." he saw her raise an eyebrow at him so he leaned down and kissed her chastely. "I'm going to mate with Crystal, I'm sorry."

Elaina saw him leave after climbing out and closing her window. She touched her fingers to her lips because the kiss might've been brief but it felt like they were still there. She was so tied up in knots she was restless the whole night.

Elaina saw the sun rising so she got dressed in jeans and a plain t-shirt without even realizing what she was doing. She threw her hair into a ponytail and walked outside only to see Ravyn sitting on the porch swing across the road. That's when a car pulled into his driveway and none other then Crystal got out.

Elaina saw her hurry up and over to Ravyn so she only headed to school. That wasn't her life. If that was true then why did it hurt so much? She sat through her classes feeling sluggish. She got a huge lunch feeling hungry beyond reason.

"Okay time to practice. We have to pick songs to sing for the cabaret." Leon said so she pulled out her CD not even seeing Blade, Larkin, and Seth sneak into the top row seats with Crystal, Ravyn, and Connor. "What number?"

"No way, you're singing yours first."

"All who want Elaina to sing raise your hand?" Leon asked and everyone rose their hands.

"You. All. Suck." she punctuated and glanced seeing the *whole* pack there with Crystal. "Need you for back up Rosa and Julie."

"Got it." They stood behind her as the song started so she kept her eyes down.

Elaina pulled out her phone as she sang and texted a message to Blade and sent it hearing his phone buzzed. She heard him scurry across the seats as she smiled as she got halfway into the song.

"Blade what are you doing? She's going to find out we're here." Larkin got out before Blade held out the phone to Ravyn who got confused before taking the phone and looking at the message. It read:

Tell the idiot (aka Ravyn) to listen very closely to the damn song.

Ravyn stared at the phone feeling hope start swelling inside his chest before he could even have time to squish it. He texted back seeing her look at her phone before busting out laughing right into the microphone. He saw Crystal look completely defeated.

"Now that I got a point across play number ten, that's the song I'm singing for cabaret." Elaina said hearing the song start before she started singing hearing her favorite three from the pack start cheering from the seats causing the others to look. She smelled the scent of evergreen pine reach her nose so she looked seeing Ravyn had actually jumped the fifteen feet to the floor and walked towards her.

"What a hottie." she heard Rosa murmur in shock as Elaina finished the song before sitting on the edge of the stage. "Is him and Elaina…"

"Who knows?" Julie asked because she'd thought they'd been mad at each other.

"So do you have something to say?" Elaina asked quietly after he stopped in front of her seeing him raise an eyebrow questioningly. "Are you playing stupid or can you seriously not think of anything?"

"I'm thinking of one thing." he answered only to see her look genuinely annoyed by him.

"And that would be…" she trailed off only to see him shrug before grinning devilishly causing her breath to catch. Elaina felt his hands cup her neck before kissing her right there in front of her friends. She heard Julie and Rosa whoop into the microphone causing her to laugh and look at them. She looked back at Ravyn wondering why she liked him so much. She felt her heart start pounding when he smiled and it made him look so much younger. That's when she realized she didn't know how old he was but it's not like it mattered. They had both stopped aging.

"Let's go." he murmured as he traced little patterns onto the palms of her hands.

"I'll grab my stuff." she murmured back before sliding off the stage only to feel his thumbs brushing across her wrists. She saw Leon trying not to laugh as she felt her face heating so badly it was almost unbearable.

Elaina looked at Julie who snickered so she grabbed her stuff and headed out of the school with Ravyn walking behind her. She saw him change directions and go to a motorcycle. She saw him get on the bike and put the helmet on so she put the other on before slinging on her backpack and getting on behind him. She held onto his waist before they left the school.

The wind whipped passed them so she held on tighter swearing she heard him laugh at that. As they pulled into the driveway she made sure that her aunt wasn't outside. Her aunt wasn't even home.

"Follow me." Elaina accepted his hand and followed him inside. She locked the door just as Ravyn started leading her up the stairs. Her heart was beating so hard in her chest as she went up the stairs one by one.

Elaina saw him lead her into his room, she watched him turn and close the door before backing her right into it. She felt her pulse leap in her wrists. She was pulled into the deepest kiss she'd ever experienced. She felt his tongue brushing against hers, a torturous dance neither of them would likely get enough of. She was pressed into the door and didn't even try to hold back the moan that escaped.

"Elaina." he breathed before pulling away seeing her eyes holding a luminescent glow and her teeth had slightly sharpened into the canines. He was sure he looked the same exact way. He sat his head on her shoulder and breath in her scent. She smelled like cinnamon and vanilla. It was subtle yet sharp, just like her. "You smell beautiful."

"You capable of compliments, who'd of thought." she teased letting her fingers brush the skin between the bottom of his shirt and the top of his jeans. She saw him look at her so she smiled impishly hearing him give a throaty chuckle. She liked his neck for some reason. Without thinking and acting on impulse she began teasing his neck. She brushed her lips up the right side before dragging her teeth down them lightly.

Elaina could feel him shudder so she decided to have a little mercy on him. She went back to those delectable lips of his. "Up." she murmured before jumping up and wrapping her legs around his waist feeling him catch her too. A deep growl reverberated in his throat as she continued to kiss him.

"Mmm. Bed." Elaina had no way she was taking charge of what they were doing but apparently he didn't mind. She watched him back up only to laugh when he nearly fell over. "Down."

Elaina felt like she was in a sauna because it was so hot in the house. He'd sat down on the edge of the bed. "Arms up." she heard him say so she rose her arms feeling him strip off her t-shirt leaving the lacy pink and pale green bra. She'd barely gotten his shirt off when her back was pressed against the bed.

"Do you agree to be mine?" Ravyn asked against her lips seeing her nod. "You have to say it like this. I, Ravyn Steel, agree to forever belong to Elaina Scotts. "

"I, Elaina Scotts," she breathed out seeing something so amazing enter his eyes. "I agree to forever belong to Ravyn Steel."

"Now I…" he started only to get pulled back into a kiss that seemed to shake the very world around them. "Have to mark you."

"What's that?" she asked before letting her teeth nip his lower lip. Elaina felt him cup the back of her head before tilting it to the side. She felt something sharp make an 'x' onto her neck seeing him look at her. "Now I mark you."

"It's not necessary."

"Yes the hell it is! You had to do that to me!" she said before rolling seeing him go to protest but she silenced him with a kiss. "Deal with it."

"Fine, you win." he grumbled and tilted his head exposing his neck.

Elaina nipped at his neck feeling him jerk so she circled her tongue around it to soothe the small sting. She raked an 'x' in the same place as he had on her only to lick the small cut feeling his hands grip her hips.

"Elaina." She looked at him because his voice had been so husky she hadn't been able to believe it. She remembered those caramel colored eyes that were so beautiful to her. She was pulled back into another deep kiss as his fingers brushed up and down her spine. She felt one arm encircle her waist as the other reached up and grabbed the back of her bra.

"You let go of that strap right now mister." she warned because she wasn't going to jump him when she barely knew the guy. She was stunned to see him pout at that looking like a puppy. "No way, we have time for that."

"Elaina." he whined softly only to make her laugh before she slipped on his shirt leaving hers on the floor.

"Don't you whine. I don't know anything about you other then your name. I'm not just going to jump the gun and sleep with you." she replied seriously seeing him go to object but she sat a finger against his lips cutting off any further protest. "You can wait, it's not like I'm going anywhere."

"Fine, come here." he grumbled before plopping her next to him seeing her smile at him. "What all do you want to know?"

"How old are you?"

"Of all questions to be first it's *this* one?" he asked seeing her nod simply. "Twenty-four."

"You're six years older than I am." she replied before thinking of another one. "Do you have family, you know, besides the pack?"

"I have a younger brother who constantly starts trouble because he can." Ravyn answered seeing her nod feeling glad she didn't delve too far into the subject.

"Your favorite color?"

"Tough one, I would have to say bronze."

"Suck up." she snorted seeing him looking completely innocent. "Good answer though. Favorite food?"

"I'm a werewolf Elaina, anything with meat." he laughed getting punched lightly in the gut. They both talked until they drifted and finally fell asleep.

Elaina woke up with a yawn seeing the sun setting so she went down the stairs after sliding out of bed to the kitchen. She got a juice from the fridge only to see Ravyn came out of the bathroom with a yawn and head towards the living room.

"Gotcha!" she called before hugging him from behind. She was suddenly tossed onto the couch seeing the guy smile. It wasn't Ravyn. He had the same hair and face but the eyes weren't caramel, they were a dark hunter green.

"A welcome home present." he said right before she screamed causing him to jump away after reaching for her.

"Elaina what's wrong!?" Ravyn asked after running in causing her to look at him.

"You never said you had a twin!" she yelled at him and pointed at his twin brother Rave. "This is so freaking embarrassing!"

"Speak for yourself." Rave said and stepped towards her only to hear Ravyn snarl. "What's up with you? Isn't she for me? I like how you remembered my taste in women. Dainty, seductive, and empty-headed."

"Speak for yourself." Elaina bit out seeing his eyes open wide so she stood and went over to Ravyn. "Not my fault I didn't know he had a twin, I thought you were Ravyn."

"And here Ravyn usually gets that he's me." Rave said before holding out his hand. "Rave Steel."

"I'm not shaking it if that's what you're waiting for." Elaina replied seriously watching him put his hand down.

"Who the hell is this anyway?" Rave asked as he pointed to Elaina who frowned at him.

"My mate." Ravyn stated seriously only to see Rave's eyes spark interest.

"I don't see a mating mark."

"What?" Elaina asked before looking at Ravyn's neck seeing nothing there. She felt her teeth lengthen so she stood on her tiptoes before marking his neck only to see it heal. "It healed."

"How is that possible?" Ravyn asked seeing her sit on the couch with a look saying she knew. "Elaina?"

"It's cause of the vampire blood."

"Vampire blood? She's a vampire?!" Rave yelled like it had to be a joke.

"No, I just happened to get dumped in the woods by a vampire after he attacked me before Ravyn bite me. I had bit the vampire to defend myself and unknowingly drank some of his blood." she explained before pinching the bridge of her nose as her head pounded. "Just great."

"So you're a mutated werewolf?" Rave asked as he pointed at her only to watch her snap her jaws. She intrigued him.

"We both are." Ravyn said seeing Rave looking stunned before Elaina stood up. "Let's go to the kitchen, I'll make us some dinner okay?"

"Kay." she murmured before leading the way to the kitchen only to freeze and look at the door right before Talon hurried in looking panicked. She hit Rave upside the head when he snarled before hurrying over. "What's wrong?"

"There's a rogue vampire in the neighborhood."

"Okay, why do you look so panicked?" she asked seriously seeing him look at Rave and then Ravyn in confusion.

"It was hanging out around your bedroom window. We could use some help tracking it." Talon said so she gave a nod.

"Absolutely not!" Ravyn yelled seriously seeing her round on him instantly.

"Don't you even start that caveman attitude with me Ravyn. Talon and Torrin have done a lot so doing this one thing isn't going to hurt. Besides, it was hanging outside *my* window." she told him off like a mother who'd caught her child sticking his hand in the cookie jar before dinner. "Now, you can either come with or stay here."

"I take back empty headed, she's a little fireball." Rave said only to see Talon frown. "Let me go too."

"No!" they both yelled at him causing him to go to protest.

"That was a reflex." Elaina replied before going upstairs and throwing on her shirt.

"Why did you go upstairs to change shirts?" Ravyn asked lamely seeing her grin.

"I fully intend to put it back on when we get back." she replied simply and brushed her finger against his hip seeing him look elsewhere. "Alright, let's go."

Elaina hurried across the road and launched herself into the tree right before Daisy poked her head out. "Hi Ellie!" Daisy piped before kissing her right on the cheek. "Are you on doggie business?"

"Shh, you aren't suppose to talk about that remember?" Elaina asked seeing Daisy put a finger to her own lips.

"Is this about the boogeyman in the tree?"

"Yeah, did you see them?"

"It was a guy who seemed like a big meanie." Daisy whispered before looking at the ground and waving.

"Did you see which way he went?"

"That way." Daisy said and pointed at the back fence so Elaina kissed her cheeks.

"Close and lock all the windows Daisy."

"Okay." Daisy said before doing just that as Elaina slipped out of the tree landing in a crouch feeling rage go through her.

"Elaina what's wrong?" Talon asked seeing her look at him showing her eyes didn't look human.

"Stay with Daisy, that vampire wasn't trying to get through my window. It was trying to get through hers." Elaina growled before going to the back fence seeing Talon following. "I told you to stay put."

"Torrin will watch her, it'll bad if the vampire isn't really a rogue." Talon replied only to watch her grunt before jumping over the fence and smelling the air as Ravyn and Rave followed.

"Big dog." Rave pointed out as it snarled at them only to see Elaina snarl back causing it to whimper before rolling onto it's back. "Is she…"

"Yep, she's the Alpha female." Ravyn finished before seeing her perk up and take off running. He felt he was the only one who could keep up with her. "Elaina wait."

"Ravyn what…what if that vampire tried to…" she started only to get pulled into a tender hug.

"It'll be fine."

That's when Elaina saw a man who was tall lunge towards them so she threw Ravyn one way while she went to the other. She jumped to her feet and hissed at the man seeing him look alarmed before a woman appeared near him.

"Please wait?" the woman asked quickly as Ravyn got to his feet feeling slightly dazed.

"Ravyn are you alright?" Elaina asked quickly after going to him as she held his face gently in her hands.

"Maybe I'll let you throw me more often." he murmured before she kissed him briefly. "You didn't have to throw me that hard though."

"I was just thinking about you getting out of the way." Elaina said before facing the other two. "Looks like we found the vampires hanging outside mine and Daisy's bedroom window."

"You guys wait up!" Rave yelled before jumping over the fence followed by Talon. "You left us with that freaking dog!"

"Oops."

"Talon!" the woman cried before pulling Talon into a hug.

"Please tell me he didn't use me to track his parents?" Elaina asked seriously seeing Talon look unrepentant. "Why you little…"

"Oh, it's not like it killed you."

"No, I was trying to kill them! You need to specify yourself, this is how crap gets started!" she yelled at him before marching over and cracking him right upside the head before looking at his mother. "Sorry, had to be done. He did something stupid."

"An interesting girl, you'd be perfect for Talon."

"I believe, Taryn, that she's spoken for." the man said as Ravyn let out a low growl so Elaina shot Ravyn a look that caused him to stop. "You must be the family my son is staying with."

"Correct."

"I'm Dracula."

"*You're* Vladimir the Impaler?" Elaina asked seeing him look a bit speechless. "I did a report on you in my World History class two years ago."

"How charming." Dracula murmured before taking her hand and kissing the top. "It's a pleasure to meet you then."

"I'm Elaina Scotts."

"And your mate?" Taryn asked so Ravyn went over and tucked Elaina under his shoulder.

"Ravyn Steel, that's my brother Rave." Ravyn said as Elaina tried to wiggle out from his shoulder so he wrapped the arm around her waist.

"A pleasure I'm sure." Taryn replied although she didn't look to happy.

"Well, we found your parents, have a nice night." Elaina replied before heading off as if everything was normal. She suddenly smelled something sweet causing her to stop and turn around only to see Dracula holding out a wrist that was cut.

"So you *are* part vampire." he chuckled like it was the most interesting thing. "I approve you as the bride for Talon."

"Sorry but I'm already mated and I like this one a lot." she replied simply seeing Taryn look like it was unacceptable.

"She's only a child, she doesn't know what she wants." Taryn waved a hand dismissively only to see Elaina let out a warning growl.

"Unlike most, I *do* know what I want and it only pisses you off because it's not your son." she replied causing Taryn to hiss so Elaina snarled. "Don't start with me lady."

"This isn't over." Taryn replied before her and Dracula vanished so she narrowed her eyes on Talon.

"You better have a good explaination on why they *approve* Talon. If you've been telling them lies I'm tearing you limb from limb." Elaina warned seeing him look at the ground. "Are they heading to my house?"

"Yeah."

Elaina changed instantly into the silver-white wolf before swiping at him getting him across the chest before heading back to the house like a bullet. She got there just as the doorbell rang so she went around seeing his parents standing there making her snap her jaws seeing them look terrified.

She got between them in the door as her aunt answered. "Elaina?" she heard Tricia ask as Elaina snapped her jaws at the couple. It must've meant they were no good so Tricia shut the door and locked it.

"I think we underestimated her. Not many turned wolves tell their families what they've become." Dracula said as she saw Connor and the others arriving so she barked seeing them turn before coming over and standing behind her.

"I think you two should go." Connor replied seeing them vanish so they left with scowls at Elaina just as Talon, Rave, and Ravyn arrived.

Elaina launched herself at Talon and pinned him to the ground snarling with such a ferocity she almost scared herself. She saw him get the picture before heading to the house and paced back and forth on the porch feeling angry. She saw Rave open the door while Ravyn talked to the others. She went to his room and changed before slipping on the shirt just before Ravyn came in. She was glad it stopped mid-thigh. She saw him hold out her clothes so she tossed them on the chair.

"Hey Ravyn can I…" Rave started only to get the door slammed and locked in his face by Elaina. "Apparently she's domineering too."

"Elaina…" Ravyn started only to see her wrap her arms around him and lay her head against his chest. He didn't want to lose her and she'd already proven that she didn't want to lose him.

"I think I know why the marks vanished."

"Why?" he asked seeing her pull him down. He felt her make the 'x' before dulling the sharp pain with the tip of her tongue. He felt it tingle before he reached up and touched it feeling the familiar 'x.' He tilted her head and repeated what she'd done seeing the 'x' there in plain sight. "Now they can't bother us."

"No, but they can bother my family." she choked out feeling his arms tighten around her. "I don't think I want to wait."

"Wait for what?" he asked only to feel her hands span his chest so he caught them. "Elaina, you are just panicked."

"Yeah I know." she grumbled seeing him go to the dresser and pull something out. It was a beautifully shaped teardrop pendant.

"This is for you." he murmured and kissed her shoulder before hooking it around her neck. "Come here, I have other plans for you."

Elaina woke the next day feeling completely groggy seeing Ravyn asleep next to her so she touched the mark on his neck before placing a little kiss to it. She slid out of bed before getting dressed…well she finished getting dressed. She slinked downstairs as she put her hair in a messy bun. She yawned as she went into the kitchen only to smack into the table.

"Walking with your eyes closed, you're going to break stuff doing that." Rave snorted only to see her shrug like there was nothing to be done about it. "You look good in guy's clothes."

"*You* shouldn't be looking at me at all. I'm your brothers mate." she replied seriously causing him to just gawk at her.

"How do you get that? There's no mark." Rave saw look at her reflection and blanch.

"How comes his stayed and mine didn't." she murmured and sat at the table feeling quite perturbed.

"Want to try marking me?" Rave saw her looking completely upset about that.

"Hell no."

"You're an intelligent domineering little fireball." Rave snorted before going towards her only to see her nails lengthen.

"Back off!" she yelled seeing Ravyn come down and pin Rave to the wall.

"I told you that she was *mine*. Stop your instigating Rave."

"Crap, it's seven-thirty." she grumbled because she didn't want to leave. She slipped on her flip-flops as the others except Connor raced down. "I have to get ready for class."

"Want me to pick you up?" Ravyn asked as she stretched up and kissed his cheek.

"If you want, I have to help decorate for the Halloween dan...damn it!" she yelled suddenly causing the others to laugh.

"You forgot to ask Ravyn to your own Halloween dance!?" Larkin laughed causing her to be grumpy.

"I'll go with you, go get ready for school." Ravyn said seeing her smile brightly before bolting from the house only to return five minutes later completely dressed.

"That was quick." Blade said after dropping his spoon seeing her straighten her outfit.

"Better hurry, bus is here in five minutes." she replied seeing them start eating faster. She went to the door only to turn around see Ravyn there so she pulled his face to hers and kissed him. She felt his hold tighten on her making her sigh against his mouth. "See you after school."

"Mmm, maybe I'll even cave and swing by during lunch."

"Uh-uh, you'll get trouble if you get caught." Elaina saw his eyes sparkling down at her so she leaned against him and breathed deep. "Not like I'll say anything though."

"Now I'm tempted." Ravyn said as he brushed a thumb against her cheek. "See you either at lunch or after school, possibly both."

"Get a room!" Rave called from the doorway as the others coughed to avoid laughing.

"Had one and had to give it up. One thing tempting me to skip class today but if I don't go then I can't go to that dance." she grumbled before kissing him briefly and hurrying out of the house right in time to stop the bus before waving for the others to hurry up.

Elaina didn't see Ravyn at lunch so when school was over she waited for Julie who showed up. Unlike her, Julie could play more then two instruments. Elaina had an electric guitar and Julie had a regular one. "Thanks for the help."

She didn't see Ravyn, Rave, and Connor sneak in.

"Ready?" Julie asked making her nod so Julie started playing since she was also backup vocals.

Elaina started singing into the microphone softly hearing Julie sing along when she needed to. She flipped on the amp as they got near the best part. Her voice got stronger right before starting with the electric guitar. She saw Julie whoop so Elaina flipped the guitar before continuing with the notes.

Elaina started one of her favorite rock songs seeing Julie roll her eyes as Rave felt stunned because she was playing a song by his favorite band and Ravyn knew it too. Elaina finished seeing Julie clap before they put everything up. Elaina was hopping when her legs suddenly felt like jell-o. She hit the ground hard wondering why her legs had given out so suddenly.

"Poor girl, you should get that looked at." Crystal said as she walked in holding some kind of talisman as well as a dagger. "Did you know that blood magic is a type of vampire sorcery. I never thought in a millions years that a pendant that could amplify old injuries would send you to the floor."

"What did you do to her!?" Julie yelled seeing Crystal smile maliciously.

"Easy, if I place this in any of her hands then her old injuries become permanent." Crystal had no idea that Julie, being a human, would slam into her sending her into the music stands.

"So glad I kept this here." Julie said before pulling out the wheelchair so Elaina pulled herself in so Julie took off running as she kept holding onto the chair.

"Jump onto the rungs in the back." Elaina said so Julie did just that allowing Elaina to wheel the chair. The weird feeling started leaving as they got out of the school seeing Ravyn rush out with Rave and Connor.

"Get back here!" Crystal yelled angrily and started running only to realize that Elaina could outrun her in a wheelchair.

"Not the hill!" Julie yelled but they were already heading down seeing the van catch up with them as Crystal fell behind.

"Get in!" Connor yelled so Julie jumped allowing him to catch her as Elaina looked at her legs. "Elaina jump!"

"I can't!" she yelled and stared at her legs right before Crystal jumped onto the back so Elaina buckled the seatbelt before slamming the brakes causing Crystal to scream as she flew over the chair and into the wall of a house.

Elaina wasn't so lucky either, the chair fell forward allowing the chair to twist before it slide until coming to a stop. She was shaking like crazy and the right side of her head was bleeding, so was her right arm but it was healing extremely slow. She needed blood and fast.

"Elaina!" she heard Ravyn yell as she continued to lay there feeling like she'd been hit by a car. She saw Ravyn start towards her right before she ripped the belt off and stood slowly.

"Oh Elaina." Julie choked out because Elaina had blood covering her as Elaina's eyes suddenly went a dark ruby. "Uh-oh, vampire came out." Julie saw Crystal screech before running at Elaina who broke Crystal's hand after becoming some kind of blur.

Elaina sank her fangs into Crystal's neck feeling rich blood flood into her mouth so she drank deeply. She took enough to sate the thirst and heal her wounds before letting Crystal hit the ground after wiping her memories.

"Elaina?" Ravyn asked causing Elaina to rub her head as her skin paled slightly.

Elaina turned seeing Julie start towards her but Elaina stepped away quickly. "Still vamped out." she heard Connor say so Ravyn went towards her and pulled her into a tight hug.

"Go ahead." Ravyn whispered knowing she needed blood seeing her go to protest but he nodded. "Let's get in the car first."

She sat in the very back seat, Julie sat in the front with Connor, and Rave sat in front of them. She threw morality out of the window before sinking the fangs into Ravyn's neck only to pull away instantly coughing.

"What?"

"I can't drink from you." Elaina choked out before wiping her mouth off feeling confused. "The blood is different, it's mixed blood."

"So I wouldn't be able to drink from you either?" Ravyn asked seeing her shake her head. "I'd like to know how she got a talisman like that."

"I think I know who did it." she bit out before wiping off her tongue multiple times.

"Here." Rave said and held out a wrist seeing Ravyn look ticked. "She needs blood and she can't drink yours right?"

"What if the same thing that happened to me happens to you?" Ravyn asked seriously seeing Rave think about that.

"Nothing will happen, that vial of blood I took from her I injected straight into my own veins. Nothing happened so I'm ninety percent positive that Rave will simply get nauseous from blood loss." Connor replied and saw Julie look at him so he grinned only to see her frown.

"It's just to help." Rave said seeing Ravyn nod seeing Elaina lean away from Rave's wrist.

"If you don't then you can't go to the Halloween dance." Ravyn said sternly so Elaina sighed and took Rave's arm seeing him looking apprehensive.

"Bon appetite." Elaina grumbled causing Ravyn to snort before she sank her fangs into Rave's wrist. The blood was more delicious then anything she'd ever tasted. She let her mouth pull against his wrist before she pulled away after the necessary pint seeing him look a bit queasy but he had another look in his eyes and it caused her to cuddle against Ravyn.

Elaina went to her house and got dressed for the Halloween dance feeling cheerful before hearing knocking on the door. She went down and opened it seeing the *whole* pack there as Julie came down behind her. "Who *is* your date anyway Julie?" Elaina asked only to gawk when Connor extended his arm to Julie who smiled at her.

"What are you all suppose to be?" Julie asked as they piled in the van.

"The men in black." Ravyn supplied but Elaina wasn't complaining, he looked drop-dead sexy in the tux he wore. Ravyn saw her look at him through half opened eyes and he had to look at the school so he wouldn't do something they'd both be embarrassed over.

"Come on Rave, let's get some girls." Larkin said after they all got in only to see Rave's eyes following Elaina so he elbowed him. "Rave, that's your *brother's* mate. It's funny taking mates of others but that's your brother."

"I'm only looking." Rave lied since he couldn't help but stare. She was beautiful for being a crossbreed. She was a hybrid and the word itself suggested she was an exotic. He liked exotics. He was happy for Ravyn but he always got the screwed up end of the stick. He wanted her. Badly.

Elaina was having fun with Ravyn only to spot Crystal by the doors. "She's here." Elaina murmured seeing him follow her gaze seeing her dressed as a fairy princess. Crystal was a beautiful girl but why did she always have the need to compete.

"I'll go talk to her. If I'm not back in five minutes then come after me." he said making her nod sternly so she continued to dance hearing a slow song come on.

"Want to dance?" Elaina turned seeing Rave standing there, god he looked just like Ravyn.

"No, I don't…"

"It's just one dance, it won't hurt." Rave replied seeing her sigh before dancing but it was more like stepping side to side. "Was that Crystal I saw?"

"Yeah."

"Wow, never thought I'd see Ravyn's ex-fiancée again. I knew she blew it when she chose her family over him but I'm glad he's moved on." Rave said only to feel her freeze and look at him. "He…didn't tell you?"

"No, he didn't."

Chapter 5

Elaina felt like her heart had dropped to the floor and all the dancers had river-danced on it. Why hadn't Ravyn ever told her about Crystal being his ex? She left Rave on the dance floor and followed the scent to a classroom where she heard voices.

"You said you'd love me always! You gave up after two months of waiting!" she heard Crystal cry angrily so she peeked in making sure to keep out of the draft.

"I did love you Crystal but a person can only wait for so long! You chose your family over me so that ended it! You didn't even look at me until you found out I might soon become the pack leader!" Ravyn snapped angrily and Elaina could tell she'd made a huge mistake.

Oh god, they both were still in love with each other!

"If I could do it over again I wouldn't have, you knew how my father was. It wasn't fair that I had to give you up. I felt terrible for what I did to you. I'm so sorry. I'm sorry I went after Elaina, she's a wonderful girl who didn't deserve anything I had done." What made it worse for Elaina was that she was actually telling the truth. "I was so mad, we're only separated for two years after being together since we were in diapers and you show up with a newly turned werewolf. I lost it, it's why attacked her so forcefully at the meet. I have every intention of apologizing."

"I appreciate what your saying but I won't do that to Elaina. I won't do to her what you did to me." Elaina only stared at the floor and could tell that she was only the rebound girl. She saw Crystal kiss Ravyn gently only to hear him growl. She knew he didn't want to but he couldn't help it. The heart wants what the heart wants. She saw him hold her just like she'd been held and tears coursed down her cheeks.

She removed the necklace and hung it on the handle before leaving. She saw Blade come out of the gymnasium laughing with Rave, Larkin, and Seth only to stop. "Elaina what's wrong?" Blade asked but she only shook her head and left only to get outside seeing Talon and Torrin arrive.

"Oh, the blood magic didn't work." Taryn stated causing Elaina glare at them. "You'll make it easier if you just accept his hand."

"People with actual feelings don't bounce back so fast! Stay the hell away from me!" Elaina snapped and marched away angrily but Rave had seen the tears spilling over.

He chased after her.

"Elaina what happened?" he asked seriously when he stopped her seeing her just look at the ground.

"I really wish you hadn't told me about what was between them." Elaina said seeing him looking confused. "They weren't over each other. If you hadn't told me I wouldn't have found him, and if I hadn't found Ravyn then I wouldn't have to watch him and Crystal…"

"Elaina I'm sorry." Rave apologized feeling angry that it had happened to her because someone like her didn't deserve that. "I'm truly very sorry."

"Doesn't matter, it's over. I didn't even try to stop it from happening, I guess I'm pretty stupid just like you said." Elaina went to go only to get pulled into a comforting hug.

"You aren't stupid. You let someone who wasn't suppose to be yours go, it takes more guts then you think it does." Rave informed her seeing her start crying silently again so he brushed the tears away. "My brother would be the stupid one for thinking that another girl could be better then you."

"That or it could that he'd prefer a girl only a year younger then him compared to someone who is six years younger." she replied and saw him grin about that before looking at her.

"Untamable hair, just like the owner. People with hair like that would be better off leaving it down." Rave said and pulled a single hairpin seeing the whole thing undo so he shook it out gently. "You'd think after sleeping with you my brother would think twice about giving you up?"

"Wait a minute! I never…I mean we never…why the hell am I telling you this anyway?!" she yelled completely flustered all over again so she started walking seeing him walk next to her.

"You mean you and my brother didn't?"

"Will you stop talking about it already?" she asked seriously seeing him point to a motorcycle and walked towards it. "Jeez, you both drive motorcycles too."

"Don't knock it." Rave tossed her a helmet seeing her looking annoyed before putting it on. He helped her get on because of her costume and then he took off feeling her hang on tightly. She was fun, young, beautiful, strong, smart, and faithful so how could his brother leave her so easily for Crystal. Unless him and Crystal were *soul mates* it was impossible.

They pulled into the driveway. "Hungry?" he asked and saw her shrug but the growl from her stomach gave her away. "Come on, Ravyn isn't the only one who can cook."

Elaina walked in and felt him slide the coat from her shoulders before putting it on the coat rack. She followed him to the kitchen where he tossed the tux jacket on a stool and rolling up his sleeves to his elbows.

"So how come you were going down the hill earlier in a wheelchair?" Rave found himself asking as he poured two glasses of wine.

"It was mine." she stated seeing him go rigid before looking at her so she took a small drink of the wine. "When I was four I was in a car wreck, my mom died and I damaged my spinal chord paralyzing me from the waist down. No one had ever met my dad so I was brought here to live with my aunt. They're the only blood family I have left."

"Paralyzed, as in you'd never walk again?" he asked making her nod as she stared at the counter.

"It's why I pretty much blocked out anyone who wasn't a girl or gay. I didn't need to see people staring at me in sympathy all the time so I found things I was good at. I had choir, swimming, and basketball…academics as well. The more I did the less people seemed to care about the fact that I couldn't walk like they could." Elaina explained seeing him forgetting completely about the food so she took the spoon and stirred what was in the skillet seeing him continue.

"What happened?"

"The Homecoming dance happened." she grumbled seeing him look puzzled. "There was one guy who kept asking me to the dance. I didn't want to go, I didn't see the point if I couldn't dance. Well turns out it was likely to be a pity date but when he showed up the day before I got a bit confused. Travis was the vampire that attacked me. I couldn't kick him so I bit him. He hit me in the head to knock me out and dumped me in the woods. It's how the others found me."

"Jesus." Rave murmured since she seemed to have a tough enough life without him in it. He had been trying to drive a wedge between her and his brother when he hadn't needed to do anything at all. He finished cooking before putting it on plate.

"What *is* it?" she asked after poking it with her fork seeing him frown. "You can't cook really well can you?"

"Ah…no." he said watching her laugh at that before going to the stove and pulling out a baking sheet. He saw her go to the freezer after preheating the oven and pull out a bag. He watched her pour them onto the sheet and waited until the bell sounded before putting them in the oven. He saw her set the timer so he scraped the plates of the inedible food he'd made. He turned only to get cracked in the head with the freezer making him groan.

"You should watch where you're going." Elaina replied seriously and rubbed the knot on his head. "Jeez, and I thought I was accident prone, it's safe to say you can no longer mess with me about running into a table."

Rave touched her hand that was touching his head only to she her go back to standing near the oven. "Did you ever think it might be why you didn't fight for him?" Rave asked quietly seeing her hands clench into fists.

"What are you talking about?"

"The reason why you didn't fight for my brother when you knew what would happen between him and Crystal. Did you think because you might like me more then him?" Rave asked seeing her look at him like he was moronic.

"No, I'm just not a selfish person. I don't see the point in hanging on to a person because it would only hurt both of us." she replied logically seeing him slam a hand against the counter.

"You're speaking like a *book*, I'm not talking about logical because feelings *aren't* logical." he replied seeing her just look at him. "A woman waking up and killing her three kids isn't logical. A twenty-three year old marrying a fifty-nine year old just because he's a great dancer isn't logical either but it happens. You can't compare something to logic when it's about as logical as a hippo wearing a tutu."

"A hippo wearing a tutu?" she asked as the timer dinged on the oven so she shut it off before pulling out the wrack with her bare hand.

"What are you…" he asked only to see her hand heal over like nothing had happened.

"You aren't logical in any way so you shouldn't be talking about things that are." she stated like it was a crime causing him to scoff.

"Fine, you want logical?" he asked seeing her nod simply so he marched right towards her before dragging her into a kiss. He felt her trying to push him away but he wasn't letting her go. He sank his teeth into her lower lip hearing air whoosh into her lungs as she opened her mouth so he deepened kiss with a ferocity know by no other. She fit perfectly against him and he liked how she felt. He finally pulled away seeing her eyes glaring at him. "Here's logic, if that had been me I would've left Crystal standing in the room by herself. I would've noticed you standing outside the door and went straight to you. I also certainly wouldn't have waited to claim you either."

"The marks kept disappearing!"

"I'm not talking about that kind of *claiming* Elaina." he smiled devilishly seeing her face go scarlet only to jump away from him. "Maybe you didn't notice how you felt because we're twins."

"Now that's stupid."

"Is it?" Rave backed her right into a wall. "Since I've been here have you had dreams about hands touching you but you couldn't tell who they belonged to? Lips kissing you without knowing the face?"

"You…" she started before shoving him away but he only stumbled away.

"I think deep down you knew, I think that's why you didn't want to bite me. You knew if you bite me then you'd know." he said only to see her swat at him. "Looks like I hit a spot."

"I don't have dreams you idiot I have nightmares!" she yelled at him seeing him look at her. "It's not easy to get over being attacked by a vampire or being in a car crash. I've *never* had pleasant dreams, I either have nightmares or I don't dream at all."

"Oh, well there goes my theory." he said before eating a couple of the pizza bites on the baking pan. "I think I know what your problem is."

"And what would that be *Chloe the Psychic*?" she asked lamely seeing him look amused by that.

"You're frustrated." he voiced simply only to watch her narrow her eyes. "It's just a suggestion."

"I'm not stupid Rave, I can *smell* you from here." she replied seriously seeing him looking like it was an every day occurrence. "Do you have any couth?"

"No, not really." Rave replied and saw her give a small smile about that. "Bet you that you can't even remember what you were mad about?"

"You invading my personal space." Elaina saw him raise an eyebrow but she only walked passed him to get a bowl.

"No use wasting dishes, just eat them off the pan." Rave said and put it back seeing her turn around causing him to drop the plate and cut his hand making him hiss. He saw her holding her breath so he tilted her head up seeing a dark red mixed in with the copper of her eyes. She hadn't taken enough blood, meaning she could've attacked someone at the dance. "You were that scared to bite me that you barely fed?"

"I took what I was allowed." she grumbled only seeing open his hand showing a red smear there. "Get that away."

"Werewolves can donate more blood then a human can but you wouldn't know that since you aren't full vampire. You need blood so take it." He said seriously because he had nearly been scared to death after seeing her when she stood up after wrecking. "You're only hurting yourself if you don't."

Elaina rose his hand to her mouth and licked the blood away feeling him tense. She gave in feeling her whole demeanor change and he could tell to. She let one of her hands curl around the back of his neck and pulled him down before breathing through her nose. She smelled cedar and black cherries causing her to trail her lips along the artery in his neck where the pulse beat frantically.

"Don't worry so much Rave, my bark is worse then my bite." she murmured as she let her teeth rake his neck making him jump. She sank her fangs into his neck hearing him cry out but it was far from being a cry of pain. She felt the blood run into her mouth and she relished in the taste. She felt him pick her up and sit her on the counter so she wrapped her legs around him pulling him closer to her.

"E…Elaina." his voice had practically fell two octaves as his hands brushed her sides.

Elaina licked the wound seeing it vanish as Rave had his head sat in the crook of her shoulder. "You need to eat." she said seeing him look up her with such fire burning bright in his eyes it almost scared her. "*Eat*."

"Don't try to glamour me." he growled only to see her look genuinely confused.

"Glamour? What's that?"

"Don't try to control me."

"I wasn't, I just told you to eat. You've…uh…lost a bit of color in your face." she pointed out only to see him start to sag so she held him up. "And this is why I didn't want to bite you again."

"Oh shut up and help me to my room." he grumbled only to get helped up the stairs and into his room. He felt her sit him on the bed and leave without a word so he sighed and laid back.

"Here, eat." Elaina watched him open one eye and look at her.

"Yep, probably dreaming already." he murmured only to jump when something pinched him.

"Guess you're awake after all." Rave sat up and took the bowl before he ate as he noticed she had her glass of wine. "You aren't old enough to drink, hand it here."

"Nope, this one is mine and I'm not going down to get yours. As for the age I don't think that should even count since I'll be eighteen *forever*." she reminded him and he felt like he'd completely lost. "If you want a drink though, I might let you have one if you ask nicely."

"Can I please get a drink before I die of thirst?" he asked seeing her hold out the glass but when he went to grab it she pulled away and took another drink. "You said…"

"I said I *might* give you a drink. I decided to sit here and drink it myself." she reminded him seeing him go back to eating.

"I don't get it." he said frustratingly and sat the empty bowl on the dresser.

"Don't get what?"

"How I've practically been throwing myself at you and you haven't even considered it!" he yelled and looked at her as if she was daft.

"I'm just not attracted to you."

"Bull! If you're attracted to Ravyn then you can definitely be attracted to me!" Rave yelled seeing her stand as she sat the half full wineglass on the dresser.

"I'm tired, going home."

"I thought you lived here with the pack?" Rave said causing her to stop and shake her head. He could smell and taste the saltwater coming from her.

"No, I live across the road." she replied only to jump when arms enfolded around her as if trying to protect her. "You should just let go."

"Ah, but I'm pretty foolish myself so I don't think I will." Rave murmured as her hand enclosed around the doorknob. "You don't have to go and I won't do anything, unless you want me to."

"You're a pervert."

"Sue me." he said seeing her hand let go of the doorknob and lower it to her side.

They laid down and just looked at the ceiling. She heard the door get opened and the last thing she wanted to hear was Crystal laughing as they came up the stairs. Elaina put her hands over her ears but it did little to drown out the noise. She heard a click before the stereo started blasting. She heard growls before there was heavy walking and then pounding on the door.

"Rave turn that off!" she heard Ravyn yell before walking in only to look at her. "Elaina? What the hell are you doing in here!?"

"Are you talking about this room or the house?" she asked seriously and saw him glance in the hallway as if to hide what he thought would be a secret.

"You shouldn't be in his room. You're my queen."

"No, Crystal is."

"Eh?" he asked and saw Rave sit up.

"She saw you two at the school and we could both hear you in you room which is why I turned on the stereo." Rave saw Ravyn glare at him. "You go ahead and have Crystal, I'm the one who wants Elaina as my mate."

"What?" Rave saw them *both* ask in shock so he sat his chin on her shoulder. "You can leave now Ravyn, you're interrupting us."

"I won't let you have her." Ravyn growled seriously before he had Rave by his throat and slammed against the wall. "She's *mine*."

"She's…not…claimed." Rave bit out and slammed a fist into Ravyn's gut making him cough and let go. "You can't have both of them and between us I think you've already made your choice or that would be Elaina in your room instead of Crystal. It's not my fault you can't make up your mind!"

"What's going on?" Crystal asked as she walked in only to stop seeing Elaina sitting there. "This belongs to you."

"You gave the necklace to Elaina?" Rave asked like Ravyn was stupid. "That goes to the….oh right, she is the Alpha female. Crystal's the *Beta*."

"Don't start." Crystal hissed before hooking the necklace around Elaina's neck before kneeling. "I'm sorry for what I did to you and what I *tried* to do. I'm asking for your blessing for me and Ravyn."

"Crystal…" Ravyn murmured in shock so Elaina stood and walked over to the guys. "You don't have any right to ask for a blessing."

Elaina detached Ravyn's arm from around Rave's throat seeing small bruises before shoving Ravyn towards Crystal. "Take the blessing and go." she grumbled seeing Rave looking speechless as Ravyn looked at Elaina. "You should go before I decide to throw you both out a window."

"A window?" Crystal asked only to watch Elaina narrow her eyes causing Crystal to scramble to Ravyn's room.

"Elaina you didn't…" Ravyn saw her give him her back meaning she didn't want him to talk to her. He couldn't blame her either, he'd betrayed her after she'd tried so hard to accept their ways. She might be the Alpha female but he had no right to call himself pack leader. He would bow to the one she chose and become a Beta like Crystal.

"Elaina…"

"I *really* don't want to talk about it so I'm going to sleep." Elaina said seriously before going over and laying down. She saw Rave lay in front of her seeing his eyes darken slightly as he looked at her. Elaina saw him scoot over and wrap an arm around her waist. Cedar and black cherries lulled her into the first dream she'd had since she was four.

Months passed and soon it was almost Christmas, meaning mistletoe was hung above doorways, presents were being bought, and snow was falling. She wondered what she should get for the pack or even if they celebrated Christmas. They probably did so when she went shopping she got everyone something. Even Ravyn and Crystal, she lived in the house now and avoided Elaina like she was the Black Plague. Things had gotten worse since her and Julie had gotten matching tribal tattoos on their lower backs that wrapped around to the front of their hips.

She also got presents for her family as well as Julie. She even got a freaking present for Torrin, Talon, and Talon's parents. How she found a site that delivered blood in wine bottles was strange enough. As for the healer of the pack who was also like the shaman, she'd heard he'd broken his athame and got him a new one. She came out of the mall with a dozen or so bags only to see Rave and the others heading towards her. The air was cold and bit at her skin but she was still warm. She and Rave were closer but they weren't dating or anything. She didn't want to rush straight into another relationship and he didn't mind taking it slow.

Talon must've talked to his parents because they had laid off with trying to get her to marry him. She'd thanked him and they'd gone back to being friends. He seemed fine with the fact that they were only friends as well.

"Christmas shopping, wonder what's in it?" Blade asked and tried to peek in the bags making her hold them behind her behind her back.

"That means she got something for us in there." Larkin said and tried to get around her.

"No I don't."

"Bad liar!" they all pointed out because she had flushed so she went to her car and put them all in the trunk. "Hey come see a movie with us!"

"I shouldn't, I mean I have a lot of stuff to do." she grumbled because she was a little overwhelmed because she was helping with the cooking in her own house, she was making a couple desserts for the dinner in the pack house since the whole pack was coming to the house. Her aunt had asked why she spent so much time over there with single guys.

Elaina had gladly pointed out that Connor was now dating Julie who was also coming to the pack dinner while Daisy was coming with Elaina, and that the pack was kind of a huge family. When her aunt looked sad Elaina had made it known that Tricia, Daisy, and Uncle David would come first before any new family. That had sent her aunt into tears.

"One movie?" Rave asked as he held out his hand.

Elaina had noticed that while he was still a huge pervert and extremely hilarious he had become less irresponsible. He had a different aura about him that caused her to feel a bit safe around him. "Fine, one movie but then I really have to go." she said and started only to hear her phone ring. "Hello?"

"Can you remember to grab the pre-made graham cracker pie crust on the way home, I need three of them." Tricia said so Elaina made a note in her notepad.

"Anything else?"

"Two bag of chocolate chips, a bag of marshmallows, three boxes of candy canes, and a container of the Hershey powder chocolate." she said so Elaina wrote it down. "Did you grab that last minute thing for you-know-who?"

"Yeah, I got it. I'll be back home in about two hours." Elaina said hearing her giggle on the opposite end before the line went dead.

"What's that for?" Rave asked as she tucked the notepad in her purse.

"Christmas dinner." she grumbled before following them in. She went to the movie with them seeing the others engrossed in the movie except Rave, he was more interested in letting his fingers trace little designs over her the tops of her hand.

After the movie she grabbed something to eat as the others branched off to go shopping leaving her and Rave. She felt him take her hand in his causing heat to race up the sides of her neck. As they walked with their pretzels she was aware of people glancing at them as he walked her to the car.

"Be careful driving home." he said so she gave a nod wondering why her heart never raced with Rave. It was like there wasn't anything there and they both knew it. "I'll see you tomorrow for dinner."

"Rave, I don't…" she started and he knew what she was going to say.

"I know. Maybe you'll find the one your suppose to be with at the Christmas dinner." he said seeing her looking doubtful so he kissed her forehead. "At least you're honest about things like this."

"I'm sorry." she choked out and hugged him tightly. She kissed his cheek before getting in the car seeing him head back inside as she drove away. She drove to the store and did her shopping before heading home. She went around the turn only to smack something sending something brown flying causing her to slam the brakes on.

Elaina got out quickly seeing a chocolate colored wolf as it stood slowly. She saw real wolves come out and surround the chocolate colored wolf as it changed into a guy laying there. She could see the wolves snarling so she howled seeing them look at her. She saw the guy look at her with tired eyes before the wolves bared their stomachs to her. She walked over and patted their heads.

"Go, I'll take care of this one." He must've been rogue because they wouldn't have attacked him if he weren't.

Elaina saw them lower their heads in respect to her decision before running back into the woods. Elaina was pretty much used to naked men from the runs so this one was no different. "Can you stand?" she asked seeing him groan and collapse into unconsciousness. She picked him up and put him in the backseat and tossed the blanket on him. "Why me?"

Back at the house she took in the groceries and presents and then came out for the unconscious guy. "Elaina is he..." Tricia started asking seeing Elaina nod simply. "I'm glad your uncle isn't back from the bar yet, I'll grab clothes and you get him to the guest room.

Elaina got him to the guest room and laid him down seeing him healing at a slower rate then she did. She put the clothes her aunt had brought on him before she went down and helped with dinner. Three hours later she heard a thump so she hurried to the guest room seeing him away looking panicked.

"Whoa, calm down there buddy." Elaina said seeing him look at her and snarled so she obliged and snarled back seeing him choke off.

"What happened?!"

"You jumped into the middle of a freaking road and I accidentally hit you with my car. Then you would've gotten ripped apart by wolves if I hadn't intervened. You're a *rogue* aren't you?" she asked after crossing her arms seeing him looking her over. "My eyes are up here."

"You're werewolf...but an immortal."

"How..."

"So am I." he said and she saw a brief red tint to his pale blue eyes. "You're a pack member. Are you Beta or Omega?"

"I'm an *Alpha*." she warned seeing his eyebrows fly up.

"Hope you aren't expecting me to bow?" he asked before the door showing Daisy who smiled brightly.

"Ellie is he a doggie too!?"

"Yes Daisy, he's a doggie too." Elaina said seeing Daisy rush forward and hold up her arms.

"Up!" she piped only to see him look completely stunned.

"Daisy let's leave the crazy man to rest. He's had a long day." Elaina said after kneeling in front of Daisy seeing her give a nod before hurrying out.

"She's human."

"So is my aunt but I wasn't hiding what I was from them." she replied lamely and headed to the door. "You're welcome to stay for a while, dinner is in an hour."

"Why are you being kind to a rogue?"

"That's what I'd like to know." Elaina heard Ravyn growl so she turned around seeing Crystal standing next to him.

"As for why you are here I could care less, who is invited to stay in this house is none of your business, and I hit him with my car going sixty." Elaina said seeing Ravyn go to step forward so she blocked him. "What are you doing here?"

"Pack is having a Christmas Eve dinner tonight." Crystal murmured from behind Ravyn.

"I am having Christmas Eve dinner with my *family*, I already told you all this, which is why I'm bringing four desserts to the dinner *tomorrow*." Elaina reminded them seeing them look confused.

"But it was to celebrate you and Rave becoming mates."

"Me and Rave are friends, not mates." she corrected seriously seeing Crystal step forward looking stern.

"You shouldn't be allowing rogues to…"

"I don't believe that's *your* choice and this is far from being your house. So unless you would like the pack to know the *real* reason why you two are mates instead of me and Ravyn I suggest you keep your snout out of my business *Beta*." Elaina warned seeing Crystal jump away quickly before she looked at Ravyn. "If you have any other business then either state it or I'll escort you both to the door."

"Dinner starts at seven tomorrow. We start opening the presents at four." he stated curtly before sweeping from the room with Crystal following him.

"I have the feeling he doesn't like me. I've never seen an Alpha male ending up with a Beta female before. How come he isn't with you?" the guy asked only to see her frown at him.

"That's none of your business, it's *pack* business. You aren't part of our pack. Dinner is in an hour." she replied seeing him look at what he was wearing.

"Whose are these?"

"My uncle's, try not to rip them." Elaina saw him look at her causing her heart to hammer but she only left the room and went to her room where she wrapped and labeled all the presents. She heard snarling all of a sudden as she threw her hair in a messy bun before running out. She saw the guy backing Talon and Torrin into a corner.

Elaina charged and knocked the guy to the ground getting him pinned to the floor. "Don't go attacking people in this house unless you want thrown out." she warned icily before jumping to her feet and heading towards them. "You both okay?"

"Yeah, why is there a r…" Torrin started as the guy stood slowly seeing her frown. "Right, none of our business. We're going to go out with Talon's parents."

"Are they coming here tomorrow?" she asked seeing them look puzzled. "What? If they can keep their fangs to themselves and out of family members then they are welcome to join us."

"Okay, no necking, got it." Talon said before they left so she glowered at the guy.

"How the hell was I suppose to know?"

"Use your head, if they are in the house then they're allowed to be in here." she replied before a knock sounded on the door so instead of going down the stairs she went over the balcony and landing right in front of her aunt who cried out.

"Don't do that! I just replaced the floors from last time! I had to lie to your uncle about what happened!" Tricia chastised her and cracked her in the head causing Elaina to laugh as she smiled sheepishly.

"Right, sorry. Julie said she was coming over for a little bit with others from school." she said before going to the door and opening it only to squeal and hug Julie who had Leon, Rosa, and Roberto with her.

"Okay, I don't know where are these really gorgeous guys are coming from but I want to go there." Leon said as she saw the rogue come down only to look like he was definitely avoiding Leon.

"Me too." Rosa murmured and looked at Elaina. "Well, me and Roberto only came to drop by really quick. We're getting ready to head to Costa Rica to spend the holidays with our grandparents. We just came to give you your Christmas present."

"You didn't have to get me anything."

"Yeah we know." Roberto said only to get elbowed by Rosa who held out something wrapped. "You have to open it now though."

"Fine." Elaina opened it only to see a beautiful picture frame with a picture of all of them together. "You guys."

"Well, we don't know where we're going after high school so we made sure you'd get something to make you keep in touch with us." Rosa said so they had a big group hug before a horn sounded. "Right, see you after Christmas break."

"Definitely." Elaina said before they left so Julie rubbed the back of her neck. "What?"

"Okay so Leon noticed how we both have been acting differently so I think it's time he finds out." Julie said causing Elaina to feel slightly panic. "I didn't tell him yet so relax. I thought you'd want to do that."

"Tell me what?" Leon asked seeing Elaina frowning at Julie.

"What? I handled it just fine, so did your aunt and Daisy."

"Daisy has always liked that stuff, as for my aunt she was fine about it the *second* time around. I've yet to tell my uncle because he's military. I can't just tell everyone, they'd have a cow."

"At least they never eat them." Julie grumbled and Elaina caught it.

"That was completely by accident!" Elaina yelled seriously only to see Julie glance at the guy and look questioningly so Elaina nodded. "You are going to drive Connor insane you know."

"A little unbalance will do him some good."

"Is that what they're calling it now Julie? *Unbalancing*?" Elaina asked causing Leon to laugh at that as Julie went scarlet.

"Dinner is ready!" Tricia called from the kitchen so Elaina led the way seeing *him* following closely behind her. "So what is your name?"

"Hmm? My name is Fury." Elaina heard him say as they sat down noticing he sat on her left. She passed the dishes around as the others laughed and talked. She wasn't in a celebratory mood at the moment.

"So how old are you?" Leon asked Fury who looked like he didn't want to answer the question. "I'm guessing maybe twenty-three."

"So you're twenty-three." Julie said since his face had given him away. "Where are you from?"

"I travel a lot."

"Leon did you know Ellie likes doggies!?" Daisy asked and Elaina thought she'd die right at the table.

"Yeah, it's cause she's allergic to cats." Leon said and Daisy went to correct him when Tricia covered her mouth.

"Daisy no more talking about *doggies* at the table." Tricia murmured as Julie laughed in her seat.

"What? Isn't she allergic?" Leon pointed out but only Julie and Tricia knew that Elaina had sneezed to keep from growling.

"Yeah, it's like she just woke up and couldn't stand them anymore." Julie snorted causing Elaina to cover her mouth to keep from spitting the juice in her mouth.

"I hate you." Elaina grumbled before going back to eating only to become aware that Fury's thigh was brushing against hers. She shifted so that she wasn't touching him. She knew what the rules were. If a rogue seduced a female pack member then they were automatically accepted into a pack. Without a female they would have to be voted in after proving themselves. They did that after hunting for the elderly for two months.

"So how did you and Elaina meet?" Leon asked as he gestured to her and Fury.

"Almost hit me with her car." he replied even though she *had* but apparently she had felt guilty which was why he was in her family's home.

"It's snowing outside." Julie pointed out seeing Leon nod but looking at Elaina like she should just stop driving.

Elaina heard a wolf howl causing her to jump to her feet because something was wrong. "Jeez, you're jumpy." she heard Leon say with a laugh. She only excused herself and left the house before hurrying across the street.

"What's wrong?" she asked and saw Larkin look at the floor. "Larkin what happened!?"

"Two of the cubs are missing and we can't track them because of the snow." Larkin said only to growl after looking at Fury. "Why is there a rogue with you?"

"I hit him with my car." That sent Larkin into hysterical laughter.

"You hit him with your car!?" Larkin laughed only to get swatted at playfully.

"Jeez, I know I'm terrible at driving. Stop reminding me." Elaina thought for a moment. "Where were they last?"

"In the backyard." Larkin replied so she hurried through the house seeing him and Fury follow before smelling the air.

Elaina walked around only to smell the sickly sweet smell of a vampire. She launched towards the fence changing instantly before running. She jumped over and she picked up the smell of the cubs. She ran faster and saw the vampire sitting under the chair getting ready to skin one of the cubs. She snarled as she pounced sending the dagger flying and causing the cub to roll out of his hands. She saw it smile sadistically before trying to bite her so she slashed its face making it screech.

"Elaina be careful!" Larkin yelled before picking up the cubs as they squeaked with fear.

"*I'll kill you.*" it hissed before throwing her making her slam into glass panes causing her to cry out.

"Elaina!" Larkin yelled as it stalked towards her and he felt the air stir. "She vamped."

"What?" Fury asked in confusion only to see the wolf stand and change back after wrapping in a sheet showing Elaina with ruby red eyes.

"*Impossible!*" it screeched before she walked towards it. It tried to move but found it couldn't.

"*You don't want to run do you?*"

"No, I don't want to run." it said as it swayed with a dazed expression before she sank her teeth into it's neck and taking what she needed.

"She's part vampire." Fury choked out like it was impossible but Larkin nodded before the thing turned to dust leaving Elaina standing there.

"So much for trying not to ruin my appetite." she grumbled and took the cubs from Larkin and holding them safely. She felt them calm down and eventually fall asleep as they headed back. "Jeez, and I thought it'd be a calming holiday break."

"Well you're an *Alpha*, and it's not like any of the females will ever fight you for it. They already know you're the right person for it. The only person being second guessed is Ravyn. You know, since Halloween." Larkin replied seeing her nod slowly. "Crystal's a Beta and always will be. She doesn't know the first thing about running a pack."

"Neither did I, did you forget I was human before all this stuff started happening?" she asked seriously seeing him shrug like it didn't matter.

"You proved yourself though. The first turning should've taken you a hour to get through, you got through it in five seconds. That's never happened before. Even Nickolas thinks you're the right person and no one *ever* second questions the healer." Larkin reminded just her seeing her just shrug. "Did you know he broke his ceremonial knife? He's trying to figure out how to get another athame before tomorrow night."

"Yeah, I knew."

"Well, thanks for helping find them." Larkin said as the mother had rushed out and held her cubs tightly. "See you tomorrow."

"Yeah, see you tomorrow." Elaina got dressed in their bathroom before heading back across the road seeing Leon and Julie had left. She sauntered to her room where she changed into her nightclothes. She headed to the kitchen and got her plate which had been put in the microwave. She slammed her fists into the counter feeling angry. She'd missed dinner with her family just because the pack didn't trust Ravyn to do anything. He was becoming a Beta making her the only Alpha meaning everyone would look to her for direction.

"It's not fair, I never asked for it." she murmured before taking it to her room and eating while she started wrapping the presents that she had left. She heard a tap on her door so she went over and opened it seeing Fury standing there. "It's the middle of the night."

"I can't sleep, and I could hear all the noise you were making." he stated simply so she opened her door seeing him come in. "This looks like a tomboys room."

"I am a tomboy." she grumbled seriously before going back to wrapping.

"Are you a perfectionist or something?" he asked while watching her do one present at a time.

"No, I just want them to look nice." she saw him walk around only to stop and look at her pictures.

"Is this your mother?" he asked as he looked at a picture of a woman and a child.

"Yeah."

"Does she know you're a werewolf?"

"No, she died when I was four."

"Oh, sorry." Fury looked back at the pictures only to see one that made him extremely confused. "Why were you in a wheelchair?"

"Will you stop nosing around and sit down already?" she got out a bit harsher then she meant to see him frown at her. "Sorry, I'm just tired and I'm trying to concentrate on getting these wrapped."

"Do you want some help?"

"Can you even wrap a present?" Elaina saw him sit in front of her and start wrapping.

"I didn't always use to be a rogue. I just lost a lot of people close to me and couldn't take it anymore so I left. I'm immortal like you but I don't have vampire in me like you do. How did that happen?" He asked seeing her stop and continue to look at the carpet.

"I got attacked by a vampire so brilliant me decided to bite him back. I was left to die after he dumped me in the woods and I got bit by Ravyn. I became a *mutated* werewolf." she grumbled only to seeing him starting a third while she was still on her first.

"And the wheelchair?"

"I was in the car wreck that killed my mom, I got paralyzed from the waist down. When I ingested the vampire blood it healed my spine while being bitten by a werewolf made me stronger. I woke up not knowing where I was and my best friend's current boyfriend thought it would be fine to come near me. I almost kicked him through the wall. We've been friends ever since." Elaina heard him snort at the last part as she saw him pour water before holding out a glass so she took drink only to feel her head spin lightly.

"Whoa, it's acting faster then I thought it would." Fury murmured before laying her down gently. "Don't worry, I'm only giving the illusion of intimacy."

"You…stupid…jerk." Elaina said before sinking her teeth into his arm making him growl only to see her eyes glowing as bright as rubies. She pushed and switched getting him pinned. "If you want to join this pack then you'll *earn* it, now get the hell out of my room."

"You're a tough cookie." Fury chuckled only to see her put the wrapped presents in the back so he stood up. "You used the vampire blood to burn off the drug."

"Yeah, tranquilizers don't work either. You know you have an odd way of showing gratitude to someone who opened the doors of their home up to you." she bit out seeing him look at the floor knowing he felt guilty. "Just go back to your room and you'll be introduced to the pack tomorrow."

"What?"

"Be glad I'm not a stuck up Alpha or you wouldn't even be getting that." she replied seeing him nod seriously. "Try not to screw things up with them tomorrow."

"Whatever." he grumbled and went to his room missing her roll her eyes and lay down.

It felt like Elaina had barely closed her eyes before Daisy was jumping up and down on her bed yelling that it was Christmas. She woke up and grabbed the presents for them and shuffled down the stairs.

"Hey watch out for…" Fury started before she smacked into the wall only to groan.

"We've told you to stop walking around yawning Elaina." Tricia giggled incessantly as Elaina opened her eyes only to close them when yawning again. "Oh for heaven's sake, sit on the couch before you brake something."

"Kay." Elaina shuffled to the living and sat down the presents for them.

"Can I open mine first!?" Daisy asked excitedly as there was a knock so Elaina went to the door seeing Taryn and Dracula there.

"Talon gave us the conditions. Thank you for inviting us." Taryn said and held out a bottle of wine so Elaina accepted it.

"Glad you both could make it. I'll take your coats." Elaina said and took them before hanging them up. "We're opening presents. You should give this to my aunt and uncle, they love wine."

"Right, you're not old enough." Dracula said and took the bottle before they went in showing Daisy opening her presents.

"I'll grab the garbage bags." Elaina went to the kitchen and grabbed three heavy duty before returning to her seat seeing Daisy jumping up and down with the new scary movie.

"David I told you *not* to get her more scary movies." Tricia whacked his arm but he only smile sheepishly. "Don't indulge her, it's bad enough Elaina had her watching *Blood and Chocolate*."

"But that's not a scary movie." Elaina said seeing Tricia purse her lips. "Here Daisy, open mine."

Elaina saw Daisy open the fairy snow globe and squeal before running over and hugging her tightly. "Thanks Ellie!" Elaina gave her a squeeze before pushing her presents into the corner and playing the music on the snow globe.

"Okay, Ellie you…"

"I'll go last." Elaina said and handed the gift she got for Tricia to her seeing her open it only to look at the locket and open showing a picture of her, Daisy, and Uncle David.

"And that will go with this." David said and pulled out a little red velvet box.

Tricia opened the box showing a beautiful diamond ring and looked at David before kissing him. "I don't understand though, this is a wedding ring."

"Ah, I thought it was time we renewed our vows." David informed causing her eyes to light up so he slipped the ring on. "We do that in the summer, Elaina has already planned it for us but she won't tell me where it is."

"You both planned this." Tricia murmured only to see Elaina looking completely innocent. "You sly little imp you."

"Me? An imp?" Elaina asked only to see Daisy giggle at that. "Well I thought I'd save where you're going as Uncle David's present."

Elaina held out the small package to him seeing him open it finding an envelope which he opened. "Three tickets to the *Bahamas*?" she saw him gawk as Tricia looked at her.

"You read my diary!?" Tricia accused causing Elaina to jump out of the way so not to get swatted. "Why three tickets?"

"You're gonna need a flower girl." Elaina replied and pointed to Daisy causing Tricia to stand before pulling her into a big hug.

"This is your *good bye* present too isn't it?" Tricia asked quietly and hugged her tightly. "It's why there isn't four tickets."

"Well, I'll be nineteen in a couple months." Elaina whispered back feeling the hug tighten before Tricia let go and wiped her face off quickly. "Stop crying already, it's too early in the morning."

"Okay, Torrin and Talon we got presents for you as well." Tricia said before they handed them a present so Elaina watched them open the leather bound journals. "I figured Elaina knew what you'd like better then me so I got you those."

"Diaries?" Torrin asked making them all laugh at that.

Elaina handed them their presents to them seeing Torrin open the ornately decorated dagger and Talon opened a red stoned necklace. "What is it?" she heard him ask only to see Dracula recognize it instantly.

"Our coat of arms." Dracula murmured only to see her hold out a small present to him and Taryn as well as a large package. He opened it seeing a signet ring as well as Taryn.

"How beautiful." Taryn murmured as she held the present she realized she barely deserved. They had a present for Elaina too though.

"This is for the two of you." Elaina said and held out a larger present seeing them open it together before opening the wooden container showing the wine bottle of blood.

"Does she always surprise people like this?" Dracula asked Tricia seeing her nod.

"A sly feat yet she's mastered it perfectly." David chuckled before pulling out about seven presents for Elaina. "Have fun opening them."

Elaina got through the new shirts and *journal* that she didn't mind having, she put on the ring from her aunt and Daisy, and noticed a small package. She opened it seeing a trip for two to Ireland. A place she'd always wanted to go. "Why are there two tickets?" she asked seeing they had paid for a whole *month*, she'd given them two *weeks* but then again she'd already paid for everything for their second wedding.

"Aren't you and that one fellow dating?" David asked only to see Tricia look at him and give a quick shake of her head.

"It's fine, thanks Uncle David, excuse me." Elaina said before hurrying upstairs with her stuff just to get away. She put it away and sat on her bed staring at the tickets. She only needed one but then she couldn't leave because of the pack anyway. She would only give them away and knew the perfect people to give them to. She'd explain why and give them to Julie who wanted to go as bad as she did.

"Elaina?" she heard Tricia ask and walk in before closing the door and sitting next to her.

"I can't go Aunt Tricia, I'm an Alpha and I'd sooner kill myself before leaving Crystal in charge of the pack. Things are just really unstable right now." she said and got a huge hug but it made her feel worse. "I can't go."

"I know sweetie, I know." Tricia murmured before they headed out seeing Dracula and Taryn there holding a gift.

"We came up to give this to Elaina, we have to be on our way."

"So soon?" Tricia asked seeing them nod so Tricia went down knowing they were vampires.

"Your gifts were very thoughtful, it's been a long time since I've seen my own family crest. Thank you." Dracula said before kissing the top of her hand as Fury started up the stairs. "You shall always be welcomed amongst our kind."

It was weird for her to have a vampire put a necklace around her neck but it was beautiful and Taryn gave her a hug. "This is for you, consider it a suggestion if you ever decide to come fully into our world. The thorns are the contract so don't touch it unless you want to be turned, it doesn't wilt either. The book you will find useful since our kind are very powerful." Taryn said before they vanished so Elaina opened the box showing a beautiful long stemmed black rose and book containing blood magic.

The smell was intoxicating so she closed the box cutting the smell off. "And people call me sly." she grumbled before putting it on the top shelf of her closet before turning only to find Fury there. "I didn't say you could come in."

"Why would they offer you to be part of their coven? Who was that?" Fury asked seeing her cross her arms.

"If you must know, that was the very first vampire Dracula and his wife Taryn." she said and saw him blanch at her. "What?"

"Dracula considers you a friend and you're a werewolf." Fury murmured only to feel warmth radiating off her skin and he could smell the cinnamon and vanilla. He really couldn't help himself. He leaned down and brushed his lips against her shoulder feeling her shiver. "You taste wonderful, sweet yet there's a bite to the flavor of your skin."

"Stop it." she said wondering why she felt panicked so she put her hands against his chest and pushed. He didn't budge until he took a step back. He was more overwhelming then Ravyn ever had been.

Fury was someone she couldn't fall for, he was a rogue until voted in. If she fell for him and he was voted out then she would be considered a rogue and the Betas would become Alphas.

He was insanely gorgeous though. He was six-foot-one with broad shoulders and a lean waist. She already knew he had a body that could make Bowflex jealous. His hair was shaggy at the moment and looked like chocolate, his skin was tanned, and his eyes were such a pale blue they reminded her of the spring sky when it wasn't raining. The only thing that disagreed with her was the beard and mustache.

Fury could smell a small amount of attraction but she didn't trust him not one bit. She was far from being stupid like the past Alphas he'd won over. She was immortal like him too… except for the vampire part. He didn't blame her for not trusting him. She might've hit him with her car but she'd made up for it whereas he'd tried to drug her to sneak into the pack.

"Out." she said seeing him leave so she got ready for the dinner while reading the book of blood magic. They had to dress nice so she pulled on a knitted black dress and black boots. It wasn't any of her new clothes though. She curled the ends of her hair loosely as she heard Tricia getting Daisy ready for the party. Daisy was her *gifter*, someone important to her to help give the presents to the pack who knew their secret. Daisy would become an official member of the pack along with Julie even though they weren't wolves.

"You look so much like your mother." Tricia said after walking in showing Daisy in a pretty purple dress with her hair pinned up. "I've given Fury an old suit that belonged to your uncle, he's getting ready now."

"Thanks Aunt Tricia." Elaina said before grabbing her long black leather jacket. She grabbed the three bags of presents and stuck the tickets in the inside jacket pocket. She led

Daisy downstairs after adding her eyeliner and a little eye shadow to cause her eyes to stand out. She sat in the living room waiting for Fury as Daisy played with her bracelet.

"I look ridiculous." she heard him grumble so she looked only to wish she hadn't. She saw him raise an eyebrow inquiringly but she only stood and slipped her jacket seeing his eyes follow her. His attraction swamped her making her stomach flip over and over again.

"You look fine." she grumbled as Daisy looked puzzled between them before they left the house. She had the presents in one hand and Daisy's in the other. She walked up the stairs and would've lost her balance if Fury hadn't steadied her. Elaina had just wished he hadn't grabbed her waist.

Elaina got to the door and rapped on it seeing Blade answer with a bright smile only to look at Fury and start to growl. She looked at him seeing him step back before sliding her jacket off. She took the tickets out of the pocket before helping Daisy with her jacket and handing it to Blade who refused to just let her hang it up by herself. She walked into the living room seeing the whole pack there, she saw Julie nestled against Connor's side looking comfortable.

"Welcome Elaina." she watched Tristan say before they all kneeled to show respect. "I see you have brought a *friend*."

Elaina saw him gesture to Fury causing the others to frown at him only to keep in a kneel. "I'll leave that to him." she grumbled before going to stand on the right of Tristan who got confused.

"He is not your chosen mate?" Tristan asked seeing her shake her head simply so the others returned to their seats. "Oh, and who is this?"

"I'm Daisy, Ellie's my big cousin!" Daisy piped causing the others to laugh.

"She's my *gifter*." Elaina said seeing Tristan grin. "Daisy can you hand me the big present in the middle bag?"

"Okay." Daisy pulled out the big present. "What's in this one?"

"Hand that to Tristan."

"You shouldn't have." Tristan replied when Daisy handed him the present so he patted her head. He opened it only to stare feeling completely speechless. He was looking at a beautiful *gold* athame with wolves carved into the handle and different stones comprised the eyes of the wolves. "Elaina this is very gracious of you."

"What is it?" Larkin asked so Tristan held up the new athame causing them to grin.

"Everyone chipped in for it, I just helped design the handle." Elaina said and got a hug from Tristan who looked practically ecstatic. Elaina called names and Daisy gave them the present and once everyone received them they opened it showing a chain. The males had a claw with the initial of their first name on the back while the girls had a small wolf head with the initial on the back as well.

"Uh…these aren't silver are they?" Larkin asked making her snort and shake her head.

"Stainless steel." Elaina saw them all look at Crystal who was red with embarrassment. Had she got them something that was sterling silver?

"Now that the presents are handed out we shall begin our meeting by welcoming two humans into out group. Julie Burns and Daisy Meadows please come stand before me and our Alpha." Tristan said so Daisy hopped to stand in front of him causing everyone to smile at her. "You two have been chosen to be accepted into our family. Do you accept?"

"YAY!" Daisy agreed and bounced on her feet causing everyone to laugh.

"I do." Julie said with a nod and looked at Connor who smiled at her.

"With these pendants you are brought fully into us, wolves of other packs will know who your family is and will welcome you with open arms unless you give them reason not to." Tristan said before putting the pendants around their necks. "Elaina your turn."

Elaina kneeled in front of Daisy and kissed her forehead. "My cousin." she said only to get a hug from Daisy.

"Love you Ellie!" Daisy giggled making the others laugh softly as Elaina moved to stand in front of Julie.

"My *sister*." Elaina saw Julie start crying silently before they hugged and laughed.

"My sister." Julie couldn't believe her and Elaina were now considered sisters.

"Let's eat!" Tristan cheered so everyone headed to the kitchen.

"Connor and Julie I have something for you." Elaina said as everyone left so they stopped and went to kneel making her stop them. "I'm going to be honest. You two are a great couple."

"Elaina…" Connor started because she'd just given them her blessing should Connor ask Julie to marry him.

"Here, I want you two to have these. It was to me but I don't have use for them and can't leave the pack when I'm the only Alpha. Even if I wasn't I wouldn't leave. So I want you two to go, hell, just bring me back a souvenir." Elaina laughed seeing Julie open the envelope and squeal before hugging her tightly.

"Seriously! A whole *month* in Ireland!?" Julie squealed while Connor stood there completely stunned.

"Great, then I can get this off my chest." Connor said before kneeling in front of Julie who inhaled sharply. "Julie Shannon Burns, will you do me the honor in marrying me?"

"Like you even have to ask!" Julie replied before kissing the daylights out of him so he put the ring on her finger. "This night couldn't get *more* perfect."

Elaina rolled her eyes as she headed to the kitchen only to smack into Fury who held the plate away so it wouldn't get sent on her. "I take it back, look who got stuck under the mistletoe." she heard Julie giggle but Elaina only headed to the kitchen. "She was never one for tradition anyway."

Everyone ate, laughed, and talked but Elaina noticed they completely avoided Fury like he was diseased. She saw Daisy sitting with him and chatting cheerfully and he didn't seem to mind her company.

"Now that we have ate we'll wait to dig into those beautiful desserts made by Elaina to extend the question as to why we have a visitor." Tristan said so Fury stood and Elaina saw him walk to stand before them. "How did you meet *our* Alpha?"

"She hit me with her car." Fury replied simply causing the others to laugh hysterically.

"I think we need to ban our Alpha from driving in the snow at night." Larkin laughed but Elaina only looked a little miffed by that suggestion. "It's like guys are better drivers."

"Don't start that crap, Julie's a better driver then me." Connor pointed out and was rewarded with a kiss.

"She's shown an immense amount of kindness to make up for it as well. I am here to extend my loyalty." Fury replied with a kneel seeing the others look at Tristan.

"You wish to join our pack simply because she showed you kindness?" Tristan asked suspiciously thinking there might be something between them. Was this a lover of Elaina's?

"I think she might've showed him more then kindness." Crystal said offensively causing Elaina to stand instantly.

"Unlike you *Beta*, I show men nothing." Elaina growled seeing Crystal shrink behind Ravyn.

"You say that and yet the rumor is it's you and Rave." Ravyn replied causing Rave to stand and look at him.

"Me and Elaina are *friends*, and I hope that isn't your jealousy talking *brother*." Rave corrected causing the pack to start yelling back and forth.

"Can I say something?" Julie asked seeing everyone looking at her and quiet down. Julie walked up and stood beside Elaina. "Look, I've known Elaina since we were five. That's practically thirteen years, and you can take my word that she isn't one to give herself easily to someone. She only started to date three *months* ago when most girls start dating as soon as they enter high school.

"She only even started to date because the guy had seemed interested her and he'd been a good friend of ours. That's when Elaina went missing. For a week I had no idea where my best friend was and it scared me. Then she came back and I could tell something had changed, she was *guarded*, even against me. Then the truth came out. The guy I had told her to go out with was a vampire that had tried to rip her throat out before leaving her for dead." Julie saw Elaina rub the side of her throat looking a bit paler. "She knows how to see the best in people but she'd *never* jump a guy just because he's good looking. She prefers to get to know someone before trusting herself to them, like how she got to know all of you."

"Then I will be blunt, Elaina have you been *intimate* with him?" Tristan asked and pointed to Fury causing her to shake her head.

"No, I really haven't." she replied and she could see Ravyn waiting for the blush that happened when she lied but nothing happened.

"She's telling the truth." Tristan said because they would smell it if she were lying. "Why, may I ask, do you want to join *our* pack?"

"Actually I would like to challenge the previous Alpha." Fury replied causing murmurs erupt everywhere.

"Over my dead body!" Ravyn yelled causing Crystal to look taken aback.

"What does that mean?" Elaina asked Tristan thought it was amusing.

"He wants to fight Ravyn for the right to be Alpha…and to be *your* mate." Tristan explained causing her eyes to widen.

"No, no way." Elaina realized it was already hopeless because Fury had already issued the challenge. She saw Ravyn glare at Fury who had removed his shirt showing the tribal tattoos on his back and chest.

"Ravyn." Crystal murmured and clutched to his side.

"I don't know what's more pathetic. The fact that you ended with a Beta instead of an Alpha that is like her or the fact that you seem to be regretting your choice of mates." Fury baited causing Ravyn to initiate the fight by slashing at him but Fury blocked.

"NOT IN THE HOUSE!" Connor roared as Elaina saw them toppling towards Daisy causing her to run and knock both of them flying into the hallway.

"Yep, she's pissed." Julie said as everyone quieted while Daisy cried causing Ravyn and Fury to stop.

"You stupid jerks! You almost hurt Daisy! Both of you get the hell out until you can act like adults!" she snapped seeing Ravyn turn and leave angrily with Crystal following behind him.

"That was a good…" Fury started only to get smacked right across the face so hard his head snapped to the side.

"Don't you ever, *ever* endanger my family again." Elaina sounded so cold she believed any worse and he would've turned into a popsicle. She went in where Daisy cried before picking her up.

"Elaina is she alright?" Tristan asked as Elaina held Daisy safely.

"Yeah, she's just really scared right now. I'm going to take her home really quick and I'll be back." she murmured seeing him nod before everyone said good bye to Daisy. She hurried over and put Daisy in bed before heading back. She heard a crunch before Crystal ran out from nowhere and rammed her with a dagger.

Elaina saw Crystal smile as she stood there so Elaina ripped the dagger out before howling. She saw the others run out seeing Fury look at her stomach which was slowly healing just because the dagger had been silver.

"I think it's time for a new Alpha woman instead! I'm challenging you to the *death*!" Crystal yelled as Ravyn came out.

"Crystal no!" Ravyn yelled since he had already conceded his Alpha status to Tristan. "We're both Betas!"

"Oh shut up! I only wanted you because you were Alpha but you're a Beta now!" Crystal snapped causing the pack to gawk since Ravyn looked sullen. "I want to be the Alpha female and when that silver finishes poisoning her I will be."

"First blood magic and then silver. Do you care about anything except power?" Elaina asked as her blood fell into the snow in a pattern as she circled Crystal seeing her glower.

"Yes, wealth. I *refuse* to let you be an Alpha." Crystal bit out as Elaina closed the circle of blood.

"I give you my back Crystal, for you aren't worth receiving anything else." Elaina said and started walking away hearing a sizzle and screech when Crystal lunged.

"What is this?!" Crystal screeched and pounded on the barrier.

"I thought you would recognize *blood magic* when you saw it since you had no problem using it on me." Elaina replied seeing Tristan stare in awe.

"You can't kill her." Tristan informed her so Elaina grabbed the pendant from Dracula before mumbling words.

Elaina saw a cage appear on the ground and frantic squeaks came from it. She went over and picked it up seeing a ferret in it. "Darn, I was going for a rabbit." Elaina got out before collapsing into the snow hearing feet run to her.

"She turned Crystal into a ferret!" Julie exclaimed in hysterical laughter. "Ravyn I believe this is for you."

"I don't want her, let Tristan deal with her." Ravyn growled only to see Fury carry Elaina into the house.

"Let's take care of this wound." Tristan said before tearing the hole larger seeing it was bleeding a lot and Elaina was getting pale. He cut the poisoned flesh away hearing her cry out in pain but Fury held her down. "It won't heal."

"She needs blood, she's part vampire so she needs blood." Rave said seeing Elaina's eyes flash open showing ruby eyes. "I would suggest Ravyn but he's like her and they can't ever drink from each other."

"Everyone can leave, I'll provide for her what she needs." Fury replied to Tristan who shrugged showing it wasn't his business before closing the drapes and getting everyone out of the living room. He closed the doors and locked them before walking over seeing her breathing was shallow.

"Get. Away." She punctuated as he kneeled next to her.

"Sorry, I'm the Alpha. Ravyn resigned while Crystal was going homicidal on you. Looks like you have to accept me." Fury replied as he brushed the hair out of her face only to get his hand smacked away.

"No." she said before standing up slowly only to stumble. She needed blood fast but when Fury caught her against him his true scent started taking over. He smelled like rain and something with a citrus smell. It was soft yet tangy. She felt his hands span her back and hold her against him. She was already changing. "Mmm, citrus."

Fury froze because her voice sounded like bells so he looked seeing her completely pale but her eyes shone like rubies. Just like the vampire stone around her neck. He felt her curve a hand around his neck and pull him towards her. He didn't know what was going on but he liked it. She had gone straight from hating him to a seductive little vixen. When her breath touched his neck he let out such a low growl only to a get reward of her teeth raking his neck.

God Almighty, he felt like an idiot because he was building with anticipation. He felt his nails dig into her back by accident but she only sank her fangs into his neck. He thought it would hurt or something but it felt incredibly erotic. The pull of her mouth against his neck had sent him breathing raggedly. He felt her tongue brush across the holes which probably healed them before she pulled away.

Fury saw her glaring at him but he only stalked forward causing her to move away from him. He lunged for her but she dodged and whipped open the double doors showing no one in sight. He ran after her everywhere in the house but still he couldn't catch her.

There was a letter from the pack saying they'd be back in the morning. They had all gone for a run. He dove in the hallway and caught one of her ankles hearing her smack the ground. He avoided a kick to the face before pulling her to him. "Will you stop running?! I'm trying to make sure your stomach healed!" he yelled seriously feeling her freeze as he flipped her around see her looking extremely upset. "Jeez, you checked on me after hitting me with your car and that was before we were mates."

"I'm not your *mate*." she bit out but he wasn't paying attention to her at all. She saw him noticed that there was a small scar but that had been because the blade had been silver.

"Hmm, she scarred you. Good thing she's ferret in Tristan's care of I'd kill her for this." Fury replied seriously seeing her start scooting away but he caught her. "Will you stop acting like I'm going to attack you?!"

"You look like you are!" she yelled at him watching his face soften causing her to find it hard to swallow.

"I thought your friend Julie said you prefer to get to know someone before committing to them?" Elaina felt slightly pleased that he'd remembered Julie saying that about her. "Which is why I have a proposition for you."

"And what would that be? You talk and I listen?" she asked sarcastically only to watch him laugh.

"No, by your nineteenth birthday…"

"I'm nineteen in two months." she replied and saw him reconsider what he was going to say.

"Okay, by July if we've dated while getting to know each other and you don't like me then I'll step down as Alpha." he said and saw her actually considering it.

"And if you win?"

"Then you acknowledge me as your mate, we mark each other, and *consummate* our binding." Fury answered as her eyes sparkled about that. "That's when you'll shut up and listen to everything I have to say."

"Yeah right, only in your dreams."

"There too. Now first things first." Fury said before leaning to kiss her only to get his face caught in her hand and held back at bay.

"I don't kiss before the third date." she grumbled feeling her skin heat and saw him smile before pointing up. She looked up seeing the mistletoe there. "I'm also never one for tradition."

"Too bad, I am."

"No!" she yelled and swatted causing him to lean away and dodge. "If I'm agreeing to this then you can respect my wishes. I won't be with someone who doesn't know how to respect my body."

"Your body shouldn't be *respected* it should be *worshipped*, which is exactly what I'm trying to do if you'd sit still long enough." he got out huskily only to see her stand up wearing a frown.

"Then *worship* from a distance." Elaina grabbed her coat and slipped it in hearing him sigh and do the same before they left. "You three can come out now, it's not like anything exciting happened."

"Busted." Seth said in unison with Larkin and Blade.

"We're having a huge snowball fight tomorrow, you in?" Larkin in causing her hold up a thumb.

"Totally."

"Awesome, bring Daisy since she can play with the other kids. Julie and Connor are coming to. We'll meet on the porch to go to the field at ten." Blade said so she waved before going to the house where she felt Fury slide the jacket off her shoulders to hang it up.

"Hands off." she smacked his hands watching him stick them in the pockets. She went to her room and locked her door before changing into her bunny pajamas and curling up and going to sleep.

Chapter 6

Elaina woke up when her alarm went off so she reached forward and shut it off before getting up. She got dressed in jeans, a t-shirt, and a thick sweater. She put on three pairs of socks before wrapping her pant legs and sticking them in the snow boots before tying them tightly. She grabbed her gloves, hat, and winter coat before going down for breakfast. She saw Tricia sitting looking excited and Elaina smelled something weird.

"Aunt Tricia, you smell weird." Elaina replied as the others came in for breakfast. "Oh my gosh, Aunt Tricia are you p…"

"Pregnant? Yeah." Tricia laughed so Elaina hugged her aunt tightly. "Two and a half months."

"Congratulations." Fury replied seeing her flushing happily.

"Daisy has been invited to go hang out with the pack. You want me to take her so you and Uncle David have some *alone* time?" Elaina asked seeing Tricia go scarlet.

"If you wouldn't mind." Tricia murmured so Elaina went help Daisy get ready.

"Will you sing while I get ready?" Daisy asked before playing her favorite CD so Elaina started singing along not even hear Fury with a couple pack members stop outside the door.

"She can sing?" Fury asked seeing Seth and Larkin nod since they'd brought a whole bunch of clothes for him that seem to fit him fine.

"Yeah. She's in choir, she's a top swimmer, and she's MVP for our school's basketball teams. She also plays piano and guitar." Seth and Larkin took turns ticking off things before Fury laced the boots.

"Ready!" they heard Daisy call only to cause them to laugh because there was no way for her to get lost with a hot pink winter coat. "Isn't it pretty? Mommy bought it for me!"

"Very pretty." they said simultaneously seeing Elaina looking away so she wouldn't laugh.

"Come on, everyone is ready." Larkin picked up Daisy who went willingly before they raced out of the house since Talon and Torrin had already left.

"Careful it's…" Seth said right before Elaina hit the ground with a grunt. "icy."

"Ellie hurt her coxcux." Daisy said causing Elaina to laugh.

"It's coccyx not *coxcux*." Elaina got out before grabbing the sleds since there was a good sized hill near the meadow.

"What the hell's a coccyx?" Larkin asked but Seth only shrugged.

"Tailbone." Elaina informed and started to slip again only to get caught by Fury who was grinning from ear to ear.

"I thought you would've thought to wear shoes with traction." Fury saw her frown so he straightened her up seeing her start forward only to slip and slide down the road on her stomach looking more like a penguin then a wolf.

"I wanna do that!" Daisy said before running and sliding on her belly so they shrugged before doing the same thing.

Elaina saw Fury stop next to her but she only got up and scooted until she got near the sidewalk. "Hurry up you guys!" she heard Julie call so Elaina waited for Daisy and picked her up as Seth took the sleds. "We'll start without you!"

"That's what he said." Elaina grumbled allowing the others to laugh while Fury blinked a few times and looked at her.

"And you called *me* a pervert?" Fury asked only to watch her hurry over.

"Snowball fight!" Connor yelled once the kids were sledding and playing. He threw a snowball at Elaina who ducked causing it to hit Fury in the face. "Oops."

"Snowball fight!" Fury yelled and threw one back at Connor who dodged making it hit Seth.

Snowballs went flying causing her to dodge and throw them as well only to hear a train coming. She checked on the kids seeing no bright pink coat. She looked around as snowballs hit her in the stomach. She spotted kids playing on the tracks. One of them was Daisy. "DAISY GET OFF THE TRACKS!" she screamed because she could see the train coming around the corner.

"We told them not to go over there!" Tristan yelled seriously as she started running only to slip and stumbled because of her shoes.

Elaina ripped her shoes off before running in her socks feeling the cold seep into her feet as she ran seeing everything blur. She grabbed all four pups and threw them into the meadow as Daisy cried.

"I'm stuck!" she cried as the train's horn sounded.

Elaina pulled seeing it open before scooping up and jumping off the other side. She felt something collide with her head and then nothing. She heard Daisy crying hysterically as the train ran passed. She barely got her eyes open seeing snow falling to touch her cheeks. Her vision was blurred as someone leaned over her. "Elaina look at me." she heard Fury say seriously as her vision cleared seeing him looking gray.

"Ow." she grumbled before getting picked up wondering why she was so cold. "Why… why am I wet?"

"You weren't looking where you were jumping. You dodged the train but when you hit the ground Daisy stopped and you smacked your head on a rock before rolling in a creek. You were *drowning* Elaina." Fury saw her just black out as tremors started wracking her body. Her body was going into shock. He picked her up as Julie got there with Connor who picked up Daisy who was wailing. "I'm taking her back, Elaina is going to be fine Daisy."

"Really?" Daisy asked seeing everyone nod so Fury ran all the way back to the house.

Fury didn't see her uncle's car so he pulled out her key and opened the door and locked it behind him. He carried her to his room since he wasn't allowed in hers before stripped the wet clothes off her. He left on her undergarments which only caused his body to burn. He stripped down to his shorts before sticking her under the covers seeing her shaking get worse.

"Damn, she's probably going to smack me." he growled before climbing in next to her and holding her against him. He felt like he was holding an ice sculpture. He felt her cling to him despite being unconscious only because her body was trying to get warm. He had almost lost her. If he hadn't started running when she did he wouldn't be holding her now.

Elaina saw her dream turn into a nightmare as she watched herself trip not getting to Daisy in time. Elaina shot awake with a gasp feeling sweat covering her. Where was she? She felt her heart pounding fast as she panicked. Where was Daisy!? What happened?! Why wasn't she in the field!? She felt like she was suffocating as she started hyperventilating.

"Shh, calm down and take deep breaths." she heard Fury say as he rubbed her back gently causing her to feel herself starting to calm. Wait, why was she in bed with Fury?

"What…" she started only to get a finger held against her lips.

"This *is* a time where you should hear my side before accusing." he replied only to see her eyes glow luminescent in the moonlight. "First, this isn't what it looks like. When you jumped the opposite direction with Daisy you knocked yourself out when your head bashed against a rock and rolled into a creek. I almost didn't get to you in time. Your body was going into shock and if you remember anatomy books if I would've thrown you in a tub of hot water it would've killed you so I used body heat. The second is that Daisy is okay, she doesn't have a scratch on her, and the last is that you'd better never do something so stupid ever again. It's terrible when the first kiss between mates is when one is giving the other CPR. Tristan is scolding the kids for not listening and going near the tracks, although he probably excluded Daisy who was wailing thinking you were dead."

Elaina saw him remove his finger causing her to look at the blanket. "So Daisy is okay?" she asked hoarsely feeling relieved when he nodded in conformation. "Thank you, for saving me."

"You should've never ran but Daisy is your cousin. I'm just glad I got there in time." Elaina felt herself shift a bit under his gaze only to feel his fingers brush against her neck so she looked at him. His eyes twinkled like stars because of the light from outside.

"So does the hero get to kiss his damsel-in-distress?"

"You did, while giving me *CPR*." Elaina saw him grin and soon her curiosity got the best of her. "Do those have a meaning?"

"Life and Death, irony, pure and simple." he answered and leaned down letting his lips brush against her shoulder. "You didn't answer my question. I answered yours so you should answer mine."

"What was your question?" Elaina couldn't remember what he'd asked as he continued to tease her shoulder. She saw him look up and grin as his thumb touched her lower lip with a pin drop of blood welling up in it.

"Kissing, is it out of the question? Or do you need another two dates?" Fury saw her eyes start glowing but it was different. He could see a red tint mixed in the luminescence of her eyes making him curious. He saw her lips barely part, it was an invitation that he couldn't resist.

Fury delved into her mouth feeling her hands grab his shoulders as if to push him away but they didn't. He felt her tongue caress his so he wrapped an arm around her shoulders. He had cheated but he really didn't care, it was working.

Elaina snapped out of the haze trying to take over and realized what was happening. If he wanted to cheat then she'd teach him a lesson. She pulled sashes out of the drawer after getting closer hearing him groan. Attraction was heavy in the air. She tied first sash around his wrist and tied the second to his other wrist.

"And what are these for?" Fury saw her eyes half open as a sexy smile curved her mouth.

"A game, do you want to play?" her voice was throaty which made his attraction even more obvious. "Is that a yes or a no?"

"Yes." he got out so she bite the tip of her tongue before licking the inside of the sash on each wrist.

"Just lay back and relax." she purred against his mouth after straddling his waist seeing him do just that thinking she was into this. She kissed him but while she did she tied his hands seeing the bedposts glow. She then repeated the same thing on his ankles and tied them. The posts glowed as she finished the spell before starting to get dressed.

"What are you doing?' Fury asked seeing her slip her jeans on and button them.

"To think I was actually really considering kissing a foul piece of crap like you. Do you think I'm stupid or something? Why would you even try using blood against me?" Elaina felt the haze of attraction he had vanish instantly as he pulled trying to brake them. "I used blood against you just like you did to me."

"This is cruel."

"No, what's cruel is that I was grateful that you were concerned about me only to use blood so I'd be affectionate. Here's a news flash, I was going to let you kiss me before you did something but now you won't ever kiss me until I believe you won't do something stupid like that again." Elaina saw the confusion vanish as he looked hopeful.

"You mean you were actually going to let me kiss you?"

"Not now, not *ever* until you learned your lesson." she replied before slipping her shirt on and grabbing the last of her clothes. She wrote a note on a piece of paper and taped it to his chest. "Oh and no one else can untie you, only me."

"What if I have to use the bathroom?" Fury saw her shrug before leaving so he struggled against the sashes only to feel them hold. "Damn it."

When Elaina woke for breakfast she saw Blade and Larkin come in the kitchen as she ate her cereal. "Where's Fury?" they asked as she took a bite of her cereal before smiling brightly.

"He's tied up at the moment, I can take a message if you want?" Elaina saw them look at each other before running up the stairs. She heard them laugh hysterically from up their.

"Damn it Elaina!" she heard Fury yell as her aunt walked in.

"Elaina what did you do?" Tricia asked in shock as she heard laughing and yelling.

"He tried to be perverted so I tied him to the bed posts." Elaina saw Tricia look amused at that as she ate.

"Good girl." Tricia replied before tossing her a poptart. "Make sure he gets something to eat."

"Yes ma'am." Elaina want up the stairs seeing Blade and Larkin doubled over laughing as Fury looked irritated. "Okay, stop picking on him you two. Visiting hours are over."

"See ya Fury." they coughed before hurrying away so she walked in and closed the doors.

"I can't believe you let them in here!" Fury was ticked causing him to strain against the restraints only to hiss when they rubbed his wrists raw.

"I didn't, they came up while I was eating breakfast. How did you feel about them seeing you like this?" she asked causing him to stop straining and flop back down.

"I felt like an idiot."

"Now you know how I felt." Fury looked at her and realized he'd made her feel like a fool. "Look, I'm a guy. It's in my nature to do something stupid but I am capable of making up for them."

"Sure." she replied before going over and untied his feet before rubbing the chafed skin gently. "Jeez, you acted like I'd leave you here for days."

"You mean you weren't?"

"I'm not *cruel* Fury, I'm fair." Elaina saw him nod slowly so she untied his left hand and then his right before she held out the poptart to him. "Breakfast, my aunt thought the *prisoner* should get to eat."

"My thanks to your aunt then." Fury ate poptart as she sat there looking out the window. She seemed a bit sullen about something. "What's wrong?"

"Get dressed, we're going somewhere." she replied and went to her room because she had something important to do today. She got dressed in blue jeans, a white camisole, and deep blue off-the-shoulder knitted sweater, and her more fashionable snow boots. She put gloves and her jacket on just in time to see him walk out in jeans and a gray long sleeve t-shirt. He slipped on the jacket before walking towards her.

"Where are we going?" Fury saw her say nothing as she went downstairs and grabbed the car keys. "It's not within walking distance?"

"Nope. Aunt Tricia I'll be back later!" she called before going to her car watching him get in the front passenger seat. She buckled her seatbelt so he followed suit. She'd already hit him with the car so she didn't need him getting hurt in a wreck. She started the car and drove off.

"So where are we going?" Fury saw her look like he just needed to be quiet and let her drive. "Okay the suspense is killing me!"

"We're going somewhere really important, you get to meet someone really important to me." Elaina got to town before parking in front of a floral shop. "Be right back."

Fury saw her go in only to come out ten minutes later holding a bouquet of orange roses. "What are…"

"You're going to need those." Elaina replied so he held the flowers before getting curious and smelling them.

"They smell good."

"Peach roses are her favorite." Elaina saw some kind of relief was over him after finding out it was a female. She got on the back roads to Pennsylvania as Fury looked at her.

"How important is this trip?"

"Very important, it's the first time I've been able to drive myself there. I didn't want to go by myself." Elaina felt his left hand take her right but she kept her face forward.

"Then I'm glad you picked me to come with you." Fury meant it to, if this trip was important for whoever she was going to see then he wanted to be beside her. However, about an hour and a half later when they started into a cemetery he stated having doubts. Who could possibly be buried here?!

"We have to walk now." Elaina said and got out of the car and started walking. She only knew he was following because of the crunch of the snow. She counted rows before heading for the angel. In the middle. She got over seeing the name was covered as Fury stood behind her.

"Who is buried here?" Fury saw her lean and brush the snow off the name.

"My mom, the flowers are for her. Today is the anniversary of the day she died." Elaina explained so Fury leaned down and sat the flowers between the feet of the angel.

"The car wreck you mentioned." he said watching her nod slowly. "How old was she?"

"Twenty years old, she was sixteen when she had me." Elaina replied feeling him take her hand and squeeze it tightly.

"When is your birthday anyway?" Fury saw her grin about that wondering if that was funny.

"Valentine's Day." Elaina saw him smile at that as she let her other hand brush the pillar of rock. It was hard and cold reminding her of how she'd been most of her life. She'd hated for acting that way but it had kept her safe. She'd never been hurt or heartbroken, she'd never cried about being stood up, but she'd missed out on everything fun because she'd been too scared to join in.

"Penny for your thoughts?" Fury asked only to see her shake her head so he took a risk and slipped an arm around her shoulders.

"Don't worry, I don't have anything to tie you up with if that's what you're thinking." she heard him laugh before pulling her completely against him. Elaina heard her stomach growl. "Come on, let's go get lunch."

Fury walked next to her on the way back to the car intending to keep the silent promise he'd made on her mother's grave. He saw her whip into a parking place in front of a *Pizza Hut* so he got out with her and went in seeing there was a handful of people there.

They were led to a booth in a back corner and Fury waited until she sat down before sitting next to her. "My name's Rachel, I'll be waiting on you. What can I get you two to drink?" the waitress asked with her eyes all over Fury but Elaina wasn't one to get jealous.

"A Sprite please." Elaina said as Fury ordered a 'Mr. Pibb.'

"Okay so you're in choir, on the swimming team, *and* the basketball team. Any clubs?" Fury asked before the waitress appeared with their drinks. "Thank you."

"You are very welcomed. Have you two thought about what you'd like to eat?" Rachel asked as they looked at the menus so she took the time to look over the guy.

"No, we'll need a few more minutes." Fury answered seeing her nod and hurry off right before Elaina erupted into quiet laughter. "What?"

"Nothing, and no I'm not in any clubs…unless student council counts because I'm student body president." Elaina answered through the laughs so Fury shrugged. "So you say you're immortal and you're twenty-three. How old are you *really*?"

"A little over eight hundred years old. I was a Celt." Fury replied causing Elaina to almost choke on her soda.

"Jeez, you're one old geezer. You look good for your age though." Elaina snickered only to hear him chuckle at that. "So what do you eat on your pizza?"

"Anything is fine, I'm not a picky eater." Fury murmured as he lowered his head to her neck not even seeing Rachel return only to gawk.

"So lucky." Rachel sighed causing Fury to go back looking at his menu. "Have you… decided on what to order?"

"A large stuff crust with extra pepperoni and cheese." Elaina could see the girl going red in the face as she wrote it down before hurrying off. "Poor girl almost died on the spot."

"Tell me the goals that you have."

"Goals?"

"For the future, whether it be personal goals or goals for the pack." Fury saw her just shrug as if there was nothing.

"I mean I've been scouted but not in any place close."

"Scouted?" Fury saw her nod slowly.

"For basketball, I've been scouted for a bunch of colleges but I don't even think that's possible with me being an Alpha. If I leave then the others have to move as well and everyone likes it there, I'm not going to make them move just to play college basketball." Elaina took another drink of her soda only to rub her head because it was pounding.

"You're a selfless person Elaina." Fury saw her just look out the window. "Sometimes it's okay to be selfish though. You aren't the only Alpha anymore."

"Okay so say I played college basketball, what am I suppose to do if I get an offer to play on a professional team in a different *country*?" she asked seeing him look like that might actually be a problem. "Exactly."

"Do you always think so far ahead?"

"Pretty much." Elaina saw him pick up her hand and raise it to his mouth to kiss her knuckles. She felt his teeth drag along them causing her to swat his shoulder because Rachel was on her way over with the pizza.

"Any refills?"

"Nope, we're good." Fury answered as Elaina went to eat a piece but he intercepted the pizza as Rachel left.

"Ugh, now I don't want it." she grumbled and let it go seeing him cock his head to the side. "I don't like eating or drinking after people."

"Anything else that irritates you?" Fury asked but she only ate her pizza.

"So what was it like being a Celt?"

Elaina saw him frown instantly and go back to eating leaving a huge and awkward silence between them. They didn't even talk on the way back to the house or even when they got there. She closed her door and went in the house after stomping her feet seeing Fury doing the seem. He seemed to be in extremely foul mood for some reason she didn't understand so she went to her room and flung the door shut.

Fury deviated from heading to his room and walked into hers seeing her booting up her computer. "You didn't knock and I didn't say you could come it." he heard her say so he went over and flipped the wheeled chair around.

"I think it's amazing at how you get angry just because I didn't answer your question." he bit out only to see that her face was perfectly calm. In fact, she seemed a bit shock that he was so upset.

"Why would I be angry? I can just look up Celts on the internet and find out myself." Elaina saw him look like that was worse.

"You should hear about my past from me."

"I'm not looking up your past though, I'm looking up your heritage." she pointed out and saw him pause as if she'd said something he hadn't considered. "You thought I was asking about your personal past? I just wanted to know what all a Celt did. I wasn't being specific Fury."

"Oh, I thought you were, I guess I misinterpreted your question wrong."

"Meaning we've been ignoring each other for nothing." she added causing him to glower at her like she should've kept it shut. "It's not my fault you misunderstood."

"You are driving me completely insane." Fury grumbled as he closed his eyes to calm down before something brushed against his forehead.

"Ah, but I don't think you really mind that much." she replied simply right before his eyes snapped open showing him looking stunned.

"Did you just kiss me?"

"Don't sound so shocked, you looked cute being all flustered like that. Now shoo so I can start reading." Elaina said before his eyes darkened causing her heart to start pounding. She leaned away when he went to kiss her. "One date to go."

"Hmm?"

"We've had two dates now, I told you no more kissing until *after* the third one." she replied before touching her finger to his nose briefly. "Unless you do something stupid again and then it'll be pushed back passed the fifth date."

"Are you serious?" He asked so she gave a stern nod. "But…"

"Don't make me break out those sashes again." Elaina saw him lay on the bed as she read everything from Celtic legend to famous battles and warriors. "Exquisite. I got a question?"

"What?" Fury groaned because she'd been reading for about two hours straight now.

"Did you carry a sporran?" she asked slyly and turned causing Fury to sigh.

"Yes, I carried a sporran."

"Then that means you wore a kilt huh?" Elaina saw him nod after covering his eyes with an arm so she plop on her stomach next to him. "I have extra skirts if you need them."

"What?" Fury took his arm off his face as she laughed quietly at him. "Why you little…"

Fury pinched her side hearing her laugh before covering her mouth. He started tickling her sides causing her to laugh hysterically. "Come on…stop…can't…breath …laughing…too hard." he watched her get out because she was practically crying from laughing so hard. He gave in and stopped tickling her ribs seeing her trying to catch her breath.

"I surrender." she said through an Irish accent and launched into another laugh as he shook his head. "Okay but seriously, so with the purse and the skirt…"

"A sporran and a kilt."

"Like I said, a purse and a skirt, did that mean you were Scottish?" she asked seeing him look hesitant before shaking his head.

"I was born and raised in Ireland but I helped fight in Scotland."

"Wow, did you know William Wallace then?"

"What did you just say?" Fury heard the name but he couldn't believe she'd said it.

"William Wallace, did you know him?"

"Yeah, I did. So now that you know me how about telling me about you?" Fury saw her look practically impish at that and he found it cute.

"I'm pretty much set in stone here Fury, I'm half werewolf and half vampire." Elaina answered and knew it wasn't what he meant but he was hiding something from her so she'd look up his name later. "So you used a claymore then?"

"We called it a *claidheamh mór*." Fury replied and heard her repeat what he said.

"What's that mean?"

"It means '*great sword*' in Gaelic." Fury listen to her say it again and smile so he leaned down and brushed his lips against her forehead. She was definitely worth the effort in getting to know.

"Hey, I said no more kissing until the third date." she pointed out and saw him look like she'd ruined the mood right before she snorted. "I was just messing with you."

"I wish you'd stop doing that."

"I know, but people in hell want ice water and you don't see them getting it any time soon." Elaina saw him gawk before she yawned and started drifting. "So does that mean you're a Gael?"

"A Gael?"

"Yeah, since you speak Gaelic you're a Gael right?" she asked tiredly with her eyes closed, she never did get the answer since she fell asleep curled up against him.

It was like she blinked and it was time to celebrate New Year's. The pack had left to go spend time with other family or their spouses while the ones across the road started planning a party. They were going to have snacks and drinks. Her and Fury were going and when Daisy asked to go Tricia quickly intervened.

Apparently the household members all had dates except for Ravyn who was still trying to deal with the fact that Crystal hadn't really loved him at all. She had loved the power that came with his name until people stopped trusting him. She spent the whole day trying to decide what to wear.

She was looking at her reflection in the mirror after putting on a pale blue halter dress right as Fury walked in. She looked finding him in black dress pants and a button up dark blue shirt. She saw him continue to tug at the collar so she walked over and undid the top four buttons before looking through her shoes seeing her silver ones so she put them on and looked at them as if deciding.

"You look beautiful Elaina." Fury murmured as he kissed her temple and unhooking the hair clip letting her hair fall around her. "Even more so now."

"Stop sucking up already." Elaina knew he wasn't but she still liked to mess with him. "That reminds me, I have something for you."

"And what would that be?" he asked before she pointed to the box on the bed. Fury felt hesitant as he looked at the Fed Ex box before using a nail to open it seeing the little Styrofoam peanuts in it. He reached in and, to his amazement, pulled out none other then a sporran. "Elaina you…"

"Well you didn't get a *pack* present or a Christmas present so I figured better late then never." she said as she put on the blackberry flavored lip gloss that she liked so much. She watched him approach her in their reflections before wrapping his arms around her shoulders and burying his face into her neck.

"Thank you."

"Your welcome." Elaina touched his arm lightly before he sat it on her dresser but she saw his fingers brushing across the surface. She could tell that it had meant more then anything to see something like that. "There's a kilt in there too."

"What is it with you and men wearing skirts?"

"I was just joshing you, as for men wearing skirts I find it hilarious." Elaina added her eyeliner before slipping on her jacket. "Ready?"

"I thought you'd never get done." Fury teased but the time was worth spent despite the dress being too short for his taste. He escorted her across the road hearing music playing so they went in and he took her coat.

"Hey! Drinks are back there!" Blade laughed merrily as he pointed as girls laughed from the living room.

Elaina went to the kitchen seeing a good bit of alcohol, she got the punch instead. It had a tangy yet sharp flavor but she liked it. She saw Fury get soda before they went into the living room. All the girls started dancing together leaving the guys to sit and talk.

"So how's it going with Elaina?" Rave asked and saw Fury nod. "I heard you woke up tied to a bedpost."

"I pretty much deserved it. I did something stupid."

"Don't we all." Larkin cheered to that as Fury looked at her dancing.

"She's a great girl." Fury said and heard them wish him luck.

"Oh cheer up Ravyn." Seth said and clapped Ravyn on the back only to see him get up and leave the living room. "Poor guy, I bet he's really regretting his decision on giving up Elaina."

"I don't feel sorry for him. He had a great girl and yet he decided to throw it away for a stupid one." Rave replied before Seth stood up.

"Drink run, anyone want anything?" he asked so everyone voiced their opinion on drinks so he hurried out.

"Why are you sitting down for Fury, go dance with Elaina." Rave gestured to her dancing with the others girls and Julie who also happened to be dancing in front of Connor.

"I don't dance." he said quickly only to get ushered towards her.

"Hey Elaina, someone wants to dance with you!" Larkin called seeing her turn and look at Fury standing there.

"Uh…no, I don't think…" Fury started seriously only to feel any protest die when she smiled and held out her hand to him. He took her hand only to walk towards her when she gave a small tug. He found himself matching her tempo as she held his hands with her own.

"See, you can dance just fine." Elaina murmured trying to figure out why she felt so giddy as they danced. She got another cup of punch after a couple hours and drank some before continuing to dance with Fury. "Be right back."

"Where…"

"Bathroom." she answered quickly and hurried to the bathroom only to find it occupied so she went to the one upstairs. She felt so much better as she walked out only to see Ravyn start out of his room only to turn and go right back in. "Ravyn are you okay?"

"Do I look like I'm okay?" he bit out only to calm down.

"Look, I'm sorry about how things ended between you and Crystal."

"I'm not, I was so stupid to believe what she said. I should've never given you up, I should've just ignored the lies." Ravyn growled causing Elaina to hear the slurs as he walked towards her. "I want to be your Alpha again."

"I don't think that's possible." Elaina saw rage enter his eyes turning them a dark red. She felt alarms going in her head but her body wasn't reacting to them.

"You *actually* like that no good piece of crap *rogue*?" Fury growled before grabbing her arms making her wince because it hurt. "He doesn't deserve you, *I* do."

"Let go Ravyn." she growled and tried to fight him off as her mind got fuzzy. "Let me go."

Ravyn flung her to the floor making her skin her hands before he kneeled and flipped her over. "I'm going to steal you from him." Ravyn bit out and started kissing her making her slap him so he cracked her back. "Stay still!"

Elaina screamed at the top of her lungs as Ravyn tried to kiss her again. She raked his face leaving four marks across his left cheek as she continued to fight him off. She saw Ravyn suddenly get flung away from her and she was picked up by Fury who looked like he could kill Ravyn and not think twice.

"Stay out of this *rogue*, she's mine!" Ravyn snapped so Fury punched him knocking him out cold as Elaina shook in his arms.

Fury went down the stairs grabbed their coats and marched back to the house without a word to anyone. He carried her to her room and sat her on her bed before going to the kitchen and making a cup of hot chocolate. He returned to her room seeing she'd changed into a tank and shorts. The torn and imbrued dress lay in tatters in the corner covered by other dirty clothes.

"Here, drink this." he said only to see her run from the room and hear her get sick.

Elaina brushed her teeth and took a warm wet cloth to her skin so hard she'd scrubbed it raw. She returned to the room and sat down before taking a sip of the drink. It scalded her tongue a little but she didn't care. She felt tears start running down her cheeks because she just couldn't help it.

"Shh, come here, I got you." Fury murmured before pulling her into his arms, she didn't utter a single protest. He held her tightly as she buried her face into his shirt. He had wanted to kill Ravyn right there but the man had been drunk causing the wolf in him to speak out what the man didn't want to say. Did Elaina feel the same way? Did she want Ravyn back now that Crystal was out of the picture? He should've asked her but he was scared to know the answer.

Elaina sat there until she wasn't crying anymore. "I didn't…I didn't think that anyone would hear me over the music." she choked out before looking up at him as his one hand played with her hair.

"You scream like a banshee, I definitely heard you." Fury replied lightly seeing her actually laugh about that despite looking shaken over what could've happen. "Are you okay though? I mean he didn't…"

"No, he didn't." she interjected quickly feeling apprehensive of what could've happen had Fury not intervened. "I'm just still a bit…shocked."

"I know."

"How do you know that?" she asked before gesturing that she was practically cradled against him. "Oh, well it's not like you're complaining."

"Neither are you, that's why I'm feeling a bit confused." Fury saw her look at her legs so he dipped his head to look at her. "Elaina why…"

Elaina was really trying to ignore the comfort, kindness, and safety she felt but it's like she'd been acting completely different ever since she'd hit him with her car. She knew she liked him, she didn't know if it was love, but she did like him immensely. So much in fact, that when he dipped his head to look at her she kissed him.

Fury sat there completely stunned as one of her hands curled around the back of his head. He watched as she pulled away slightly and bit her lower lip. "What…did…" he got out seeing her rub the back of her neck.

"Guess I like you more then I was letting on." she murmured shyly and Fury felt like he'd just won the lottery.

"So you like me?"

"I already said that." Elaina said and playfully hit him in the gut. She looked at him right before she was pulled into a deep kiss that promised everything she could think of. This kiss didn't just electrify her, it also made her feel that she was on fire. It was like he knew every place Ravyn had touched her because she could feel his fingers brush against every single offensive spot she'd tried to get rid of.

Her tongue danced with his as she let one of her hands unbuttoned the shirt he wore. She found her finger tracing one of the many tribal tattoos. That's when the kiss went from calm and collected to demanding and urgent.

Fury angled her head against his to deepen the kiss between them. When a moan escaped her he found himself shifting to lay her on the bed under him. He stretched her arms up before letting his hands run up them and clasping her hands. That's when she squirmed to get out from under him. He looked down seeing her looking like she wanted to crack him.

"What did I do now?" he grumbled after letting go of her hands.

"I'm not going to sleep with you." she said seriously seeing him maneuver to lay on his side. "Well, not in a literal sense anyway."

"Not in a literal sense." he repeated and saw her nod as he heard her stomach growl. "Hungry?"

"Yeah." Elaina saw his eyes lighten considerably as she sat up and kicked her feet over to slip her feet in the slippers. "You can come down with if you want."

"Like you had to tell me that." Fury heard her laugh at that so he walked behind her as he held her hands.

The house was dark and quiet as they tiptoed downstairs to kitchen where she got a small pint of ice cream. She grabbed a spoon before hopping onto the counter letting her feet dangle above the floor. She hummed to herself as she opened the container as he searched for spoons as she took a bite of the ice cream.

"Where are the spoons?" He looked at her seeing her holding out the same spoon she'd used with ice cream on it. He walked over and lick the ice cream from the spoon. "I guess this'll work."

They sat there in the dark alternating between bites of ice cream. They talked more and Elaina noted that he didn't mind standing in front of her. She was holding out ice cream and he was leaning down when the light flipped on causing him to jump. She felt the ice cream land on top of her thigh.

"What are you two doing in the kitchen?" Tricia said before yawning and looking at them suspiciously. "It's almost three in the morning."

"Early morning snack." Elaina said and held up the pint of ice cream.

"Whatever, make sure you don't make a mess." Tricia said after grabbing a juice and going back out after flipping the light off.

"I thought she'd yell or something." Fury saw Elaina shake her head before seeing the glob of ice cream causing him to grin at her.

"What are you…" she started only to feel her breath catch as his fingers curled around the bottom of her leg before licking away the ice cream.

"I don't think I need a spoon now." Fury murmured after finishing only to feel the heat radiating from her face. He knew she was flustered but in a good way. Grinning he leaned down and nibbled on her lower lip only to kiss her when she parted them. Fury saw her pull away to catch her breath as her hands rested on his shoulders. A laugh rumbled in his throat as she calmed only to look at him accusingly but he feigned innocence.

"You did that on purpose." she grumbled before crumpling the empty ice cream carton and tossing it seeing it go into the garbage can. Elaina slid off the counter and barely had room to stand there because Fury was directly against her.

"Come on, you're tired." Fury murmured after she'd stifled a yawn. He led her to her room where they laid down and curled up under the covers. As he fell asleep with Elaina in his arms he knew all his questions had been answered. She was *his* and his alone. If Ravyn tried anything like what he had done earlier then Fury would rip his into shreds.

Chapter 7

As soon as school resumed Elaina found that she didn't have as much time to spend with Fury who had moved out of her aunt's and gotten a small apartment. She had so much to do that she could barely grasp what day it was until she got to school.

Elaina sauntered into the salon after school feeling exhausted since the choir was getting ready for the huge school-wide talent show, the school was being decorated for Valentine's Day which was approaching fast, and the gym was set up for it. It was a formal dance that everyone was excited for, it was *almost* bigger then prom. Elaina needed to get ready for that one too.

Elaina got her hair highlighted and trimmed to make it more healthy looking. She got her nails manicured before they were painted with a Valentine's Day design. She also got a pedicure and had them painted a deep magenta. She drove to the mall and met up with Julie to go dress shopping.

"What do you think about this one?" Julie asked and held up a hot pink dress causing Elaina to make a gagging noise. "Thought not."

"I can't believe they gave a color code for dresses. Some people don't like wearing white, pink, red, *or* purple." Elaina said as she saw deep pink dress with a purple hue in it. She grabbed it seeing it was actually her size so she went into the changing room and slipped it on before walking out. "Yay or nay?"

"Yay, it looks really good on you Elaina." Julie said as she looked at the halter styled dress. It had a rhinestone strap that went behind the neck and an empire waistline. "You should definitely wear it."

"Okay, this one it is." Elaina replied before going in and changing.

Elaina helped Julie pick one out before they bought them and headed out of the store seeing Bethany and her little clique on their way in only to stop. "Looks like we shouldn't shop here, the loser squad got here first." Elaina saw Kimberly say. "So are you to going to the Valentine dance together since you couldn't get dates? That'd be cute that way you two aren't the only ones sitting by the walls."

Elaina saw them laughing right before the pack started by only to see Fury stop and turn to look right at her. She realized she must've been staring because Bethany and the others to turn.

"Oh my, who are *they*?" Kimberly said as Fury and Connor headed for them. "Completely gorgeous."

"Julie what are you two doing here?" Connor asked causing Bethany and her friends to turn and gawk at them.

"Dress shopping for the dance. Shouldn't you be looking for a tux to wear?" Julie asked only pause and cock her head to think for a moment. "Why are you all here anyway?"

"We're here to get a p…" Connor started only to get elbowed by Fury since Elaina was there, they saw her look suspicious instantly.

"What dance?" Fury and Connor asked seriously only to watch both girls cross their arms in unison and frown.

"Uh-oh, we must've forgot something important." Connor said right before Julie looked at Elaina.

"Let's go get something to eat and leave them to think about something they forgot." Julie said only to see Connor give a fake pout. "Damn, he does that better then me now."

"Julie." Elaina groaned as Fury tried the same thing but she couldn't find it cute on him, it looked ridiculous. "That's not going to work Fury."

"Ouch." Julie snickered as Connor looped an arm around her shoulders so she put an arm around his waist. "Looks like Fury isn't getting forgiven as easily."

"Wanna bet?" Fury asked before pulling Elaina's head to his letting their lips meld together causing Julie to laugh because Bethany and her friends had went scarlet. He pulled away slightly seeing Elaina pinken slightly. "You're even wearing your blackberry lip gloss."

"Now *that's* determination." Julie giggled before Fury obviously got forgiven by Elaina who was tucked under his arm.

"Wait a minute, these are your boyfriends?" Kimberly asked like there was no way it could be possible.

"Actually I'm Julie's fiancée." Connor corrected causing Bethany to signal the other girls to go into the store.

"So how's your grandma?" Elaina asked and saw Bethany smile.

"She's great, I'll see you at the dance. Bye, Elaina. Bye, Julie." Bethany said before heading into the store like she could possibly own the place.

"Who is she?"

"That's Bethany, us three are *frenemies*." Julie replied seeing him and Fury look puzzled at that. "In the public eye we pretend to despise each other but really we're friends."

"Why?" Connor asked seeing them both roll their eyes.

"Boys." they said before walking off without them.

"So what dance is it?" Fury asked after they caught up.

"The Valentine's dance. All the girls with dates wear pink, red, or purple while girls without dates wear white. The guys either wear a tux or dress pants and a dress shirt. Elaina and I were here to get our dresses." Julie informed seeing Fury look at Elaina who looked elsewhere. "Elaina? You haven't asked him yet?"

"No, she hasn't." Fury replied causing Elaina to flush so dark she almost went purple herself.

"I was planning to ask later." she grumbled feeling his hand take hers. "Wanna go with me?"

"Of course I'm going with you." Fury murmured before kissing her knuckles noticing that Julie and Connor were grinning at them like idiots. "Where are you two doing now?"

"We have to get shoes." Julie replied so the guys accompanied them to the shoe store before sneaking off to do something. "Hey, wouldn't it be amazingly romantic if Fury proposed to you on Valentine's day?"

"Julie…" Elaina started only to see Julie look at her, she watched Julie's eyes widen.

"Elaina, you love him don't you?" Julie asked seeing Elaina start crying silently so she went over and sat next to her. "What's wrong?"

"I got accepted to a college Julie." Elaina informed only to a huge hug from Julie who squealed excitedly.

"That's so great! I'll be going here and so will you!"

"No Julie, I haven't gotten an acceptance letter for the college, it's in Australia." Elaina murmured and watched Julie yank away showing a deep frown. "So far it's the only college I got accepted to."

"Why so…"

"Hey, we're back. Why is Elaina crying?" Connor asked as the rest of the pack waited outside while Fury stood next to him.

"It's a girl thing." Julie lied and could tell they didn't believe her but they accepted it thinking it was a *personal* issue. "We got our shoes, lets go."

Julie walked next to Connor and couldn't believe that her best friend and pack sister would likely be leaving and going to a completely different country for college. She saw Fury give her a questioning look but she only shook her head before tightening her arm around Connor's waste. What would Elaina do if Fury *did* propose to her on Valentine's Day?

"Could I ride with you?" Fury asked seeing her nod simply but it almost looked as if it was on reflex, like she'd heard what he'd said but she wasn't really paying attention. "Elaina?"

"What?"

"What's wrong?" Fury saw her shake her head but he knew something was bothering her. He got in the front seat of her car as she buckled herself in. He saw her go to start the car so he stopped her. "What…"

"I don't want to talk about it okay!?" she yelled seriously watching him look wary. "Please, just drop it!"

"I think I'll walk." Fury got out of the car hearing her start swearing to herself but she didn't come after him. Maybe she was starting to regret picking him and wanted Ravyn back? If she wasn't going to fight for him why should he fight for her? He decided that he wasn't going to. He'd let Ravyn have her if they wanted each other that much.

Elaina drove to the house and made dinner only to see that Fury didn't show like he was suppose to. Maybe he needed to cool off? She got a shower feeling herself calm down about the whole college situation. She curled under the covers but she was restless. Either she'd been staying with him in his apartment to sleep next to him or he'd come over and sleep next to her.

Elaina woke up after only three hours of sleep but she continued to lay in her bed staring at the ceiling. She had decided to tell Fury about her getting accepted when he came to get her tonight for the dance. Elaina spent the day watching television until four before going to the salon to get her hair done.

It was curled and pinned up elegantly causing her to smile before driving back to the house. She stood in front of her mirror as she did her makeup for the dance seeing the purple smoky eye look great so she added the blackberry lip gloss since it seemed to be Fury's favorite. She got in her dress and zipped up the side before slipping the heels on.

"Happy Birthday!" Daisy said and popped into the room with a bouquet of red roses.

"Awe, thank you Daisy." Elaina murmured before smelling them. "They're absolutely beautiful."

"You look pretty too Ellie." Daisy said before Tricia came in and put little gemstones in her hair.

"Now we wait for your prince in shining armor to arrive." Tricia giggled so they went up and watched a movie.

Elaina felt excited when the doorbell rang so she walked to the door and straightened the door only to frown seeing Ravyn there in dress pants and shirt. "Ravyn what the hell are you doing here?" she bit out seriously since she no longer had sympathy for him anymore, not after what he had tried to do.

"I'm here to escort you to your dance."

"I already have a date, who I happen to be waiting for."

"Fury isn't coming, apparently at the next meeting he's resigning as Alpha." Ravyn informed only to see her bare her teeth at him.

"Stop. Lying." she punctuated with a bite to her words seeing him smile slowly.

"I'm not lying, come the next meeting you'll be *mine*." Ravyn heard her snarling deep in her throat and it was so feral he moved away from her quickly.

"I won't *ever* be yours Ravyn." she hissed icily and slammed the door in his face as her heart started breaking in her chest. She saw him go back to his house so she pulled on her coat and left the house.

Elaina took off running and got to the apartment complex only to smell his scent leaving the complex. Had he planned on meeting her at the dance? She followed it quickly only to get to a biker bar causing her to feel her insides sink. Elaina heard cheering inside so she went in only to see Fury doing a body shot off a girl she didn't know and could care less about.

"What a pretty little thing you are." one guy started only to back away when she glared at him. "Jeez, no one can take a compliment."

"Kiss! Kiss! Kiss!" the crowd started to cheer and she saw Fury actually do it.

Elaina felt tears start running down her cheeks as the bartender looked at her and then Fury. "Hey man, is that your girlfriend?" the bartender asked as he tapped on Fury's shoulder before gesturing to Elaina.

Elaina saw Fury look only to look at her like she wasn't even really there. "Not anymore." she watched him say causing her to be so mad she stomped over and hooked him right in the jaw knocking him to the floor.

"Nice punch!"

"Shut up!" she snapped at the guy she didn't even know before look at Fury. "You stood me up for my school dance on my *birthday* to come here!? I *hate* you!"

"What a jerk." the girl he'd kissed said before moving away from him as if he was diseased or something.

"You're disgusting." Elaina said before spinning on her heels and leaving as tears blinded her. She ran from the bar only trip over something causing her to tear her dress and skin her knees and palms.

"Elaina!" she heard Fury yell angrily as she stood slowly only to keep walking away. "Elaina stop!"

"Why? Want me to watch you kiss someone else!?" she yelled after turning causing him to stop instantly. "I can't believe...actually no, apparently once a rogue always a rogue right?"

"What's wrong? Ravyn not show up to take you to your little dance?"

"Yes and that's the whole problem! I'm here waiting for you and that stupid jerk shows up!" she yelled seeing a couple peek out. "Get back in the damn bar you bunch of eavesdroppers!"

"Yes ma'am!" they yelled and closed the door quickly.

"Well I'd thought I'd let you go to the dance with the person you really wanted." Fury bit out only to watch her glower.

"What made you think I'd want to go with someone who...who tried to..."she choked out angrily watching his face soften and take a step towards her but she moved away shaking her head. "You're stupid."

"You're the one hiding things from me! At least if I screw up I do it in front of you!" He snapped causing her to realize that she might love him but she didn't want to be anywhere near him now. "I just wanted you to tell me what was so upsetting!"

"I was going to tell you tonight!" Elaina saw him look confused. "Might as well say, I got accepted to a college."

"That's all that was bothering you?" Fury didn't understand how she could be perturbed about that.

"Yeah, well, the college is in Australia," Elaina saw him gape like he couldn't have possibly heard right. "but it doesn't matter now."

"Why? You turned it down?"

"No, I *was* going to turn it down…until now. If I'm going to be stuck with Ravyn I'm stepping down as Alpha and going." Elaina saw him go to say something but she only gave him her back. "What a great birthday this turned out to be, good bye Fury."

Fury saw her leave and felt like he'd just lost everything important to him. "Damn it!" he yelled and kicked the dumpster only to see a couple guys come out.

"Fury, chase after her. You might think it's over but it's never over even when she's completely out of you life. If you don't go after her she'll just think you've agreed to everything she's said and don't care." he heard the girl from the bar. "Trust me, I know these things. It's what every girl wants, jeez, we aren't perfect either you know."

Fury had a small bead of hope form before he took off running seeing Elaina walking along the side of the road carrying her shoes in her left hand. He ran faster seeing her pause before turning and he saw the surprise in her eyes.

"What the hell…" Elaina started but that's all she got before he swept her in his arms and kissed the common sense out of her. He tasted raw and the faint taste of whiskey laced his tongue. She felt her feet leave the ground after he picked her up feeling as if her body didn't even belong to her as she tangled her arms around his neck.

"I'm sorry I hurt you Elaina. I am completely stupid but it's like you said, I'm a rogue so I can't help but question how you feel about me." he said as she looked down at him. "You said you didn't want to be tied to a jerk like Ravyn, how about an idiot like me? Is that okay?"

"Huh?" she asked before she was sat down and he pulled a small velvet box out of his jacket pocket. "What…"

Elaina saw him flip it open showing a beautiful diamond ring sending her heart fluttering in her chest right before he kneeled in front of her. "Elaina, will you do me the honor of becoming my wife?" she saw him ask and she felt tears start falling from her eyes. "Are those uh…tears of joy or rejection."

"I don't know, I think the adrenaline rush is finally wearing off." she sniffed and noticed he was close to laughing. "Of course I will you big idiot, I love you."

Fury felt like he might've heard wrong only to see her looking a bit embarrassed about it. She *loved* him. She loved *him*! Fury caught Elaina against him and spun her around so suddenly that her shoes went flying. He heard her laugh before he sat her down and slipped the ring onto her finger. It fit perfectly, just like how she fit against him. He enfolded his arms around her.

"To the dance?"

"I ripped my dress…and cause of you I lost my shoes." Elaina saw him tug the fabric taking the sheer purple hue from the dress leaving the magenta.

"And now it's fixed." Fury gathered her shoes before slipped them onto her feet. He kisses the scrapes on her knees that were still healing and then kissed her palms feeling her fingers brush against his face. "I do too you know."

"Do too what?"

"I love you too." Fury said before carrying her to the bar and sat her in the car.

"Oh, I think I dropped my purse in the bar when I punched you." Elaina said right before the girl came out and held the small silver clutch out to Elaina who was driving. "Thank you."

"Have fun, aren't you glad you listened to me and went after her Fury?" the girl asked and winked at Elaina who gave a small smile before driving to the school.

Elaina heard music pounding as they pulled in and got out of the car. She checked her dress noting it didn't look that bad as she walked hand and hand with Fury into the school. She handed over the tickets to the teacher who looked wary at the sight of Fury.

She proceeded inside seeing her friends spot her and run over instantly. "It's about time you got here!" they exclaimed before pulling her into a group hug. "What took you so long!?"

"Elaina is that what I think it is?!" Julie cheered causing Bethany and her friends to look over with their dates. "AH! He proposed!"

Elaina felt herself flush as Julie, Rosa, and Leon all started looking at the ring.

She smiled up at Fury who grinned boyishly causing him to look only two years older then her instead of five. She saw him look at her hair and grumble, she felt her hair tumble down after he pulled out a bobby pin. "It took forever to get my hair like that." she complained but Fury only ran his hands through it.

"Mmm, it might be true but I like your hair down." he murmured causing her to darken even further before she heard her favorite song start playing.

"Come dance with me." Elaina led him to the dance floor seeing the eyes of people widen in shock as she danced with Fury who looked a bit embarrassed. She sang along with the song softly as they danced letting her right hand rest over his heart. She felt his had brush against her side before he gave her a small turn and pulling her back to him.

"A rough start but a nice ending." Fury saw her smile before fast music started causing him to go only to feel her catch his hand.

"Nope, your dancing." Elaina laughed watching him looking horrified.

"Lets dance!" Julie said as their song came on so Julie danced with Connor so Elaina danced with Fury.

Elaina couldn't believe that he was barely moving at all. She had her back directly against his chest and had one of her arms draped around the back of his neck. "Hey, is Fury okay?" she heard Connor ask so she turned seeing Fury with his eyes almost completely closed.

"Fury?" Elaina saw him look at her showing bright glowing eyes.

"You can't keep dancing like that." he warned seriously so Elaina thought for a moment before leaning into him.

Elaina thought she'd might as well go all the way since she'd already agreed to marry him. She beckoned him down with her index finder hearing him grunt before leaning down. "I want you to claim me Fury." she murmured against his ear letting her teeth graze his neck feeling him shudder.

"Elaina you don't know what you're asking." Fury exhaled so fast as her fingers brushed the opposite side of his neck.

"Yes I do, that's why I'm asking." Elaina saw him look at her so she nodded.

She felt him grab her hand before they left the school heading straight for the car. She got behind the wheel and drove to his apartment complex. Elaina laughed as he jumped over the side of the car and walked to her side. She got out when he opened her door following him up the stairs to his door, which he opened letting himself step in.

"Are you sure?" Fury asked seriously as Elaina looked at the doorway knowing there was no turning back if she walked in.

"Positive." she replied as she walked in closing the door behind her and slipping off her shoes. She watched as his hair got shaggier, his eyes started glowing, and his teeth lengthened. She knew she looked the same too. She walked towards him watching as his eyes sparkled with humor.

"Trying to scare me off are you?" he chuckled only to watch her quirk an eyebrow as a smile crossed her face so he scooped her up into his arms.

"Me? Scare *you* off?" Elaina only sat her head against his shoulder allowing her to nuzzle his neck. She was more ready then anything knowing she wouldn't mind being with Fury forever. She reveled in it. She could feel her fangs sharpen so dangerously that they ached to bury themselves in the side of Fury's neck.

"I love you so much." he murmured against her ear after laying her down only to dig his hands into the sheet when she rose slightly to nuzzle the spot above his carotid artery. "Elaina…" he choked out before marking his neck as she sank her fangs into it.

It was going to be a very long night.

Hours later Elaina laid curled up against Fury feeling deliciously sore. She had her head resting against his chest as she drew small designs with her hand. "How are you feeling?" she heard him ask after he had taken her hand and kissed the inside her wrist.

"I feel amazing. You?"

"Fine, despite the many bites I've suffered."

"Sorry." she apologized meekly causing him to laugh. "I didn't know I'd get like that."

"You *are* half vampire so it's only natural Elaina. It's not as though I didn't enjoy it." he pointed out seeing her face heat slightly. "Still blushing, I thought you'd never be embarrassed after the things we've done."

"So? Just because it happened doesn't mean I no longer have any modesty." she said quickly seeing him grin at her so she brushed her thumb against his lower lip. "Can I ask you something?"

"About my past?"

"Hmm, how'd you know that?" Elaina saw him sigh like it was bound to be brought up again. "You don't have to tell me anything you don't want to. It's just that I don't know much about you and I want to know you."

"I thought that if I told you my past then you wouldn't allow me near you. I mean I remember seeing you briefly after you *accidentally* hit me with your car and thought I'd made you up in my own mind. You seemed too beautiful to be real." he said as his fingers brushed down her arm.

"Fury, I'm not going to see you differently because of what happened in your past. Times were different back then and people did things like that to survive. I'm not going to hate you, it's pretty impossible to after all you've done for me." she saw him looking speechless so she raised up on her arm and kissed him. "Give me credit will ya?"

"Okay, what do you want to know?" he asked softly feeling his heart expand when she smiled. He had fallen for her at first sight, he would've back then as well.

"Were you born a werewolf or were you created?"

"Born, there were a lot more but most were male…only a few women were werewolves." he explained and thought that would be understandable.

"Okay, have you kept the same name through the years?" she saw him nod seriously as another question plagued her. "What kind of things did warriors have to do?"

"Eat, drink, fight in wars usually pillaging in the process, and other things I'd rather not say in front of my mate. You have to understand that it was in the twelve hundreds though." he stated seriously and saw her think a moment before frowning.

"You basically slept with other women correct?"

"Why did you have to ask that?!" he complain and started to move but she pinned him and he could only groan. "Yeah, that too."

"See, it wasn't that hard to admit." Elaina stated watching his eyes open and look at her. "Fury, I was never the kind of girl to get jealous besides, I have you now."

"I'm suddenly wishing we had those sashes." he grumbled seeing laughter dance in her eyes.

"So what did you look like back then? Same as now?"

"No, I had longer hair with usually a braid or two in it. I didn't have the tattoos yet, well I did but they were painted on so they usually washed off. I usually kept my face clean shaven unlike the men who followed me." he explained as she seemed to be soaking in every word.

"How were vampires treated back then?"

Elaina thought she'd never see him go so pale and terrified. "I'm a lot more relieved that we met in the present then in the past. Vampires weren't considered people Elaina, they weren't considered *anything*. When we found vampires we acted first and thought last. We usually killed the men and while I would never harm a woman the others didn't feel the same way. They were raped by the men and then killed."

"That's terrible."

"This is why I didn't want to talk about it." he stated only to feel her squeeze his hand.

"I'm not blaming you Fury." she murmured and placed a kiss over his heart wondering if things could've really been that bad. "Okay, say something in Gaelic."

"Hmm, if I would have to say anything then it would have to be that you are my *sonuachar*." he stated so she thought about it for a while as if trying to figure out the meaning by herself.

"I give up, what does it mean?" Elaina was curious as ever and she nearly lost her train of thought when he pulled her into a deep and sizzling kiss. She saw him lean away so she gave a little pout hearing him laugh. "So what does it mean?"

"You'll find out eventually."

"I'm suddenly curious, were you the *only* immortal in the whole group?" she inquired only to see him frown instantly.

"No, I wasn't. There were many of us but with the constant wars between us and enemies for land, and then ones between us werewolves and vampires a lot of my brethren died. A day doesn't go by that I don't think about them." he murmured as saw her looking sad for him. "Mind you these are the same men who helped pillage."

"They were important to you though, it's never easy to lose people close to you. Trust me, I know how hard it is." she said before curling back against him. "It must've been terrible."

"It was." he said more to himself then her before they fell asleep in each other's arms.

Elaina shot away feeling hostile eyes on her so she looked around before turning on a light seeing Ravyn there with a vampire. "What…" she started only to get thrown into a wall making her cry out in pain seeing Fury snap awake but it was too late. Elaina watched in horror as the vampire plunged her fist through Fury's chest and ripped out his heart causing her to feel her heart drop. "NO!"

"Looks like I'm the Alpha now." Ravyn said and Fury died in front of her eyes.

Elaina snarled at the vamp who back away in horror before Elaina tackled her to the ground and ripped the heart from the vampire's own chest. Elaina jumped onto the bed seeing Fury laying there causing her to cry hysterically as she cradled his body to her as Ravyn left. "Fury don't die!" she screamed, begging him to open his eyes, but he was gone and she knew it. Elaina felt rage engulf her as she threw on her dress not caring the vampire's blood covered the front. She removed Fury's necklace that he had ever since they met and slipped it around her neck.

She was going to kill Ravyn.

Elaina ran not bothering with shoes as she ran after him with her arms pumping at her sides. She saw him go into the pack's house so she went to her room and pulled out the book of blood. She packed a few skirts and dresses in a bag with shoes before tossing in her tooth paste, tooth brush, and her daggers. She looked up a time traveling spell seeing it was a bit complex but she'd get it to work.

She pulled out the athame and headed over to the house not bothering to change. She kicked the door in seeing Rave come out of the living room with the others. "Where is Ravyn!?" she screeched as her nails lengthened into sharp points.

"He's up stairs, what happened? Why are you covered in blood?" Blade asked only to see her hold the bag tightly before stalking up the stairs making them follow her.

"Elaina what happened?" Rave asked seeing her eyes so dark a red they seemed like blood themselves.

"I'm going to kill him."

"What!?" they yelled only to look confused.

"You can't!" Rave yelled seriously only to get thrown into the wall.

"He killed my *mate*!" she snapped watching the color drain from their faces. "Fury forgave him when he tried to rape me on New Years but I'm not going to forgive him Rave! I'M NOT!"

"Please don't kill him, let the pack handle the retribution?" Rave begged and she knew he didn't care about his brother. He didn't want Ravyn to die by *her* hand.

"I'm not promising anything but I still need his blood and that I'm going to get no matter what." she said before kicking in the door seeing Ravyn packing frantically so she ran before throwing him into a wall. "You're going to help me get him back Ravyn whether you like it or not."

"You can't! He's dead! There's no way to get him back! You're stuck with me!" Ravyn laughed only to get punched in the nose sending blood onto the floor as it gushed.

"I'll be back as soon as possible." she replied before murmuring the spell seeing the blood rise from the floor and open showing a portal.

"NO! You have to love me!" Ravyn yelled before ramming her in the gut with a dagger. She could tell it was steel and not silver.

Elaina raked his face seeing him stumble to the others who tied him up. "Use silver chains, they'll weaken him so he can't break the ropes." she stated seriously before Rave hurried forward.

"Here, drink before you go." he said so she took enough to sate her. "Where are you going?"

"About eight hundred years into the past." she replied and then she was gone. She thought of Fury's homeland and of his face. She held those thoughts as she fell before she collided with something sturdy. She opened her eyes seeing the sun high in the sky partly covered by clouds.

She could smell blood, smoke filled the air meaning something was on fire, and she could hear yells of triumph. She held her pack after standing and looked down the hill seeing people screaming and running. That place was under attack! It wasn't by Fury either.

She saw soldiers notice her and point before yelling. She shot into the woods only to get tackled to the ground. "Got you!" she heard him yell triumphantly. "What a beauty you are! You will make our lord pleased!"

She was dragged to her feet before her hands were bound and she was led back to the village seeing them looking at her in shock. "How beautiful." The people murmured as she started walking with the others seeing a soldier look at her in outrage.

"What fool is making a beauty like herself walk! She should be on a horse that is being guided!" he yelled seriously before getting off his horse and cutting the rope binding her to the others. "Allow me milady."

She was sat on the horse and led seeing a small child walking with her mother crying that her feet were hurting. "Will you let the child to ride with me? She is in pain." Elaina said seeing the man look hesitant. "Please? Can you not see her suffering?"

"You are not Scottish, you're *English*!" he exclaimed in shock like she shouldn't even be a captive.

"The child if you will?" she asked seeing the woman look at her in gratitude after child was sat on the horse behind her. "Thank you."

"Of course." he said as the woman walked next to her.

"Thank ye for letting my child ride with ye." the woman said so Elaina lowered her head slightly since she still had her modesty.

"It was no problem I assure you." Elaina stated politely realizing they all looked stunned. "What?"

"I beg ye forgiveness, we seldom run across *English* such as ye. My I ask as to why ye are in Ireland?" the woman asked and Elaina felt sadness engulf her. "It is a painful subject?"

"I'm searching for my *sonuachar*." she hoped she said the word right and when they looked at her with bright smiles she knew they understood.

"We wish ye all the luck in the world."

Elaina rode on the horse quietly feeling her ears perk up when sticks broke seeing nothing at all. She couldn't sense anything either. "We'll rest for a while." she heard the man say so she was helped off the horse.

"Don't untie her!"

"I have no weapon, if you wish then tie a long rope around one of my wrists so that I won't run. I do need to go into the woods though." she said and shifted slightly since she had to use the bathroom really bad.

"Ye need to change ye clothing, why are ye covered in blood?"

"I was attacked by a very large animal. This is the animal's blood because a man rescued me only to lose his own life in return." she altered the story slightly so she was led into the woods by a man to a stream where she washed the dried blood off her skin, she'd already cleaned her mouth before she had left the pack's house. She opened her bag and pulled out a white floor length white skirt along with and orange t-shirt. Saw the man refuse to turn around so she put the shirt over the dress before pushing down the top of her dress. She pulled on the skirt before unzipping the dress letting it fall to the ground so she went by the tree where she was tied to it with a rope as other women were tied to trees.

She saw them leave before she went to one side to use the bathroom before sitting on the other side. She suddenly heard growling before a dark gray wolf sauntered out causing the other women and children to panic. This one wasn't a werewolf but it knew what she was. She saw it bear its belly to her so she patted it gently.

"Ye must have a way with wild animals."

"You could say that." Elaina said as the wolf curled against her protectively so she patted it's head. "Good boy."

"Okay, time to leave!" a soldier yelled causing her to look at the wolf.

"Find a werewolf named Fury. Tell him these people need to be freed and to bring help with him." she whispered watching it nod in understanding before smelling the necklace since it had Fury's scent on it and taking off.

Elaina was led back and sat on the horse with the child and that's where they remained until they got to a castle like building. She saw a hole big enough in the side for dogs but that was it. So that was how they're likely to get it. She was removed from the horse and led inside with the others.

"Your Highness we have a special gift for you! I believe I have found the most beautiful woman in the world!" the man cheered before she was pushed forward seeing the man looked old enough to be her father.

"Lovely, I will bed her to show that she is mine. No one else should have her." he said and started down so she made up a story.

"I wouldn't." she voiced seriously as a story formed in her mind.

"And why not?"

"My body is cursed. No man shall touch or know my touch for it means their lives if they try. I have lost some of the most daring and handsome suitors because they did not heed my warning. They tried to take what was not theirs by force and died an agonizing death." she explained knowing it may or may not work.

"I believe no such thing!"

"I even have a mark that cannot be removed from my body. It is the mark of the curse." she stated suddenly feeling glad that her tattoo was a tribal. "Raise the back of my shirt and look for yourself if you don't believe me."

She turned and felt them raise her shirt and gasp in horror. "She is cursed! Kill her!"

"Why kill me? I have many talents."

"Such as what?"

"I can cook, sew, and I can also sing and dance." she replied seriously watching him actually think it over.

"Let me see this dancing." he said knowing she'd have to use her ballet if she wanted to live.

"May I have some space, a bird has more room in a cage." she stated seriously so the soldiers backed away so she began to dance letting the gracefulness of the vampire come out.

"Beautiful." she heard the man say. "It is settled, you will dance for me and my men!"

"It shall be my honor." she stated before being led out with the other women and children.

"Mommy I'm scared." a child cried softly once they were in the room.

"Help is on the way, I'm sure of it." Elaina found herself saying because they had to be helped.

"I hope so." the woman said as night fell before Elaina was removed to bathe but didn't wash over the claim mark and she made sure to remove the necklaces.

Elaina was put in a beautiful brown dress that fit her torso like a glove but the bottom was loose. She removed the sleeves because they were too tight. She put her necklaces on and tucked them in the dress. Her hair was plaited with dozens of small gold coins before she was led out as the woman held her bag for her.

She was led to the hall of men seeing them cheer so she gave a deep curtsy when really she wanted to rip them to shreds but that would give her away. "MUSIC!" she heard the man in charge yell so she began dancing right before the door was thrown open seeing soldiers bringing in men.

"Your Highness, these men claim to be a traveling act. They demonstrated and are quite good. What shall we do with them?"

Elaina felt her heart start pounding because she could smell them and they were indeed werewolves. Right in front was Fury looking humble seeing him wearing a kilt. She had to look at the floor to keep from laughing.

"I want to see *her* dance! Sit them aside until she needs to rest!" the man roared before clapping causing music to begin playing. "Start dancing!"

Elaina began dancing watching every eye following her as men even forgot that they were eating. She pirouetted letting her leg give her more force to continue spinning until she sat it down making her stop watching the men cheer so she looked elsewhere only to glare at the floor.

"What a beautiful woman!" a man said and grabbed her arm so she pulled but his grip tightened.

"Let go of me!" she yelled before he was thrown away by two soldiers.

"Have you lost your mind! She is a cursed woman and you wish to instead lose your life with only seconds of pleasure!?" the man yelled before the man scuttled away. "Are you alright milady?"

"I'm fine." she said and was made to dance a few more times before being allowed to sit down. Elaina found herself sat directly next to Fury who only glanced at her and shifted slightly. She could feel heat raising up her neck without even knowing why.

"Bring me wine!" the man in charge called before giving her a devilish grin causing her to turn her head in gag.

"Ugh, gag me with a spork why don't you." she bit out quietly because it was disgusting.

"Ye are English?" she heard Fury ask in confusion but she only glanced up feeling her heart take off like crazy. "Why are ye a captive?"

"I'm certainly not here willingly." she grumbled before crossing her arms wondering why she had the spur of the moment of coming back in time. She was probably screwing up the flow of history right now without a care. "I shouldn't even be here."

Elaina felt her heart ache as she looked at the floor wondering it felt like she was being selfish. She sighed as the men ate and chatted while drinking their wine. She watched as a man carried over a tray with a single goblet before presenting it to her.

"A drink for you milady."

"I don't drink wine." she replied simply despite the odd smell coming from the cup.

"Surely you wouldn't be so cruel as to refuse?" he asked so she rose an eyebrow at him.

"But if I drink how do you expect me to dance?" she countered watching every man object to giving her the alcohol. Elaina was made to dance more and she felt her calf muscles start hurting.

"Bring out the women!" the man cheered and she saw women and *girls* about fourteen be dragged out against their will in the clothes they came in.

"Let go!" a girl screamed as a man grabbed her and pinned her against the wall. "Mother help me!"

"Let go of her!" a woman demanded as Elaina heard a crack before the girl cried harder.

"I want this one for myself!" a man laughed with a slur before grabbing Elaina's arm painfully. He spun her around and as he did she hooked him in the jaw sending him to the floor yelling in pain.

"Keep your god damn hands off me you stupid good-for-nothing pig!" she snapped before she could help it hearing everything go silent.

"A lady shouldn't talk in such a way." one replied and went to restrain her so she kicked him in the groin causing him to fall to his knees before kicking him in the head with the opposite leg sending him to the ground unconscious.

Elaina stood there completely enraged because they acted like damn barbarians. She felt the anger die as fast as it had started causing her jump away from both unconscious men.

Why was she so irritated? She knew why, she couldn't watch these women get forced into such relations against their will.

"Just keep calm, panicking isn't going to help you or anyone else here. Just stay calm." Elaina murmured quietly as her head pounded making her feel a bit out of it.

"She's knocked him out." a man complained angrily after checking on the men. "No woman should raise their hand to a man!"

"He shouldn't have touched me." she bit out seriously without remorse before walking down the stone steps and seeing the man move away from the girl. She touched the mark on the girl's cheek gently before leading her back to the bench where Fury and the others were.

"I suddenly could care less about this curse of yours. I think a few minutes in your arms would be worth the death." the man said after stopping his men from coming after her. "Take her to my chambers, this one is mine."

"I'll never be yours." she murmured as she was led out by two soldiers and tossed into a room.

Elaina looked for a way out heading straight for the window and looking down. There was a moat but it was about fifty feet below and she didn't know how deep it was. She heard the screaming start before the man burst into the room and closed it.

"We are going to be killed!" he yelled as she heard a howl knowing it was Fury and his men. "I shall kill us both to save us from such a terrible death."

"Your death is already terrible." she replied and when he turned around with a confused look she plunged the small knife into his chest. She saw his eyes widen as the smell of blood wafted around her. She was suddenly very hungry. She saw the door fly open showing Fury standing there with a dark black wolf standing next to him. Another man suddenly came up behind Fury who was looking at her with disappointment.

"She's a deadwalker!" he yelled but she only ripped out the dagger letting it fall from her hand. "Kill her!"

Before Elaina could say anything the man lunged with the sword causing her to dodge as she heard the girl from earlier screaming. She took off running dodging between Fury and the wolf knowing they were following her. She saw a staircase so without hesitating she got to the first step and jumped causing her to jump the whole staircase only to land silently in a crouch. She heard a growl so she looked seeing the wolf snarling at her with Fury standing next to it.

She took off running when she heard another cry so she ran feeling herself panicking now. She got to the hall only to see a disgusting looking creature slinking towards the girl and her mother.

"Get away from them." she warned after picking up a sword not seeing Fury and his pack walk in. She saw it freeze before turning to look at her showing bright ruby eyes.

It was a vampire, a tainted one at that. She felt the evil rolling off of it causing her to press a hand to her mouth as it chuckled.

"You dare raise a weapon to me? Learn your place." it hissed before attacking but she blocked before spinning as she sliced hearing it hiss in pain before snarling at her so she glanced at the girl and her mother.

"You should be running you know?" she suggested simply seeing them hurry to the door. When the vampire went to attack she pounced and tackled it to the ground. "Don't even think about it."

"You should new better." it hissed before slashing into her shoulder causing her to kick it in the gut and getting to her feet seeing her shoulder bleeding badly It licked the blood from its nails only to freeze. "What are you?"

"Nothing you'll ever live to see." she hissed before moving quickly and slicing the head from its shoulders but she didn't do it without getting unscathed. She had felt its nail rip into her stomach causing her to double over. She heard a snarling knowing it was the wolf so she straightened up seeing the dress she wore no getting soaked with blood. She felt her teeth lengthen causing her to grit them tightly. She was getting hungry.

"She's hurt!" the girl cried and started running towards her causing Elaina to move away so quickly to girl looked hurt. "You need help."

"I'll be fine."

"If you don't get bandaged then you'll never find your..." the girl started causing Elaina to felt her chest get tight as anger rushed through her.

"It's not that simple. People can't accept you when you're different." Elaina stated seriously to the girl who looked confused but she could see Fury looking at her closely. "They always see the bad, never the good."

"You saved us though."

"You remind me a lot about how I used to be." Elaina replied simply and started passed the girl sitting a hand on her head. "Don't be scared, embrace every day as if it's your last...or you'll miss on a lot of things that should've been yours."

Elaina was sneaking out when one of the guards who had obviously escaped apprehended her. She was pushed against the wall with a dagger held to her throat. "Don't move." she saw him order so she remained still as he lowered the dagger.

That's when she attacked. She was hungry and couldn't help it.

She sank her fangs into his neck and drank deeply feeling her wounds heal themselves only to see the girl and her mother walk out. She saw them look at her in horror.

"DEADWALKER!" the girl screamed in terror but Elaina only let the guard drop to the ground as Fury and the others ran out. "She...She's a deadwalker!"

"Don't sound so obviously terrified, it's not like you're the one I got my teeth into." Elaina shot back watching the girl whimper and jump behind her mother who just looked at her.

She saw something move out of the corner of her eyes and there was a sword suddenly through the right side of her chest. "Go to the devil where ye belong." she saw a guy with black hair say calmly and she felt her body shutting down.

She felt herself hit the ground as her eyes remained open but her breathing stopped so he body could heal itself. She saw the girl cry hysterically as the woman looked away. She saw the others walk off but Fury remained behind and she watched him kneel next to her.

"May ye find peace, wherever ye are." he said only to see a tear slip from the eyes staring up at the sky without holding an ounce of life. He wondered why he felt like she shouldn't have been killed. She had risked her own life for humans, why would a deadwalker do that? He closed her eyes before hurrying for the others so they wouldn't come back.

Chapter 8

Elaina woke up sucking air into her lungs next to a small rock before running into the woods near by as the sun rose slowly in the sky. She listened closely hearing a stream and knowing that there was likely to be a lake around if she followed it. She ran happily seeing the woods open up to a beautiful lake. She dropped her bag and removed the bloody clothes from her body.

She jumped into the lake and swam around for a little while making sure to wash off any trace of smell. She found herself once again touching Fury's claim mark. It was the most beautiful thing in the world to her. She brushed her fingers against it gently before sitting in the shallow end and crying hysterically as she remembered when the world was taken from her.

"Hey do ye hear the wailing? It's got to be a banshee!" she heard someone exclaim so she got out of the water.

Elaina threw on her undergarments before slipping on the skirt and putting on the shirt not even knowing that the back of her shirt hadn't come down. She grabbed her bag and went to run when Fury and his men entered the clearing causing her to feel irritated.

"We killed you!" the guy with long black hair snapped like she was a pest that couldn't be gotten rid of.

"I say we have a little fun with her before we behead her this time." a guy maybe three years older then Fury suggested causing a snarl to rip from her throat before she could stop it. "She's a feral one, probably likes to bite."

"You'll never know." she stated before taking off running as she slung her bag onto her back. She didn't need to bother with shoes. Her feet were already tough enough thanks to Fury making her run all the time in human form in her bare feet.

"Get her!" she heard someone yell but she was running like it was no one's business.

Elaina felt a hand grab her shoulder and that familiar warmth washed over her but she had to ignore it. It wasn't the same Fury. She tore away instantly when that thought hit her like a sack of bricks to the gut. She could feel tears rolling down her face as she ran. She couldn't look back. She couldn't go to Fury because he had no problem letting someone thrust that sword into her chest. He could let them kill her and not even think twice about it.

She'd already lost him once, she didn't need it to happen twice. She couldn't stay there in the past, she had to get back to the future where she belonged. Elaina suddenly tripped and tumbled down a hill. She felt something knick the side of her head before she landed at the bottom.

Elaina looked up seeing them running down the hill so she took off running knowing she wouldn't be able to out run them on foot…at least not in human form. She went through bushes ripping off her clothing before launching into a stream before changing into wolf form.

She took off running with the bag clenched between her teeth only to pause in some bushes. "Where did she go!?" she heard one yell in anger as she peered out of the foliage around her seeing Fury pick up her torn clothes and smell them.

"I don't get it." Fury mumbled seeing his men looking confused so he tossed the clothing to his right hand man. "What do ye smell?"

"I smell a human, but we saw her eyes Fury. She's a deadwalker. There's no in between with them. All I know is that if we donna find her there'll be bodies piling up." he stated seriously but she only moved further into the bush only to step on a stick. "She's over there!"

Elaina watched the shrubs get yanked and thrown away only to see Fury stop his man. "It's only a wolf Baron!" she watched him yell causing her to back away snarling.

"What's that in it's teeth? Looks like a bag." another said and reached for it but Elaina only moved away with a warning growl. "It has some chains around it's neck. I wonder if it has an owner."

Elaina watched Fury kneel in front of her causing her stomach to start doing cartwheels because the compassion in his eyes was deeply moving to her. She saw him reach towards her neck and hold up the necklace that looked exactly like his.

"What in the name of…" Fury started saying so she bit his hand causing him to jump away allowing her to take off running.

"Did that wolf have the same pendant as you?" Baron asked causing him to nod. "Is it your sister?"

"No, I remember her scent. The scent of this wolf is entirely…different." Fury stated wondering why his mind kept going back to the deadwalker. When Baron had plunged his sword in her chest the betrayal in her eyes confused him, and the tear that rolled down her cheek nearly undid him. How could he be attracted to that kind of monster?

Elaina got at a safe distance and decided to travel towards a close village. She saw night start falling so she changed back and dressed before walking to the village that seemed a little too perfect. She saw eyes look at her while the mouths belonging to the people remained quiet as she walked into what had to be an inn.

She sat at the bar seeing women shake their heads in disgust as men glared furiously at her. She noted the pale skin, the dark eyes that seem to have a reddish tint.

"Your kind isn't welcomed here wolf." a guy said after sitting next to her so she looked at him square in the eyes.

"You don't know what my kind are, vampire." she replied seriously before pulling out a coin and twirling it between her fingers.

"We donna carry stuff for wolves and humans."

"Did I ask for it?" she asked seriously before a glass of blood was sat in front of her. She smelled it before wrinkling her nose. "This blood is foul, pulled from a dead man five days ago. You'll only poison yourself with that."

"Ye had better…" the bartender started causing her to glare letting her appetite become visible seeing him stop in his tracks. "What are ye?"

"Nothing you've ever seen." she replied seriously before standing up and leaving the inn. She needed to find some place else to sleep.

That's when the screaming started, she growled because she was tired of changing back and forth. She went behind the inn and removed her clothing before slipping it in the bag and changing knowing she made the right choice when she heard Fury yelling to his men to pillage the small town. She slunk around in the shadows until she got to Fury seeing he had yet to change forms. Her blood sang in her veins as the wolves fought the vampires. They tore through the men who seemed more vile then the women.

Elaina saw a vampire sneaking up on Fury so she charged out seeing him look at her right before she launched into the air and latched her teeth around the vampires head and twisted it off with a sickening snap. She felt his hand rub the top of her head so she looked up. The smile on his face was appreciative.

"Thanks, I owe ye one."

Elaina backed away from him knowing he was confused as to why but when a vampire lunged towards them she did the most reasonable thing. She tackled Fury to the ground feeling the sword slice into her back causing her to cry in pain but the sound was only wounded barks. Elaina rounded on the vampire before chewing it's stomach hearing the agonizing yells before Fury beheaded it turning it to ash.

"VICTORY!" the men cheered so she hurried as fast as possible causing her to feel her back stinging.

"Fury where are you going!?" Baron yelled as Fury hurried into the woods so they all hurried after their leader.

Elaina could hear Fury following her as she held the bag between her teeth but suddenly she couldn't walk anymore. She collapsed to the ground so she curled up behind a boulder knowing she was probably going to die now. She couldn't stop her body from changing back into her normal self. She should've left instead of sticking behind to see him.

"Ye little wolf where's ye…" Fury started as he came around the boulder following the smell only to see a female form curled up at the base. Was it really his sister!? Fury felt hope as he kneeled in front of her and reached over slowly only to get his hand smacked away. "Ye donna have to be scared. I'm not going to hurt ye."

Elaina knew it was too much to hope for as she curled her arms closer to her body as she felt his finger hook underneath her hair and move it away. She thought he would likely have a heart attack by the amount of shock that crossed his face. She murmured the spell under her breath before clothing appeared on her body causing him to jump away.

"It's impossible that ye are a wolf." he stated only to look even more angrier when she didn't reply. "Ye aren't a wolf! It's not possible! Ye are a deadwalker!"

Elaina moved away instinctively when he reached for the sword balancing on the balls of her feet with her fingertips against the ground. She saw him pause and when he did she bolted. However, she didn't get far because she was wounded and had already needed blood to begin with.

"Stop ye moving!" Fury yelled before rolling her over seeing the necklace as plain as day hanging around her neck. He felt her fist collide with his gut but he only pinned her to the ground only to feel guilty when she hissed in pain. He'd forgotten about her back. He'd forgotten she'd even saved him from not one but two vampires. He looked down at her seeing the tears already welling up but she was holding them back. She wasn't going to cry in front of him.

"Ye got her! Ye got that damned deadwalker!" Baron cheered as William looked from him to her.

"Why isn't she dead yet?"

"I owe her." Fury growled seriously only to get kicked away by her and she jumped to her feet.

"You don't owe me anything you piece of crap!" she snapped before glaring at him as she moved away from him and his men.

"Why do ye have the same necklace as myself!?" Fury demanded but she only shook her head.

"It's not worth telling."

"Let me kill the deadwalker?" Baron offered and it ticked her off to no end.

"You think all of us like being like this!? You think all of us go willingly!? That we all have a say in becoming one!? You are insane if you think that!" she yelled seriously as the cut finally started healing on her back.

"Ye are spouting nonsense, of course ye wanted it or ye would've killed ye own self." Baron bit out causing her to shake her head as she rubbed her temples.

"Nothing is ever that easy." she murmur and remembered Ravyn causing her to clench her hands into such tight fists her nails bit into her palms. She suddenly went rigid when a sword went into the right side of her chest again. "It won't do anything, you obviously don't know the first thing about killing a deadwalker."

"Maybe it's part of the curse?" William offered so she decided to use that as a cover up.

"I think we got us a prisoner." Baron bit out since it was obvious they weren't going to kill her. He put shackles around her wrists but she only looked at it.

"Really? You think these are going to keep me restrained? You're a moron. Exactly how many times were you dropped on your head as a child?" she asked seeing him aim a slap at her face but she dodged before snapping the shackles into little tiny pieces. "Don't ever try to hit me or you'll go from being Baron to being a Baroness."

"She is going to drive me out of my mind."

"Can't injure something that isn't there." she shot back before she froze feeling eyes watching her. She started scanning as the others argued. She didn't realize that Fury was watching her closely. She focused her eyes before red eyes were suddenly staring into hers. "Come here."

"Kill her, she's trying…" Baron started only to see a vampire walking out with a dazed look as Elaina remained focused. Elaina started forward only to get restrained by Fury.

"What are ye up to?"

"Eating, I seriously doubt I'm going to find volunteers." she shrugged off his grip before leading the vamp behind a good sized tree. She was a bit shocked that Fury followed with a stern face. "What are ye up to?" she mocked wondering if a corner of his mouth had twitched up.

"Making sure ye donna try to run away."

"You couldn't catch me even if I did." she grumbled back as her fangs extended painfully. She didn't even hesitate to sink them into the dazed looking vampire. She felt the blood pour into her more so she drank realizing this one must've just fed because it had a lot to give. She opened her eyes seeing Fury watching in disapproval but she only pulled away as she erased the memories of them ever being seen by the vampire causing it to hit the ground.

"Ye are cursed." Fury found himself mumbling as he looked at the vampire sprawled on the ground.

"Donna worry so much wolf, ye aren't my type anyway." she imitated the brogue perfectly causing his men to gawk like she couldn't have just said that.

"Like ye would have a type when it comes to blood." Baron bit out so she decided to cross her arms.

"I do actually, blood is more delicious when the partner is heated." she replied simply before running the tip of her tongue against one of her fangs before they vanished. She saw their jaws drop and they gawked at her but then she only followed them seeing Baron tie her wrists with rope so she didn't break them. Apparently it was to make him feel secure.

"So ye are English but why are ye here if ye aren't with the kings men?" William asked as they headed back to the village.

"I'm here to find someone."

"Is it someone important?" one with a scar down the side of his face asked simply.

"You could say that." Elaina didn't say anything after that but she could only rub her chest when it ached.

"Who is it ye are looking for? Maybe we can help find them?" William offered causing her to just walk with her eyes forward. "So who is it?"

"I'm searching for my sonuachar." she finally answered watching them freeze but she only kept walking. "The one who carries my heart with him."

"An English deadwalker searching for her sonuachar? I've seen everything now." Baron replied sarcastically as they caught up to her. "What is this man's name?"

"That I won't say, I'll know it when I see him."

"So he'll know ye when he sees ye then?" Fury asked but she couldn't help but feel disappointed because if he was asking then he hadn't figured it out yet.

"No, he won't know me when he sees me. You see," Elaina started and wondered how she should phrase it. "he has already died so I came looking for him."

"Ye are insane, why not just settle with someone else?"

"I don't want anyone else!" she yelled seriously causing William to jump away so she forced herself to calm down.

"Ye are chasing a bloody ghost."

"I'm not, he's alive. I've already seen him so shut up." Elaina bit out and marched off only to see them stop in a clearing and make a camp. She sat there as everyone except her, Fury, and Baron fell asleep.

"Tell her to sleep Fury, she's scaring me."

"Like I'm going to risk anything to make you feel comfortable." she replied lamely only hear a crunching before the familiar wolf padded out and sat next to her. She leaned against it and sighed as she stared into the fire. It felt like everything was falling apart.

"I won't be able to sleep unless she does!" Baron complained causing William to wake only to groan.

"Milady please sleep so the barin will sleep and stop crying?" William asked so she stood and ran at the nearest tree before catching a branch and swinging herself onto it.

"Fine, but I'm not sleeping down there." she said and climbed up halfway and let herself get lulled to a deep sleep. She was swamped by nightmares causing her body to hit something hard making her to snap awake gasping for air.

Elaina had fallen out of the tree and hit the ground. She realized that the sun was shining, Fury and his men were watching her warily, and she was covered from head to toe in sweat. She stood shakily and took a deep breath before letting it out slowly.

"A deadwalker that breaths, and I thought they were completely dead." William said but she only walked over and sat down. "So how did he die?"

"His heart was ripped out by a vampire." she bit out as her nails sharpened dangerously causing him to look confused.

"Vampires?"

"It's the correct name for deadwalkers, spending an eternity of life alone drinking blood to survive." she said emptily and shattered a rock by squeezing it.

"They're disgusting creatures." Baron voiced only to see her frown.

"Yeah, well it was hired to kill my mate through a damn werewolf." she growled back seeing them look unable to believe it.

"A deadwalker working for a werewolf is unheard of." Fury stated seriously but she only looked at him.

"Unheard of but not impossible." she replied as she felt hungry again. She stood up and stretched her arms seeing them looking puzzled.

"What are ye doing now?"

"Going hunting, I'm hungry." she replied watching them all go to reach for their sword but she only snorted. She removed the rope and started walking through the woods and took off at a light jog before breathing air in through her nose. She spotted some deer and saw them grazing without a care.

"Deer? Ye are hunting deer?" William asked quietly causing her to get irritated when the ears of the deer perked up causing them to shift nervously.

"Be quiet." she warned as Baron looked at her.

"Ye aren't hunting the deer!" he yelled accusingly thinking she was just trying to make them think she was different causing the deer to start running.

She growled and took off running seeing the deer try to outrun her but she was faster. She tackled a deer to the ground and snapped its neck painlessly before slinging it onto her back seeing William looking close to laughing. She carried it back to the fire and proceeded to field dress it without so much of a word to the others as they watched her closely from the opposite side of the fire. She didn't like them watching her like that at all. It made her nervous to know they refused to take their eyes from her.

She made a spit and proceeded to cook the deer meat she'd carved. She rotated it feeling bored out of her mind as she wondered how long it was going to take. "I like mine rare on the inside." she heard Baron say and go to touch it causing her to smack his hands away.

"This isn't for you." she replied seriously since she hated that he assumed she was going to share with them. They hadn't even helped her with any of it.

"I'm hungry."

"You didn't help therefore you don't get any...especially talking like that." she bit back her eyes warning him to just stay away from her meal.

"Um...may I please have some?" William asked along in unison with the one everyone called Seamus.

She sighed in defeat since they'd asked so nicely watching them grab a couple pieces and eat like everything was normal. They had forgotten what she was so easily and she hated that all she had to do was feed them.

"How can ye ask for it so politely as if she's not a deadwalker?! Ye ought to go finish ye selves off instead of letting the monsters do it. Where's ye pride?!" Baron yelled causing Elaina to see them pause and stick the meat back on the spit.

"I think you're confusing pride with having manners. You think just because someone is dead they have no right to be treated with decency!?" she snapped as she stood seeing Fury shift. "You have no right to talk to them like that when they were simply doing what everyone does, asking politely!"

"I doubt ye have any feelings." Baron growled causing her to pull out Fury's sword before anyone could stop her and slashing slicing a thin cut across Baron's chest causing him to stumble away.

"You're right, I found that incredibly easy to do." she replied with a calm face and marched towards him and pinned him to a tree by his neck. "Don't forget this, I don't have to drain your blood to kill you."

She threw him to the side before slashing at a huge tree with the sword watching it slice through like a hot knife through butter. The tree fell over and crashed onto the ground. She felt anger swarming through her so badly she felt herself shaking with it.

She marched over and sat down and only when she was positive Baron didn't get blade happy, she gave Fury his sword back. "Aren't ye going to eat?" William asked and pointed at the deer meat.

"I'm not hungry anymore, personally I think I'd rather starve then keep company with those who'd kill me the first chance they got." she said before going back to the tree and climbing into it. She sat there refusing to come down no matter how much they yelled for her to come down.

"Please come down?" Fury asked and saw her frown at him before her wolf ran forward and let out a whine so she jumped down watching it hurry over and sit obediently by her side.

"Good boy." she murmured and scratched the wolf behind the ears seeing it make a lazy face. She saw Baron come forward with a rope only to see William and Seamus stop him.

"She could've left any time and she didn't, I don't think it's necessary." Seamus replied and saw Baron look angry as ever when they looked like he should just forget about the rope.

"I don't care, the people in the village should know what she is so they avoid her." Baron bit out and went to grab her wrists so Fury stopped him.

"It'll be fine Baron, we'll watch her closely. If she looks like she's going to attack then stop her by any means necessary." Fury replied simply only to see her look he should've kept his mouth shut.

"Great, I'll go to talk to someone and get a sword through me. What a nice way to be welcomed to a country." she stated lamely and sarcastically uncaring as how him looked at her like she should keep her mouth shut.

She was surrounded by all of them as she walked towards the village seeing kids running around laughing and having fun causing her to smile warmly at them watching them giggle and hurry back. She saw Fury glance at her so she wiped the smile off her face and looked forward ignoring him completely. She saw people glance at her, the men murmured about how beautiful she was and the women murmured as if trying to figure out why she had guards.

She could hear their questions ask if they were yelling them. She didn't like to be able to hear everything. She followed them to the inn where they got rooms noticing a man there looking her over and it caused her to be uncomfortable. She followed them up to the multiple rooms.

"You get to stay in the room, we're going to the celebration." Baron stated making her roll her eyes like it was stupid anyway but she already had a plan to sneak out once they left. "Don't even try to sneak out, we have people watching for you should you come downstairs."

"Whatever, just go so I can relax." she grumbled like they were probably going to be bored anyway. She saw them leave and instantly took a quick bath before getting dress in the black floor length billowy skirt and a purple shirt. She left the coins in her hair causing her to pull it back into a ponytail not even thinking about the claim mark.

She jumped out of the window into a tree and remained still when someone came around the side. They were smart to have someone patrol outside. She would give them credit for that but she only slinked in with the shadows using them for cover as she went to the celebration. She decided to walk up behind the others.

"I can't believe we brought her here. She's gonna cause us nothing but trouble and ye know it Fury. We should just kill her and get it over with…before one of these two idiots get attached to her." Baron said and gestured to Seamus and William who frowned at him.

"We aren't attached her, but it's nice to have someone to talk to that doesn't always say how weak we are for having feelings." Seamus corrected as she stood there without moving an inch.

"She's only being kind so we lower our guard and then she'll kill us. She's getting into ye heads to make ye relax around her." Baron sounded as if she was the scum of the earth causing her to hear the music stop.

"Anyone else have a song?!" a man cheered so she snuck around to the front seeing the man look at her. "Ye got a song do ye?"

She got on the stage seeing Baron start to yell so she started tapping her foot. She began singing hearing everyone stop talking. She felt something inside of herself as she sang and found her eyes glance at Fury who was watching intently. She saw the band start with a good beat and people dancing as she heard her voice get louder. It rang out like bells at church on Sunday morning. She jumped off the stage and spun causing everyone to have fun as she finally finished the song causing them to applaud and asked for another song but Baron was full on glaring at her. She didn't care if he was glaring cause the man from the inn was by the inn door watching her. She didn't like the look he was giving her.

She felt herself step back unconsciously seeing the others look at the man who had suddenly vanished. She found herself rubbing the inside of her wrist. It always comforted her when Fury had done it and it sort of worked now but not as much now.

"You look like you've seen a ghost." William said when they got near her and she felt her head start pounding.

"No, it was a man that had been at the inn when we arrived. I don't get a very good feel from him either." she answered seriously only to see Baron look like she was crazy and to keep her mouth shut. "Fine, don't believe me. If he starts killing people then don't come get me to help get rid of him."

"I bet you were a handful for your parents, they were probably as terrible as you are." Baron bit out only to see her freeze.

"I wouldn't know, my father left my mother when he found out she was pregnant with me and my mother died when I was four." she answered missing Fury shift about that. "I've always done things by myself, you aren't the only one with pride…but at least I still keep my dignity."

"You don't know anything about pride, your heart doesn't even beat." Fury murmured thinking she hadn't heard so she walked over and stuck his hand against her neck so he could feel the pulse.

"Really? Then I guess I have one for nothing then." she bit back before removing his hand and heading back to the inn.

"Her…her heart was beating." Fury choked out making Baron look like it couldn't be but Fury's reaction said it had.

"If she has a pulse then she can't be a deadwalker…then what could she possibly be?" Seamus whispered and wondered why it felt like eyes were watching them. He looked around and the feeling vanished, right before he heard a scream and people rushed from the inn.

"She's exposed herself." Baron growled so they hurried in only to pull up short when they saw a man lifting her off the floor by her neck.

"I've been looking for you. You're the one who killed my brother in the village raid. We told you to stay out of our village wolf." the man hissed before throwing her into a wall making her brace herself right before she hit the floor. "Tonight is the night you die."

"You think I'll go so easily? You are sadly mistaken." she laughed and stood up showing reddish-orange eyes as her joints started popping causing her limps to lengthen. "I'll put you back in your grave."

"Don't be overconfident, you're only a wolf." he chuckled only to see her stop changing as if she flicked off a switch.

"That's what you think." she said as her hair fell out of the ponytail sending her hair around him while her nails and teeth lengthened. She saw him lunge and slash getting her across the face before jumping away watching it heal instantly.

"Impossible!" he roared causing her lunge and tackle him to the floor letting herself change all the way.

"Holy…" Seamus started because she didn't look like a normal wolf at all. "What did she just do?"

"You won't kill me!" he yelled and rolled away before jumping out a window so she chased him without thinking.

Elaina followed him through the woods seeing nothing but she could hear the others following her. She suddenly smelled mixed scents, all of them were vampires. She turned as the others caught up. She roared right when some kind of hook went through the lower part of her arm. It was silver.

She screamed as she changed back causing her clothes to hang on her in a somewhat intact shape. She felt the chain get pulled causing her to grab the chain and pull back hearing more then one person grunt.

"What…"

"Get out of here!" she snapped at them seeing them pull out their swords…even Baron. She felt another hook go through her arm causing her to scream in pain. The silver was starting to enter her system. She felt herself start stagger and when they pulled the chains she was pulled forward. She felt like she couldn't move. She heard chuckling as about five men walked out with smug faces.

"She's a werewolf alright." one snorted and held up the silver chains making her snarl and snap her jaws. "This one has a bite, she'll make a good pet."

"I'm not a pet." she bit out and rushed forward swiping the head from one causing the others to jump back so she ripped the silver from her skin with a yell of anger.

"Milady ye need to calm down." William murmured only to get rounded on seeing her skin pale and her eyes become eyes of the deadwalker when she turned around. He stumbled away as everything animalistic about her vanished leaving her there looking like a vampire completely.

"Kill the werewolves and skin them, I could use a nice pelt." one ordered so three rushed forward.

"Stop." she said in a hypnotic voice seeing them freeze instantly. "Don't you remember, you don't work for him. He's using you, you were ordered to kill him. Right?"

"Right, we were ordered to kill him." they said back before turning to face their boss and heading towards him.

"You idiots, she's the one who is suppose to die! What are you doing! How can you betray your creator!" the man yelled as they surrounded him causing her to look as cold as ice.

"Just shut up and die." she said watching him yell as he was slain by his own kind so when they were done she went over and sank her teeth into one neck after another.

"She's drinking from them!" Baron yelled causing one to snap out of it and run at him. He didn't have his sword out either. No one did. He braced for impact but he suddenly saw a hook emerge from the front of the chest making the deadwalker stop.

"You should know better then to attack people I'm around. I might hate that one but it doesn't mean to kill him." she replied and pulled the chain causing it to screech as the heart flew out of the chest causing it to crumble to ash. She suddenly remembered it was the same way Fury had been killed causing her cover her to move away because she didn't need to remember.

"Are ye okay? That was pretty amazing, how ye pulled it's heart form its chest." Seamus said and went to pat her on the back only to see her staring at the pile of ash with haunted eyes.

"No it's not amazing, no one should have to die like that." she choked out and touched the mark feeling calm but she still felt so far away from Fury. She couldn't stop the tears rushing down her cheeks as the pain just engulfed her completely. She covered her face and just cried hysterically.

"Is that how ye mate died?" Baron asked quietly and saw her look up.

"I would've given anything to trade places with him, he didn't deserve anything like that. We were suppose to be married…and now he's gone. I don't think I'll ever get him back." she choked out and covered her face because Fury was standing three feet from her.

"What did ye like about him?" Seamus asked and saw her lower her hands.

"Well it didn't start out like that, I hated him at first. He was a rogue trying to get into a pack the easy way but they wouldn't allow it. He was kind though, he didn't mind what I was." she murmured as she touched the ring on her finger and looking at it. "They killed him on my birthday."

"What?"

"I couldn't do anything to stop it and they did it right in front of me." Elaina rubbed her temples and found herself smiling. "He did the most idiotic things ever! He had this habit of checking his nails to make sure they weren't broke before he went hunting."

"That's funny, Fury does the same thing!" Seamus howled with laughter right before he noticed the claimed mark. Seamus recognized that mark anywhere causing him to see her glance at him in confusion as to why he suddenly stopped laughing. "Um…he claimed you?"

"Of course he did, why wouldn't he?" she asked simply before touching the mark remembering what that night had been like and she felt herself go red in the face just thinking about it.

"Well let's head out, we got a lot of ground to cover." Fury said so they went a good ways from the village despite paying for room and made camp near another lake. He woke suddenly seeing feet go passed him so he looked up seeing her walking to the lake. He stood as the others slept before following her down. "You should be sleeping."

"I don't want to sleep…I see it happen every time I close them." she replied simply and stepped into the water feeling more relaxed then she had.

"Then don't think about it."

"That's very hard to when I see him…" she started only to trail off before she could finish the sentence that would end everything so she didn't say it. She just shrugged like it was pretty simple and walked around in the water. She was suddenly splashed completely with water causing her to go rigid because it was still cold. She spun around only to get splashed again. She wiped off her face seeing Fury looking completely innocent so she kicked water at him.

"No, no, no!" she yelled when he came at her causing them to both slip and fall in the water getting completely soaked. "Cold, very cold."

"Sorry, didn't intend for this." he said and stood up before helping her to her feet bringing them so close that there was an inch between them.

She could feel her heart beating frantically in her chest as his blue eyes looked at her like there was something he recognized about her. "We should go get dry before we get sick or something." she murmured and headed to the fire where she sat down only to get Fury's blanket wrapped around her. "What if you…"

"I don't get sick." he replied simply seeing her give a small nod wondering why she was being so quiet all of a sudden. He saw her looking at the fire and soon she was dry and he was still soaked.

"Here, I'm dry so you can have it back." she murmured and handed it back.

"It's not even damp from ye having it around ye." Fury could tell something had happened that he'd missed but his eyes kept going back to the necklace she had around her neck. "How did you get a necklace like that anyway?"

"It was given to me." It was all Elaina would say about it and she saw him shift but when she turned her head to look she noticed that his face was close to hers.

"I was trying to look at ye claim mark." he said and suddenly felt a huge urge hit him hard. Why did he suddenly want to kiss her? He started leaning towards her but then he heard someone clear their throat.

"How about you stop using your evil magic on my friend?" Baron asked and Fury knew it wasn't deadwalker magic but how could he tell his men that he was the one becoming attracted to her.

"I wasn't doing anything." she replied defensively but Fury only leaned away from her.

"Ye heard Baron, either stop with the magic or ye will be bound in silver." Fury felt guilty for saying that to her when he was to one who had been leaning down to kiss her. He saw her move away from him wearing a frown before climbing into a tree.

"You should be ashamed of yourself." she murmured knowing he'd heard her. She closed her eyes but she refused to go to sleep.

"I can't believe she used magic on ye!" she heard Seamus yell in disgust all of a sudden right before she saw someone in her dreams lunge at her with a sword. She thrashed instantly causing her to fall from the tree and slam into the ground. She coughed a couple times only to feel someone step on her back. "We should end her life now for doing something like this!"

"Doing what?" she asked in confusion wondering why it hurt so much.

"Don't play innocent, ye used ye magic on Fury last night. Baron even saw ye do it!" William said before kicking her in the gut causing her to roll and hold it.

"You two stop!" Fury ordered but they weren't listening to him at all and saw Baron standing there with his arms crossed. What had he just done? He saw William drag her to her feet by her hair and stand her up looking outraged.

"We were trusting ye and ye do something like this! Baron was right, all of ye deadwalkers are the same! It'd be better if ye all were dead!" William yelled and pulled out a dagger but she twisted away only to see her hair fall to the ground.

He'd sliced her hair off to her shoulders causing it to fall out of the braid she wore it in. She reached up slowly and touched it realizing like Fury, it was gone now too. She saw Baron pull out his sword and walked towards her.

"For the use of magic ye will pay the price, ye life." he stated seriously right before lightning crackled causing her necklace to start thrumming.

"What…" she started before she heard yelling causing her to get confused before something landed in the woods. She smelled the air only to jump to her feet instantly. "Impossible, I closed it so no one could follow me."

"Closed what?" Baron asked right before she took off running like crazy. "Catch her!"

Elaina got to a clearing and peeked out seeing that it was either Rave or Ravyn laying in the clearing. She saw the others catch up before she tiptoed out carefully since she couldn't smell anything but forest. She kneeled next to him and shook him gently. She heard him groan right before the eyes opened showing caramel colored eyes that narrowed instantly.

"You…" he started before throwing her like a rag doll causing her to slam into a boulder with a grunt only to stand slowly as he got to his feet. He snarled angrily before his nails sharpened so she snapped her jaws. "Where the hell did you bring me Elaina!?"

"I didn't bring you anywhere. You should've stayed there and away from me." she hissed venomously before they lunged at each other and started fighting like cats and dogs. They were matched though because they were of the same species. For every cut she received she dished out. She had fed recently compared to him though because she healed faster.

"I'll kill you just like I did your mate! You should've chose me!" he snapped before grabbing her by her throat and squeezing.

She hadn't wanted to change into her second wolf form but it was necessary. She changed with a blink and roared before ripping into his shoulder and throwing him into a tree. She screamed in rage causing it to come out in another roar before she pounced.

"Elaina don't do it!" she heard Rave yell seriously as she held Ravyn pinned to the ground so she looked. She saw him just as scraped up as she felt, hurrying into the clearing.

She saw him look pleadingly so she smacked Ravyn's head against a tree hard enough to knock him out for a while. "Um…you look a bit creepy right now."

She grunted before he tossed her his shirt so she caught it and went behind a tree. She changed back while slipping on the shirt and finally buttoned it. She felt glad it at least went to her knees. She stepped out as Fury and the others came out slowly only to freeze after looking at her.

"Rave, what are you and your brother doing here?" she asked seriously without looking at Ravyn because she really wanted to kill him right now.

"I don't know. We were fighting, I cut him, his blood hit the floor, and then we fell out of the damn sky landing here." Rave explained with a shrug wearing nothing but a pair of jeans and boots. "It seems Crystal escaped from the cage you put her in and then got attacked by a bunch of stray dogs. The pack buried her yesterday."

"Pack?" Fury asked in confusion only to see Rave look at him and do a double take.

"I think I'm hallucinating." Rave grumbled and looked at Elaina who shook her head. "How far back again?"

"Eight hundred…maybe a little more, I was never precise." Elaina replied as Rave groaned before picking up his brother and slinging him over his shoulder.

"Peachy, I'm guessing I'm stuck here too?" he asked causing her to look apologetic so he walked over and sat a hand on her head. "Don't worry about it, you look like you could use someone on your side anyway."

"Thanks." It was the truth too.

"Well, you're the pack's only Alpha so it's natural that you need someone to protect you…especially from idiots like the one I'm carrying." Rave informed lamely as she turned, the look on Fury's face was priceless.

"Pack? Wait, she's your packs Alpha?" William asked in confusion so Rave gave a confirming nod. "But she's a deadwalker."

"A what?"

"Vampire." she murmured to Rave who quirked an eyebrow.

"Actually she's a hybrid, she's half deadwalker and half werewolf. She started out human though which was a huge shock to me when I first met her. At the time she was to be mated with the idiot over my shoulder but then he messed up big time and ended up a Beta. He's lucky he didn't become an Omega…or even shunned by the entire pack." Rave explained quickly causing her to just stand there shaking her head like he was the worst. "I'm surprised she hasn't killed him yet."

"Only because you keep stopping me damn it! Do you really think I want to be around him!?" she snapped seriously before stomping off to get her backpack.

"I think it's that time." Rave saw the one with a scar down his face say but Rave shook his head.

"No, she wants to kill him because he killed her mate. Actually, he hired a vampire to kill him just to be the Alpha. She has yet to kill him because I ask her not to even though I don't have the right to." Rave said before following them to the campsite seeing Elaina had already dressed.

"Here's your shirt." she grumbled and tossed it back before pulling out the book.

"You aren't going to turn him into a ferret like you did to Crystal are you?" Rave asked after slipping on the shirt seeing her hold up a finger.

"Trying to focus here and you aren't helping." she stated before snapping the book shut and putting in her bag. She let her fangs come out before sinking them into her wrist. She started murmuring under her breath causing the blood to stop midair and start floating to Ravyn's body seeing markings appear on the left half. She saw the markings become permanent before she collapsed to the ground feeling completely drained.

"What did you do?" William choked out in horror and poked Ravyn with a stick causing him to snap away before lunging at Elaina. He saw the werewolf get restrained by some force that couldn't be seen before he yelled in pain as he got electrocuted.

"Elaina…" Rave started seeing her look apologetic.

"It'll keep him from attacking people. It's not just to protect me, it's to protect everyone. You don't want to leave him behind right?" she asked and knew that Rave understood that it was necessary. "It only stuns him…temporarily."

"Okay, now what are ye?" Fury asked warningly showing he didn't want to be lied to. "Are ye some kind of deity?"

"Deity? Elaina? No, she's just her normal self. Where'd the book come from anyway?" Rave inquired in confusion and pointed to her bag which she held to her chest. He also noticed her hair was shorter and she was covered in dirt. A few feet he noticed the rest of her hair was there in a pile haphazardly.

"It was a gift from Dracula."

"Ye know the infamous deadwalker!?" Baron roared in anger causing her to nod slowly. "This is terrible!"

"You don't even know his story. He became a vampire to find his wife after she'd killed herself. Souls that die are born with no memories of their past lives. I wonder if he's found her yet?" Elaina wondered as she tapped her chin only to feel sad because hers sat across from her and she couldn't do anything. It upset her to a point where she was irritated.

"Speaking of mates, how come you haven't…" Rave started only to snap his mouth shut when she looked at him warningly and Fury saw causing him to be confused. Rave held up his hands in surrender before she just opened the book and continued reading.

"Ye are brave to travel with a cursed woman. I can't believe ye haven't been tempted." William voiced seriously looking like Rave was impressive.

"What?" Rave asked in confusion causing Elaina to snort because she simply couldn't help it. "Elaina what the hell is going on?"

"Nothing you need to know." she replied simply and patted him on the top of his head like a parent would a child causing him to wrinkle his nose at that.

"We should start moving. Let's go." Fury said so they all started off as Ravyn was carried by his brother.

"We should get a horse for that one." Baron replied simply causing Elaina to grit her teeth. Why should Ravyn be treated with kindness when Baron had been trying to kill her before Rave had arrived.

"He should just be dragged." she bit out quietly as Rave looked apologetically but she only sighed.

"Elaina." Rave said seeing the others look between them looking curious.

"What?"

"Your eyes are red again." he pointed out but she only continued to walk without a word. "You need to…"

"I know what it means Rave so please stop pointing it out. I can go days without it so it doesn't matter." she replied so he shrugged his shoulders as she continued to walk.

"It must be really painful." he said after looking at Fury right before the others looked at him but he was already looking at her.

"You have no idea." she got out calmly despite a choking feeling gripping her so quick that it caused her to pinch the bridge of her nose. "It's almost like it never happened, but even then its not the same."

"It'll get better." he saw her look completely doubtful but she said nothing. "So how come you cut off your hair?"

She saw the others pause in their own conversation. "I only left it long for him and since he's dead there's no point in keeping it long anymore." She saw that Rave seemed to accept that reason only to pause for a moment and look hostile.

"You're lying." he pointed out and grabbed her wrist. "What's been going on here?"

"Nothing you need to worry about." she said and started forward only to hear his quick intake of breath. She felt him touch her back, it had been the same place William had kicked her. She went rigid from pain and gritted her teeth against from crying out.

"Who hurt you, whoever it was hit you hard…it looks more like you've been kicked." Rave bit out seriously and saw two in front of them go tense. He sat his brother onto the ground before a snarl ripped from his throat causing them to freeze and look at him. "You dare put your hands on our Alpha out of violence!?"

"She was using magic against Fury!" William yelled defensively but Rave knew a lie when he heard one.

"Elaina would never do that, he life was ripped from her own hands and I know she wouldn't do that to someone else." Rave bit out as Elaina remained quiet. "Since it's obvious that she won't tell me who it was then I'll just hurt all of you."

"Ye probably don't even know her that well!" Baron snapped only to get tackled to the ground easily and realized this werewolf was incredibly strong.

"I know Elaina better then her own friends. You're the one judging her because of what she is instead of who she is. Elaina's the kind of person who would lay her life on the line for people she didn't know whether they're human, wolf, or deadwalker. She's never brought shame to our pack, if anything she's revered by every pack who has done business with us." Rave bit out and saw Baron's eyes sparkle at that.

"You sound as if you love her."

"I do love her and I'm not ashamed to say it. She loves someone else so I'm content with being her friend instead of her mate but I won't let anyone hurt her in front of me so be warned. Any of you touches her then you'll deal with me." Rave bit out seriously and stood seeing Fury looking at him. "You could've stopped it by telling the truth and you let it happen. Keep your hands off her in fact, don't even bother looking at her or I'll gouge your eyes out."

"Rave that's enough." she murmured simply because she didn't need him making threats on her behalf.

"I recognize lackeys when I see them, that I could smell traces of your scent on her. You're the ones who hit her so I'm going to hit you to give you a warning." Rave bit out and she felt glad that he was still so protective of her but she didn't need him doing something foolish.

"Rave, stop."

"I'm not going…"

"That wasn't a request." she warned watching him snarl at William and Seamus before returning to her side and picking up Ravyn.

"How long am I going have to deal with the idiot pack of Scotland?" Rave asked seriously and saw Baron go to retort but think better of it when Rave glared.

"I'll try to figure out a way to send you both back, no matter what." she promised but he looked worried about that. "No worries right?"

"Yeah, no worries." he said but her eyes were empty as she looked forward. She must've loved Fury a lot if it had effected her in such a way. He saw Fury look back and from him to Elaina and look irked about something. Was this Fury developing feelings for Elaina? He hoped so, he missed her smiling and odd humor. "When do we eat?"

"We usually just hunt down anything. So ye name is Rave?" the guy with the scar said so Rave gave a nod. "I'm Seamus, nice to meet ye. So ye and ye brother are twins right?"

"Unfortunately…sometimes it came in handy though." Rave grinned at that but Elaina only rolled her eyes. "Hey, don't go rolling your eyes!"

"You caused more trouble then the pack ever wanted to deal with so don't be telling me not to roll my eyes." she said seriously but he only looked at her sheepishly. "Seriously, don't start."

"Start what?" William asked in confusion as they stopped to take a break. "So how do ye know each other anyway?"

"Oh, well it's a long story so to put it simply her and the idiot over my shoulder were suppose to be mates. She thought I was my brother and grabbed me from behind and when she realized I wasn't him she jumped away and screamed." Rave explained simply causing Elaina to be peeved about that when William looked at her curiously.

"I only screamed because he called me his 'welcome home present' and I didn't like it." she grumbled as she looked at the lake they had rested near. She wanted to be in the water.

"I really want fish." Baron found himself grumbling and Elaina thought that would be really good.

"What are you doing?" Rave snorted as she stood up and looked at the skirt.

She murmured something under her breath seeing the skirt change to a pair of shorts. "I'm going fishing." she replied simply before taking off running towards the lake and jumping from a rock and diving into the water feeling the cool water feel like heaven.

She swam down to the bottom lazily seeing everything looked fine and peaceful. She didn't need to breath if she didn't want to but she preferred to so it was natural that she wasn't drowning. She stood on the bottom and when a fish swam close she snatched it. She started walking and snatching fish as she went.

"I wonder if she's dead?" Seamus murmured since she hadn't surfaced for a while. He felt guilty about how they had acted that morning when she was in the lake getting food for everyone.

"No, she doesn't have to breath."

"But she does." Fury pointed out and Rave thought it was obvious.

"She breaths out of habit, it makes her feel normal. She never asked to be like that, it just happened." Rave replied simply as he saw the surface waver before she walked right out of the lake holding fish in her hands. "How was the water?"

"It was great!" she replied cheerfully smiling brightly causing the others to gape but she only tossed the fish into the net Seamus was holding. She went over and proceeded to wring the water out of her hair. She saw him shrug like it was fine before him and William fixed a fire while Seamus prepared the fish for roasting.

She picked up a stick and started drawing stuff in the dirt. That's when she heard a groan from Ravyn causing her to jump away without hesitation as Ravyn started coming around. "I'll distance myself."

"Ye aren't going anywhere!" Baron warned seriously causing her to narrow her ruby eyes on him instantly.

"Get the hell out of my way." she bit out seeing him change but she only bared her teeth.

"Let her go, it's hard enough for her already." Rave said feeling responsible because he always seemed to be causing her pain. He saw Baron change back and narrow his eyes.

143

"Only a fool would trust a vampire."

"She's also a wolf! And she has been our only Alpha leading the pack single handedly putting all of us first instead of herself! I'm sorry if I don't share your outlook on vampires! Some of them where we come from are worth trusting!" Rave snapped back after standing causing Baron to start forward but suddenly Elaina was between them.

"If you lay a hand on either of them I'll rip you apart. They are under my rule so stay out of it." she warned seriously causing Baron to pull up short because she was serious.

"Damn Elaina, do you always have to interfere with every fight?" Rave groaned like it was annoying causing her to grab his ear painfully and yanked his head down.

"This is how you cause so much trouble. Starting fights when I am capable of handling it myself. Stay out of these things and make sure your brother doesn't kill anyone." she ordered watching him go to complain but nod since it was clear she wouldn't hear another word of it. "Understood?"

"Yeah, sorry." he replied with a nod so she let go of his ear before Ravyn jumped to his feet so suddenly she barely had time to shove Rave out of the way before something sliced into her stomach and burned like crazy.

A silver blade.

Without thinking Elaina slammed Ravyn into the tree and sank her teeth into his neck and drank despite her body protesting. She was poisoning herself to get rid of Ravyn. She looked into Ravyn's eyes. "Forget." she said and erased every memory about her from his mind as he yelled painfully after she let go of him. She removed every memory about herself despite his screaming as he held his head.

Elaina saw her skin visibly paling so fast as her legs gave out from under her. "Elaina open your eyes already!" she heard Rave yell so she peeked out.

"Calm down, it's not like I'm going to die." she croaked out before she sent herself into a sleep to heal. She felt something trickle into her mouth and knew it was blood. She turned her head away from it instantly, she didn't want it and she didn't need it either but she did need to sleep.

Elaina dreamed of her and Fury.

Elaina didn't know why this kind of dream felt so strange as she noticed she wore a beautiful pale green dress. She walked forward through the woods when she noticed a figure in the fog. She was confused when the fog thinned and then vanished seeing Fury there looking as puzzled as she felt.

She saw him turn around and look at her only to move away. She could only blink a couple times and looking around. "What are you doing here?" she asked seriously and it seemed to throw him off his own thoughts.

"Why are ye here?" he countered and she realized what he hadn't. Either she was in his dream or he was in hers.

"I'm waiting." she replied simply like it was obvious seeing him realize who she was waiting for.

"How did ye get that necklace?" Fury was surprised when he walked over and picked the necklace up that looked identical to his own.

"It was given to me." Her answer was always the same as she felt the back of his fingers suddenly touch over her collarbone.

"Ye are warm."

"I'm always warm." she stated simply like what he said didn't make sense.

"Impossible, ye are a deadwalker." he replied only to watch her face go red with anger. He'd never seen a deadwalker do that either. "Okay, so what are ye then?"

"I'm half werewolf and half vampire. I mean, I'm alive but I just don't need to breath if I don't want to." she replied simply right before he reached out and touched her face. She was a bit uncomfortable by that but he seemed to be amazed by that. She saw him step closer and she felt her heart start pounding in her chest.

"Ye are still cursed." he murmured only to watch her snort. "What?"

"I had to think of something to keep men from trying to take advantage of me." she replied lamely wondering why he grinned at that. "Besides, this is only a dream."

"Nay, it feels too real to be just a dream."

"That's all it is, nothing more." she couldn't mess with him in his dreams because he would likely remember them when he woke and freak out. She went to go when his hand caught her own making her look at him. "Let go Fury."

"How do ye know my pack name?" he asked seriously only to see her move away a bit quickly. He wasn't understanding why he was dreaming of the deadwalker but since it was only a dream he might as well make the best of it. He stalked towards her causing her to move back just as quickly. "Why are ye running away from me?"

"I'm doing this for your own good." she replied seriously seeing him shake his head before trapping her against a tree.

"Only I know what is for my own good. Now stop moving." Fury wrapped an arm around her waist seeing her face go red. "What a beautiful color."

"A closet romantic." she replied lamely right before he held her chin between his fingers. She tried to lean away but she missed it, she missed the arms holding her now. She connected her eyes with his right before his lips descending upon hers. It was just like she'd remembered.

Fury was expecting her to shove him away and complain about how she was a lady. She did the exact opposite. She was the one who deepened the kiss between the two of them. He felt her arms wrap around his neck and he realized she fit perfectly against him.

He felt the wolf in his raise up causing him to rip away instantly seeing her flushed from head to toe. He saw her give him a knowing look before walking forward and taking his face into her hands. He felt strange and she closed her eyes before breathing deep. The bright warm smile she gave him sent his heart beating crazy in his chest.

"You don't have to be careful with me Fury. I'm not human remember?" she reminded him causing his eyes to start glowing phosphorescently so she leaned forward and kissed him. She felt him crush her against him causing her to moan as the kiss became more demanding.

"Fury wake up." she heard Baron groan irritably so she pulled away noticing the disappointment on Fury's face.

"You need to wake up now."

"I can sleep for a little while longer." Fury murmured against her neck as he leaned forward to taste the flesh there. That's when he felt a tiny shock pass through him. He looked down and saw a claiming mark on her neck. He felt his finger brush over it right before his eyes collided with the necklace that looked like his. "Who is ye sonuachar?"

"You aren't ready to know the answer to that question." she murmured softly but he felt like he didn't need to ask. "It's okay, like I said, this is only a dream. If you don't want it then I will leave. It's completely up to you."

"So if I wake and want ye to leave then ye will leave?"

"I will, no matter how much it hurts."

"Wait, ye told us ye sonuachar died." he replied seriously only to see her face look completely tortured.

"I couldn't protect you, you had protected me all the time and I couldn't even save you. I'm so sorry." she couldn't help but cry at that because it made her chest hurt just thinking about it. "I loved you so much and I couldn't even protect you!"

"Shh, don't cry." he murmured and went to touch her but she only shoved him away.

Fury snapped awake seeing Baron looking at him like he was annoying so he sat up and looked around the camp seeing Elaina laying on the ground. She was unmoving, her skin was still pale, and she wasn't breathing. He saw Rave pull out a small knife from her bag before kneeling in front of her. He didn't even know why he suddenly had Rave by the throat glaring at him.

"Fury what's going on?" William asked in confusion thinking he knew something about them that they didn't.

"Let me go, he cut her with silver. I have to open the wound to get the poison out or she's going to die." Rave said and knocked Fury away before he saw Fury looking at her worryingly. Did he know? Rave sat on one side before raising her shirt a little showing the cut was getting infected. He heated the blade in the fire before he swiftly cut away the poisoned flesh hearing her cry out in pain but she didn't wake. That's when he saw inside the cut. He felt his heart sink in his chest because the silver likely combined with Ravyn's blood and it had spread throughout her whole system.

Elaina was dying.

Rave sliced open his wrist and held it over her mouth and she drank a little before she started convulsing. He saw his wrist heal as Elaina thrashed. He saw the others finally stand looking at her in horror.

Elaina felt terrible as she woke up slowly seeing Rave looking down at her with the saddest face she'd ever seen him wear. She knew what it meant, she had succeeded in helping Ravyn but she had damned herself. She felt her stomach roil so rolled to her side before getting sick to her stomach seeing the blood was clotted and a greenish-black.

"What's wrong with her?" Baron asked thinking she had some kind of disease only for deadwalkers.

"She's dying." Rave choked out and Fury felt his heart drop. "She always was such a selfless person."

"How can she be dying?" Seamus asked because he didn't understand.

"Her and Ravyn were the same, hybrids. Their blood is poisonous to each other. She drank his blood so that she could erase his memories. His blood combined with the poison from the silver and spread through her body." Rave explained as his saw the black lines spreading showing her veins.

"How long does she have?" Fury asked seriously so Rave looked at them.

"Until sunrise tomorrow, maybe less. It depends on how fast the poison spreads."

Elaina sat up slowly seeing the lines spreading over her slowly. She could feel it draining her energy faster then anything. "Rave…need to talk…now…private." she said watching him look confused. "Book."

"Right." he said before holding the book in front of her seeing her movements were sluggish and clumsy.

Elaina looked through the book and found the page she was looking for. The return spell. "This…home." she was so exhausted she couldn't even say whole sentences so she opened her mind.

Rave can you hear me? she asked seeing him look at her and nod. Okay, listen carefully. This spell will send you and Ravyn back…but I'll be sending you to the time before I get bit by the vampire. Don't let Ravyn bite me, you do it instead. Make sure that I don't fall for Ravyn or this will happen all over again. Now, to get back you have to kill me.

"WHAT!?" he yelled seriously only to see her looking serious.

Ravyn's blood is key to getting you back but he would've had to been killed to get us both back. You would never be able to kill your brother and so I decided for myself. This is my last order to you as an Alpha, Rave, at midnight I want you to kill me. The portal will open instantly so go in. Elaina saw him look at the ground but she only closed the book as he looked mad at that. Don't let Fury see.

"I won't." Rave sat her against a tree seeing her just sitting there quietly as he saw Ravyn still laying on the ground. "How much is he going to remember?"

Nothing. He won't even remember biting me in the first place.

Rave gave a small nod while the others looked confused about what was going on. "You should tell him you know." he murmured only to see her look like it would be pointless.

"What is wrong with her?" Baron asked wondering if it was the curse.

"She's going to die, and she knows she doesn't have that long either. What do you think is wrong with her!?" Rave snapped seriously causing Baron to jump away.

"Ye really do love her don't you?" Fury stated wondering why he wanted to tear the wolf apart.

"Yeah, well, she didn't love me in the same sense. It's not like I was going to do to her what my brother did. She didn't love me as much or the same way she loved her mate." Rave saw Elaina look apologetic about that but he knew she didn't need to. "Her mate was everything to her, he meant so much that she'd risk everything just to see him again."

It was as simple as that and they both knew it. Rave might've loved her but they would only be friends. She was meant to be with Fury and he knew it deep down. He walked over to Fury and gave a small nod before going to the lake.

"What was that about?" Baron asked only to see Fury looking at Elaina as if he recognized her. "Fury?"

"Ye are her sonuachar aren't ye?" Seamus asked seriously but Fury could only feel disappointed. "I am sorry. It must be hard to see her die like this. I had a thought when I saw the claim mark on the side of her neck."

"Can you three go down to the lake? Take that one with you." Fury said as he pointed to Ravyn so they obliged and went down. He walked over to Elaina and picked her up before he took off running.

"Where…going?" he heard her ask in confusion right before he got to the waterfall surrounded by a field of flowers. He carried her over to the small pond and sat her down in the flowers gently before sitting next to her.

"I'm sorry I didn't realize it sooner." he apologized quietly as the sun shone down on them.

"I'm…sorry…didn't…tell…sooner." she replied softly as she leaned against his shoulder. She felt herself sag against him because she was so weak. She saw him move to cradle her against him. She smelled his scent wash over her and her mouth started to salivate but she couldn't bite him.

Fury? She asked mentally feeling him jump before he looked at her. I'm sorry that you have to see this happening to me. I really am. You should know something about me though.

"What?"

Technically I'm not even born yet. I met you in the future…about eight hundred years into the future. She replied seeing him look like that couldn't be possible. She gave his hand a small squeeze since that was all she was capable of.

"How is that possible, I couldn't possibly live that long." he said and she realized something about him that he'd never told her before.

I think this was suppose to happen. If you accept my blood you'll become immortal. If you become immortal then you will meet me again. That's only if you want to. she saw him hesitate as she felt him tracing the black lines that were slowly spreading over her body. I need to tell you something before you do though.

"What?"

I've ordered Rave to kill me.

"Why?" he looked like he didn't understand.

It's painful, I'm able to hide it but it hurts. Don't be angry with him when he does. I won't hurt anymore and it'll get them both home. Rave has already promised not to let this happen to me again. She felt his arms fold around her protectively so she sat her head against his shoulder and slowly rose her arm up. If you do then you should drink now before the lines spread further.

"Won't they spread if I drink from ye?"

They will but I'm willing to risk it if it means I can meet you again. It was true to. She would fall for him all over just like he had fallen for her. She might be doubtful at first but she'd warm up to him.

"How close were we?"

I'll let you handle that the next time around. Third times the charm. she laughed so he accepted her offer. She saw him raise her arm before biting into it causing her to gasp slightly. She saw him drink deeply until she yanked her arm away before the black lines could get to the cut.

"I don't feel any different." he murmured and she knew he wasn't really suppose to.

You won't. If you wish, you can share this with your pack but tread carefully. Give your blood only to those you completely trust. she replied seriously seeing him nod before they laid in the flowers and just rested. She saw the sun start setting as she got hungry but she couldn't feed or the others couldn't get back.

"Are you alright?" Fury asked slowly seeing her just give a slight jerk that looked like a nod. "We should get back."

"Mmm." she felt him pick her up right before her arm shattered causing her breath to hitch in pain and tears rolled down her face.

Get to the camp, quick. She said so he ran as her arm continued to get jarred.

"Rave!" Fury called so they hurried up and she saw Rave look stunned at how much Elaina had changed.

"What's wrong with her?" Rave asked quickly because she was crying and her arm looked incredibly weird.

Rave you have to do it now, I'm not going to make it to midnight! she cried out in her head seeing him hesitate. Do it now. It hurts! It hurts Rave!

"Okay!" he yelled before she looked at Fury who sat her down.

Fury, please don't forget me. Don't forget Rave either, you two are going to be really great friends. She said seeing him looking more tortured then she felt. I love you so much.

"Shh, this isn't 'goodbye' remember?" he murmured seeing her nod slowly so he leaned down and kissed her briefly.

Rave saw Fury move away so Elaina used the last of her energy and magic to create the seal for the portal. He felt his hand start shaking so she looked at him. He wasn't sure if he could really help her by doing this. How could he kill the woman he loved?

Remember Rave, you have to pierce my heart with the sword. She saw him nod before she felt herself collapse onto the ground. She saw Rave poise the sword over the left side of her chest. Thank you Rave, you've truly been a great friend.

"I...can't." Rave got out as his hand shook because he was looking at the girl he had fallen in love with and she was asking him to kill her.

This is only minor for me Rave, we'll meet again. Please end my suffering? She asked so he took a deep breath to calm himself but it didn't work.

"I'm sorry Elaina, I really can't."

"Have to...home. Have...home." she said as she cried because the pain was getting worse. She felt her left leg shatter into pieces and she felt cold seeping into her. "Hurry."

Baron, can you hear me? She asked seeing him go from looking around to looking directly at her. Take Rave's hand in your own and push the sword through. Please do this. It... is becoming unbearable and I don't want Fury to see me suffering. Look at him.

Baron looked at Fury and saw him using every bit of control to hold himself in place. He could tell Fury was going to snap soon and stop it from happening if Rave didn't go through with it quickly.

Please Baron, not for me but for Fury. Please!? she begged because she was already choking on her own blood.

"Fine!" Baron yelled suddenly causing everyone to get confused. Baron marched forward and grabbed Rave's hand that held the sword.

"What are you..."

Baron pushed the sword through her chest in one swift movement hearing her breath hitch in her throat. He looked at Fury apologetically and only saw a look of gratefulness in his eyes. Had Elaina already told him? He guessed so if Fury wasn't attacking him.

"Thank...you." she choked out before Baron pulled the sword out seeing blood spread out from underneath her. She felt her bones popping as she resumed the body of a beautiful silver wolf. She saw the portal form from the blood.

Hurry...go...Rave. Rave heard her say that so he picked up his brother who would have absolutely no memory of anything and stopped by her side.

"You'll always be an Alpha to me Elaina." he said and brushed a hand across the fur on her neck before he jumped into the portal thinking about the time before Elaina got asked out to the homecoming dance. He would do as he was ordered.

Fury saw the portal close before rushing forward and kneeling next to Elaina. "How will I ever find ye?" he whispered after leaning his head down and burying his face into her neck.

The…book…has…my address…in it. she got out as she felt her vision start dimming. Don't…forget…me.

"I won't forget ye, I promise." he murmured right before he sat back to look at her. That's when her body started glowing before erupting into lights that faded before he swore he felt fingers brush against the side of his face. He looked at the book and opened it seeing her name and some kind of number and other things with it.

"Do ye know how long ye have to wait?" Baron asked causing him to nod slowly.

"About eight hundred years." he replied right before his nails got pointy and his vision sharpened. He felt slightly different but the same nonetheless. "I'll find her, I swear I will."

"We'll help." Baron swore causing the other to nod seriously and he felt like with his pack he could do anything.

Chapter 9

"Elaina get up already!" Daisy laughed as she jumped up and down on Elaina's bed making her groan so Daisy dog piled on her.

"Okay, Okay, I'm up already." Elaina grunted before sitting up and stretching her arms. She stood up and went to the bathroom where she brushed her teeth.

"Good morning Elaina." her aunt said so Elaina gave her a hug as Daisy jumped up so Elaina picked her up and kissed her nose. "Daisy stop pestering Elaina.

"It's fine." Elaina laughed before they ate breakfast, that's when a knock sounded on the door. She hurried over and opened the door seeing Julie with Connor and Rave with Blade and Larkin. "Morning."

"Morning." they said as she noticed Connor looking at Julie.

"Come on in, we're having chocolate chip pancakes." Elaina snorted seeing Blade rush in with Larkin and Julie. "Connor I don't see why you just don't ask her."

"Elaina we are suddenly out of juice, could you go to the store and get some please?" Tricia asked after sticking her head out.

"Yeah, you two go enjoy breakfast."

"You want company?" Rave asked but she shook her head. "You're doing a great job as alpha Elaina, especially by yourself."

"Oh, thanks." she replied brightly before running off to the store. She ran feeling great as her feet beat against the pavement below her. You see, Elaina use to be human. Now she was a very complicated creature to figure out. She was sort of half vampire and half werewolf. It was pretty cool, what was even cooler was that she was the only alpha of a pack of werewolves. They were letting her be the only alpha until she found someone she wanted as her mate.

Elaina got in the store and headed straight to the juice section. "What kind of juice did she want?" she grumbled so she mind melded with Rave.

Hey Rave, ask my aunt what kind of juice she wanted. Elaina said only to catch the smell of something pleasant. She would've followed it but she had to get juice.

She said orange juice with no pulp. He replied as one of her favorite songs came on. *She also needs more syrup, Larkin and Blade got a bit out of control with the pancakes.*

Elaina took off running to the aisle with the syrup only to turn the corner and run into something solid. She thought it wouldn't have been so bad if the carton hadn't gotten crushed between her and whatever she'd smacked into. She felt herself start to slip right before an arm wrapped around her waist and steadied her.

She felt the intoxicating fragrance wrap around her so she looked up slowly only to feel completely stunned. She knew Rave was very handsome but the guy looking down at her in shock was gorgeous.

"Hey Fury…" Seamus started asking only to drop the cookies he had in his hand in shock when he saw Elaina. "Elaina?"

"Do I know you?" she asked and put space between her and Fury quickly. She could tell they were werewolves instantly. She saw two more come behind the one and stare at her in shock. She heard her phone suddenly ring so she answered. "Hello?"

"Hey, we got a huge problem!"

"What is it?" she asked quickly because Seth sounded urgent.

"We got some trouble. Tristan needs you at the pack house now!" Seth yelled so she hung up before grabbing the syrup and grabbing another carton of juice.

"Damn it, always having to rush." she grumbled before hurrying out of the store and running to the pack house. She got there and breathed deeply to catch her breath.

"Where'd you run from?" Seth asked in confusion thinking she was home.

"At the store, run these to my house please. You might as well eat while there." she replied seeing him nod and hurry over with the groceries. She went into the living room seeing Tristan pacing looking troubled. "What's wrong Tristan?"

"I've been walking around town and there are scents of wolves that I've picked up that aren't familiar to me. There are four of them." he said causing her to gawk as she remembered the ones from the grocery store. "What?"

"I met them, when I was at the grocery. They all looked at me like they knew me but I've never seen any of them before." she said as Rave came in only to freeze.

"They recognized you? Are you sure?" Tristan asked so she gave a serious nod. "And you didn't know any of them?"

"No, but I felt a familiarity despite never seeing them before." she answered wondering why she felt like she knew the one. She shrugged since it was only a matter of time before they left. "I need to go for a run and clear my head."

"That isn't a good idea." Tristan saw her look like she needed to run or she was going to go insane. "Be careful."

"I will." she replied before going out the back and stripping off her clothes. She changed into a wolf and jumped over the fence before running into the woods where she felt adrenaline star pumping through her veins. She loved running in the woods because it allowed her to clear her head.

Elaina lopped through the underbrush and started running through the woods. She jumped over fallen logs reveling in the feel of soil underneath her paws. It was likely the best feeling anyone could ever have in their life.

She was running when something suddenly clamped around her front right paw causing her to scream but it only came out in wounded barks. She looked down seeing a metal trap and the teeth were through her leg. Who the hell put that here?!

"Well look what we got here!" a man laughed as him and another walked forward causing her to snarl. "See! I told you I saw some wolves running through the woods!"

"What a beautiful wolf, we'll get a lot for her pelt." the other said as he pulled out a hunting knife.

Elaina saw one reach so she sank her teeth into his hand only to get her side sliced with the knife. She tried to bite him causing the poacher to jump away. She felt fear start blossoming in her when the one pulled out a gun and aimed it right at her.

"You can't shoot it you idiot! You'll ruin the fur! Just slip the leash around it." the poacher bit out and the other slipped the collar around her neck so tight that it practically started choking her. She was removed from the trap and practically dragged through the woods causing her to yelp and try to tug the other way.

"Stop fighting!" he yelled and kicked her in the side causing her to collapse onto the ground. "You stupid mutt!"

She felt the foot collide with her again and the pain was completely unbearable. She knew she had probably just got a few ribs cracked by the idiot dragging her like she wasn't even an animal. Elaina needed to escape quick before they pulled out the daggers and started slicing at her.

Elaina growled and snarled as she was dragged through mud, underbrush, and anything else that littered the forest floor. She thought it was impossible for her to ever hate the forest that her and the other wolves held dear but at the moment she hated it. No one would find her until it was likely too late. She tried to strain against the leash but the more she pulled the more it hurt. She could feel it cutting into her skin from struggling so bad.

"Tie her to the tree so we can go get something to eat already." the third yelled annoyingly as he sat next to the small little tent.

Elaina was latched to a metal chain link that had been snapped around a large tree trunk. She saw the third walk towards her and smile in such a twisted way it made her nauseous. She was going to die by their hands.

"This is a nice catch. Let's go get something to eat, then we'll come back and finish up with this mutt." the man bit out so they left meaning that they probably lived close.

Elaina waited until she was sure they had left so she tried to change back only to feel the metal in the chain start burning her neck. A silver chain!? How could they possibly know to use a silver chain?! Maybe it was just a coincidence? Anyway, it was useless to change back into her human form. At least the fur on her neck prevented the silver in the chain from poisoning her.

Elaina needed to rest to build up her strength so she fell into a light sleep. She felt hands touch her causing her to snap her jaws around it hearing the poacher scream in pain.

"I'll hold it down and you cut it off!"

Elaina was flattened to the ground causing her to scream and yell because he was too heavy and she couldn't expose what she was by changing forms. She felt the knife cut into her side again making her kick hearing the guy swear.

"Snap it's freaking neck, it's too rowdy."

Elaina felt the hands grab her neck right before she heard snarling so she looked up seeing a brown wolf with pale blue eyes. She saw three more arrive behind it causing the guys to stand looking terrified. She saw the one reach for his gun so she sank her teeth into his ankle making him scream in pain.

"You stupid dog!" he yelled and kicked her in the side of the face causing her to cry out in pain despite it healing shortly after.

She was likely to still have a good sized bruise though.

Elaina saw the brown one snarl before tackling the guy to the ground and snapping him jaws, but he didn't kill the poacher. She saw them run off as fast as possible which wasn't that fast since they were overweight. She saw him change into his human form causing her to move away instantly because she didn't know why she felt comfortable around him.

"Is she alright?" William asked causing Fury to shrug since she wouldn't let him close enough.

"You three go alert her pack what happen, they shouldn't be running through the woods. God knows how many of these traps those poachers have set." Fury said so they nodded and took off running after changing back so he looked at Elaina once they were gone. "I'm not going to hurt you."

Elaina knew it was the truth so when he approached her she sat down despite her arm still in the trap. She saw him reach forward and open the trap with little to no difficulty so she lifted her arm out only to groan from the throbbing. She changed back and held her arm because it hurt.

"Let me see." he said and held out his hand so she sat her arm in it slowly. "It could be worse."

"No kidding." she replied seriously and went to tug her arm back but he hand wrapped around her arm gently so she looked up seeing the pale blue eyes looking at her with worry. Why would a stranger be worried for her?

"I hate to be the one to tell you this but it's no longer safe for you and your pack to be here. If poachers are after you then you need to leave." Fury saw her frown at him showing she already knowing that. "Are you okay to walk?"

"I'm fine to walk." she replied but didn't stand. "What are you and your pack doing on our territory?"

"Hmm?"

"Why are you and your pack here?!" she yelled seriously and saw him look sheepish about that. "How do you all even know me!?"

"It's a bit complicated." he murmured like she might not believe him so she stood slowly and turned to leave only to feel his arms wrap around her shoulders. "Please don't run from me, I've been looking for you for a long time."

"Looking for me? Why?" she got out with difficulty right before she was turned to face him wondering why those pale blue eyes felt so familiar to her. She felt like she couldn't break eye contact as she looked at him. All she felt were his fingers brushing against her jaw gently and her heart started pounding. "Who are you?"

"My name is Fury and I have been waiting for you for eight hundred years Elaina." he murmured before leaning down and brushing his lips across her cheek. That's when Rave arrived with his pack brothers. "Hello Rave."

"Fury, I thought you weren't suppose to come until next month?" Rave asked in confusion but Fury only shrugged.

"He couldn't wait at all." William replied lamely causing Elaina looked at Rave.

"You know them Rave?"

"You did too, at one point." Rave grumbled but she looked puzzled more then anything. "I'll leave the explaining to Fury."

"Okay so how do I know you?" Elaina asked seriously so they others walked away to give them some privacy.

"We're mates."

"No we're not." she replied in a matter-of-fact tone watching him rub his temples as if knowing she was going to say that. "I'm not mated to anyone, let alone *you*."

"And what is wrong with *me*?" Elaina went to say only to look elsewhere because she didn't know him well enough to say something like that. "Don't you even want to get to know me?"

"Get to know you?" she repeated since most males had only tried to get her to sleep with them.

"It's not like we don't have the time. After all, neither of us are ever going to age." Fury replied simply causing her to freeze, how had he known that she wouldn't be aging anymore.

"No, I don't think that would be a good idea." she murmured and went to step away but one of his arms curved around her waist. "What do you think you're doing?"

"Elaina? Don't run from me?" he asked and the longing in his voice was almost too much for her to bear. "I don't care how long it takes for me to win over your heart, but don't leave without even considering it."

"How could you say something like that without even knowing me?" she asked seriously hoping this wasn't some kind of prank put on by Rave. He had always been messing with her about how she needed to get into the dating ring but with all the decisions she'd need to make alone as the only alpha she never had the time. She suddenly realized that his thumbs were brushing against the mark around her neck made by the chain. What's worse is that it was likely to scar too.

With a sigh she removed his hands from her neck and pushed them away from her because she had to put the pack before herself. "Elaina, you don't have to do everything by yourself." she heard his words and they touched her deeply but there was no reason for him and his pack to help hers. She could handle doing everything by herself. Even Tristan agreed that she was the best Alpha they'd ever had for a very long time.

It's because she was selfless where others hadn't been.

"I'm sorry but there's no possible way something could exist between us." Elaina felt terrible when he gave her such a downcast face but she only sat her hand on his shoulder. "You have my gratitude and the gratitude of the pack for saving my life. We owe you a great deal."

"You don't owe me anything Elaina." he replied seriously before taking her hand and kissing the inside of the wrist. "I'm glad I made it in time."

Elaina took off running seeing Rave break from the others and join her to go back to the house. She could feel tears running down her face and she didn't understand why. Why did she feel so sad when she hadn't even know him.

"Elaina what's wrong?" Rave was confused as to why she was crying but she only shook her head. "Did something happen?"

"No, nothing happened. Nothing will ever happen." Elaina felt her heart ache at those words but she forced herself to keep running until they got to the house. She grabbed clothes that she'd left in the pack's house when they went on runs before going up to the bathroom and getting a nice hot shower. She scrubbed offensively at her face and shoulders but no matter how hard she scrubbed it felt like she'd never get rid of Fury's fingers brushing against them.

She stepped out of the shower and wrapped the towel around her as she walked to the mirror and wiped the fog of it. She looked at the scar around her neck and sighed. She'd never gotten scars like this until she became a werewolf. She rubbed her head feeling a migraine start but it was probably because of the silver chain. It was going to make her a little sick but it hadn't touched her skin long enough to poison her.

She dried off and got dressed quickly letting her hair hang loose behind her so she went down the stairs seeing Rave had gathered the pack. She saw him give a small nod showing everyone was ready. She walked into the room hearing the loud talking and chattering hush immediately and the others showed their respect by kneeling down and exposing their necks.

"Rave said something happened while you were on your run." Tristan stated only to see a scar around her neck. "You've been exposed to silver."

"It's time for us to leave this state. We need to go to a state where it's normal to have wolves." Elaina saw everyone look like they couldn't possibly leave their homes. "I'm sorry but there are poachers gathering in the woods now. It's not safe for us here any more."

"Your family and friends are here though." Elaina looked at Ravyn's mate Fern. "How are we going to leave without our alpha?"

"You won't have to, I'm coming with you."

"Elaina you can't…" Rave started only to see her hold up her hand so he snapped his jaw shut.

"I can't stay here and put them in danger. If a poacher were to see what we really are, *who* we really are then they wouldn't be safe here either. I'd rather leave and know they'll be safe then to stay and risk something happen to them. That's something I can't do." Elaina was completely serious and they could all tell. "Fern and Ravyn?"

"Yes?" they asked so Elaina faced them.

"I want you both to find a new home for us. Somewhere that we won't stand out of place. A place that has a lot of land for sell that we can live peacefully." Elaina saw Fern smile warmly with excitement before running over and hugging her tightly.

"Of course! We won't let you down!" Fern exclaimed quickly and ran back to Ravyn who bowed before they left with Tristan to work everything out. "Blade, Seth, Larkin, and Rave?"

"Yes?"

"I want you all to help the elders and people with children pack up. We need to get out of here before any more poachers show up. I want *everyone* to stay out of the woods until we leave. It'll keep everyone safe but make sure you all start packing right away because we need to be out of here before the next full moon. That's a week and a half away."

Everyone nodded so she went to the store with the women to buy containers and boxes to pack everything in. She was walking out when she saw Fury and the others heading towards the store. She wasn't surprised when one pointed her out causing Fury to look from the packing supplies to her.

"What a gorgeous wolf, looks like he's interested in you Elaina." Fern giggled but Elaina only shook her head quickly.

"You all head back to the house, I'll see you there."

"If you say so." Fern murmured wondering who they were to Elaina.

Elaina walked over and stopped a good three to four feet away from Fury. "You're leaving with the pack aren't you." She could only nod despite it not being a question. "It's because of the poachers."

"Yeah, I can't risk anyone's life just to stay here so we're leaving."

"How can you leave your family?" William asked only to see tears suddenly well up but they vanished showing she was refusing to dwell of the matter.

"I'm only going to put them in danger by staying here. I can't do that, I have to leave." she replied like it was the only object. "I keep trying to convince myself that I can live normally with them but I'm not normal. I'll never be normal ever again and endangering them is something I wouldn't be able to live with."

"You'd rather be unhappy know your family was safe."

The air seemed to swirl around them as she looked at him.

"Where are you all moving to?" Fury asked only to see her give a small shrug.

"Somewhere we won't feel out of place, where wolves won't stand out. Probably out west I believe." she saw him nod as he closed the distance between them. She could feel the body heat radiating from him. How could she feel safe or relieved with him just standing there in front of her, she had to be losing her mind.

"Will I ever see you again?" he asked and the look on her face said that it was unlikely to happen. "I mean once everyone has settled in and there's no longer any danger from poachers."

"I doubt it."

"Ah, but if it does happen you might have to go on a date with me." he replied simply and Elaina looked like he had to be kidding. "You do owe me for the rescue remember?"

"What ever happened to being a *Good Samaritan*?" she asked but he only chuckled at that, she couldn't stop the smile that crossed her face.

"We aren't human, we're wolves. We have our own sets of rules. There's no such thing as a Good Samaritan in the Were world." Fury snorted as he tried to make her see that it probably wouldn't be that bad but she seemed to be resisting the charm.

Elaina, is everything alright? Rave asked in her mind and she forgot he wasn't near her causing her to nod.

Yeah, it's fine. I'll be back in a few minutes. she replied quickly and wondered if the uneasiness in her tone. She knew she would feel like that until they got to their new home. She wanted to get there as fast as possible so that no one else would have to go through what she'd went through a hour or so before.

"Well, goodbye."

"This isn't goodbye." Fury murmured as he watched her hurry back to the pack house to help with the move. How was she going to explain to her family that she had to move?

Elaina was exhausted as she walked back to her aunt's house hearing Julie and Daisy laughing in the kitchen. She got in the doorway seeing Connor making faces at Daisy while Julie laughed. "Hey you guys." she saw them look up right before Connor jumped to his feet.

"Is something wrong?" he asked causing her to give a small nod.

"We're leaving."

Elaina felt terrible at Connor's pained face showing that he didn't want to leave but going against the pack would make him a rogue. She knew he wanted to stay here with Julie and she wanted him to.

"Why are you leaving?" Julie seemed puzzled by the idea as to why since there were so many things that they'd planned for the future after high school. Like going to the same college, going to parties, seeing movies, and having sleepovers.

"Yeah, why are you leaving Ellie?" Daisy asked as she cried so Elaina kneeled in front of her.

"There are people who want to hurt us doggies."

"Poachers?" Connor asked so she gave a quick confirmation.

"None of us are safe in the woods anymore, they sat down bear traps." she saw Julie look like she couldn't believe that. "I think it might've been coincidence but they have silver chains. I couldn't even escape because I'd get poisoned."

"That's inhumane, how could they use bear traps for *wolves*?" Julie asked and hugged Elaina tightly as Tricia came in only to pause.

"Did something happen?"

"Julie can I talk to you for a bit?" Connor asked so Julie followed him out while Elaina explained the situation.

"You're leaving?!" Tricia couldn't even believe it because she'd already received her acceptance letter to a local college. "Why do you have to leave?"

"It's necessary, please don't try to stop me Aunt Tricia. It'll keep you and Daisy safe, we can't risk letting others know what we are. I told you, Julie, and Daisy because you're the only family I have. It's time for us to leave though."

"I knew you wouldn't be able to stay here forever but I was hoping for it." Tricia was going to miss her niece, but she knew it was for the best because it would keep Elaina safe. That's all she hoped for.

"Anyways, I have to go back over to the pack house for a little bit to help but I'll be home tonight."

"How long until you move?"

"A week." Tricia pulled her into a tight hug since that was too soon. "We have to leave before the next full moon."

The days flew by as they got everyone situated to move out of their house and onto the new property that was located in Choteau, Montana. Montana was a very large state, it was heavily forested with mountains and plenty of games for when they went on the full moon runs. It was a perfect place for a pack of wolves could live without being exposed.

"Everyone the vans are here!" Blade called so Seth and Larkin started carrying down their stuff. The other pack members were already on their way to Montana. They had stayed behind because Tricia insisted on having a 'goodbye' dinner for them and they were never ones to complain about a free meal.

"I'll go tell Elaina!" Larkin volunteered as Rave walked down the stairs only to pause for a moment.

"She already knows and is on her way out now." Rave replied a few seconds later so they stated loading up the trucks seeing Elaina loading up hers.

"Hey Rave, how come you haven't told Elaina your feelings?" Connor asked suddenly but Rave only looked else where. He didn't see why there were only three vans when there should've been six. "I told Julie how I felt, we would be going out if we weren't moving to Montana."

"Yeah, about that Connor…you *aren't* moving to Montana." Elaina said causing him to stop short and pause.

"Wait, how come?!"

"You have officially become a rogue." Elaina stated watching the color drain from his face. "Just kidding."

"Then why aren't I going with everyone?" he asked seriously before Julie walked out of the house and gave a small wave. "Wait, I'm staying here?"

"Yeah, but under specific orders. Make sure you protect my friend. As for what pack you'll be apart of, I called in a small favor." she stated seriously so Fury and the others came out of the house as well. "My aunt has agreed to let them stay with her and Daisy. You and William will be roommates."

"Yo." William said with a small wave so Connor went over straight to Julie and pulled her into a kiss that caused Elaina's face to flush.

"Oh for crying out loud, get a room."

"He has to move in first." Julie pointed out teasingly so Elaina started putting her stuff into her personal truck since the whole pack decided to get her a house for herself. It was all one level but the pictures of it were beautiful and she thought it would be perfect. "Here, I want to help too."

Elaina sighed in defeat since Julie was handling the move in her own little way. She saw Fury come over and help her as well while his pack members helped hers. It was annoying her that she seemed to notice every time his arm brushed hers, when he was close, or when he seemed to be looking at her.

"Hey Elaina, Rave has something to say to you!" Larkin laughed hysterically as Rave tried to shut him up and she heard Fury give a low growl.

Elaina felt shocked that he had sounded so feral but she ignored him and followed Rave into the house. "Something wrong Rave?" she asked and when he shook his head she saw him looking embarrassed pretty quickly.

"Look, I'm going to say this as simple as possible." Rave watched her give a small nod so he took a deep breath. "I love you."

"Eh?" Elaina couldn't believe those words had just came out of his mouth because she thought he'd be the last person she'd ever hear say that.

"I love you, and I at least wanted you to know before Fury proposed." he stated seeing her confusion get even worse at that.

"Why would a complete stranger propose to me?"

"You are soul mates Elaina. You are meant to be with Fury." Rave thought it was obvious but she stood there looking at him like he was insane. "Anyway, I just wanted you to know before you became his mate."

"I don't know anything about him, I'm not going to be his mate."

"You will, in time." Rave said and just because he couldn't help himself he kissed her. It was just like he remembered, empty and completely pointless but he just wanted it to happen. "I'm sorry but please act like I never said it."

"Act like you never said it?" Elaina hurried from the house seeing Fury look up and frown before going back into the house. She wasn't going to chase after someone she didn't know anything about. She went back to packing as Julie kept asked her what was wrong but no one needed to know. She hadn't even needed to know. She wished she didn't.

"Well we're all packed up." Blade stated triumphantly as he slammed the back of the moving truck shut.

Elaina gave a small nod so she went over to her aunt and gave her a huge hug as well as Daisy before heading to the van the pack would be riding in. They had already agreed to come and see her when everyone had gotten settled in. She sat in the front passenger seat next to Larkin who was driving and waved out the window.

"Let's go, we don't need to be here longer then necessary. We're already cutting it close to the change anyway." Elaina said so Larkin started away and she just watched as her family got smaller and smaller until they were finally out of sight.

"You don't always have to be so strong for us Elaina." Seth voiced seriously but she wasn't going to let them see her cry. She would see her family again so she didn't need to cry.

"I don't know what you're going on about but thanks anyway." she replied like he'd said something entirely different. She sat in the chair as they started down the road to the interstate. That's when she heard barking. "What…"

Elaina looking in the side mirror seeing a chocolate brown wolf chasing after the car and her heart soared in her chest. She squashed that feeling, which sent her heart aching instantly. "Does this car go any faster?" Elaina saw Larkin nod as the wolf started catching up. "Can you drive faster please?"

"Hey, one of the wolves from that guy's pack is following us." Seth pointed out when Larkin went to hit the brake she growled.

"Just keep driving."

"Elaina…" Rave started but she didn't need someone else around her…let alone someone else that she had the risk of losing.

"I said to keep driving." she ordered and Larkin could do nothing but step on the gas and drive even faster. She watched the wolf try to keep up but she only blasted music to drown out the barks that were pleas in her ears.

Elaina saw the walk fall behind and then finally stop before howling up towards the sky in agony. It tore at her but she only clenched the door handle to keep from opening it and jumping out.

"Why did you do that?!" Rave yelled seriously only to see her look at him like it wasn't his business. "Don't you get it Elaina, he loves you!"

"I get it Rave so stop talking about it! It's my choice not yours!" she snapped back before looking forward as tears spilled over and these one she couldn't stop because she didn't have the strength to. She'd just killed some part of her and knew it was unlikely to ever return to her. At least she'd have a clear mind of what to do for the pack.

"You should've stopped the car."

Elaina didn't know how much Rave's words would haunt her. She didn't know what was expecting her in Montana but did know it wasn't what she got.

Chapter 10

Elaina ran through what seemed to be an endless forest. She could hear water trickling but no matter how far she ran she could never seem to get to a creek, river, or stream. Not even a lake existed. There were no birds, no insects, not even a small animal scurrying under the leaves and foliage that littered the ground.

"Hello?!" she called, not even her voice echoed like one's usually did when you yelled at the top of your lungs. She was all but screaming and even then doubted anyone would hear it. She was all alone, and it scared her. "Hello?!"

Nothing. Not even the wind stirred.

Elaina ran and ran, never getting tired or hungry or thirsty. She ran silently hoping to reach something but even then she didn't know what she was reaching for. It seemed hopeless. She finally screamed at the top of her lungs.

Elaina snapped awake and stopped the scream she'd been emitting while sleeping. She looked around the large room seeing nothing in the shadow's, nothing outside her window, and no sound was made except that of her air conditioner. It was nice and cool in her room but she was covered head to toe in sweat.

She was scared of nothing. There had been nothing in her dream but a forest she couldn't seem to escape. She sighed and picked up the small blanket in the chair in front of her desk and went out the front door to sit on the porch. What was she so scared of?

She took a seat on the porch swing after wrapping the blanket around her that was more for protection then warmth. She was always warm, she was a werewolf. She sat there watching the sky lighten at first and then the sun rose slowly showing the beautiful landscape of Montana. She felt herself give a small smile.

The pack loved it here, she couldn't believe it had already been three months since they'd moved. She'd been having the dream ever since she'd left the house though. No one knew about it, she wouldn't tell them if they asked.

Tristan believed that it was time for her to get a mate to help her run the pack so they would be having a fight for the younger eligible males. Whoever won would become her mate, and the second Alpha to the pack. It would be happening tonight in her own backyard. She hated the idea of people fighting because of her, was it that big of a deal for her to have a mate? Why couldn't she just stay single?

She stood up and stretched wondering why she couldn't just run the pack by herself. Tristan knew it didn't bother her but he wanted everything to be easier for her. The pack even took a vote and while the women thought she was fine the men wanted a chance to win her hand. She doubted she'd accept any of their hands if they won anyway.

Elaina went in her house and made a simple omelet for breakfast. She sat at the table eating and drank a glass of juice before she went to her room and put on a lavender sundress. That's when she heard horn honk letting her know that she had company.

Elaina went out only to feel stunned when she saw a huge van that she didn't recognize. "ELLIE!" she watched Daisy pipe after the side door was opened. Elaina picked her up and spun her around. "Are you surprised!? Mommy thought it would be nice to visit!"

"I am surprised. I've missed you a lot Daisy." Elaina laughed before sitting her down only to freeze instantly when a certain scent wrapped around her. She glance up and saw Fury getting out of the van causing her to feel completely stunned. "Why…"

"We heard that there is going to be some kind of fighting tonight. We came to watch." Baron laughed thinking it was boys trying to prove they were men. "I can't wait to see who become new members of the pack."

"It's not an initiation." she replied lamely as her aunt hugged her.

"What else could there be a fight for?" Tricia asked through a laugh only to see Elaina look elsewhere. "What are they fighting for?"

"To be my mate." she growled and stomped into the house feeling completely irritated. She didn't want any of this to happen. She wanted to pull her hair out until all the guys thought her too insane to be mated to.

"Wait, you're going to be getting married?!" Julie yelled like it wasn't possible but Elaina only slammed her fist into the table causing it to splinter. "Whoa, someone is not in a good mood."

"DAMN IT!" Elaina snapped and pinched that bridge of her nose. "That's the second table this week."

"How many have you broke since you've been here?" Connor asked but she only shook her head.

"I've lost count and it's better then putting holes in the walls. Those won't be as easy to replace." Elaina plopped into a chair only to hear it creak but it was sturdy…unlike the table.

"What does the pack have to say about this?" Tricia asked only to read the answer on Elaina's face. "I am not letting people you've only known for a few months decide your future for you!"

"It's already been decided, I don't have any choice but to go with it." Elaina saw Connor nod seriously when Tricia looked at him. She saw Fury look angry at that but he didn't say anything. What could he possibly say to the fight? If anything he'd ask to participate in and in which case she'd kindly point out that he had no right to get involved in her matters.

"When is it, maybe we can stop it?" Julie offered only to look at the calendar seeing today circled with a black marker.

"It's tonight. The whole pack is going to be here, plus guys from other packs." Elaina stood up and went to her room before curling up under the covers. She had locked her door and didn't bother answering it when anyone knocked. She couldn't go against the pack's decision and she didn't like how they could act like they weren't feeding her to the wolves.

Literally.

She heard a knock before the smell of deer wafted under her door to her nose. Deer was her absolute favorite. She went to the door and opened it only to see Fury standing there holding a basket.

"What..."

"I figured with everything going on you'd want to get out of here for a while. Does a picnic sound good to you?" he asked and she didn't look fooled for a second but he knew she liked deer. Rave had told him how accustomed to it she'd become to a point where she liked it more then any other meat.

"Fine." she grumbled and closed the door so that when she opened it a second time she was wearing plain jean and a t-shirt with tennis shoes.

"Great, let's go." he stated simply before they went on a small hike to a little outlook that gave them a view of the whole farm. "So how are you adjusting out here?"

"It's fine, I mean I don't really like the heat much so my air conditioner is always on when it becomes too unbearable." she replied casually trying to figure out why it felt so comfortable talking to him.

"So what's your favorite part about it?"

"It's so open, there's so much room to run and the mountains are pretty comforting... despite the mountain lions but they don't really bother us since they can sense we aren't normal." she said as she opened the basket seeing a lot of food in there besides the deer. She took a piece and started eating a little bit at a time. "So where are you from?"

"Scotland."

"Eh?" she asked and saw him nod right before she started laughing seeing confusion cross his face. "You wore a skirt?!"

"It's a kilt!"

"Skirt!" she argued with a laugh because it was too funny to think about. "A guy like you wearing a skirt, I just can't seem to picture that!"

"That is my heritage you're making fun of."

"Sorry, it's just that it caught me off guard a little. Is your whole pack from there or just you?" she inquired carefully and saw him look hesitant to answer her.

"We all are from Scotland but unlike you being a created werewolf, we were born werewolves." he retorted and saw her cheerful face vanish instantly leaving a furrowed brow.

"Well sorry if I used to be human." she bit back and went to stand only to get stopped.

"That's not how I meant it so sit down an let me explain." he said watching her sit down slowly as if debating on whether or not she wanted to really stay. "Back in our time there were a lot of born werewolves but they were mostly male so they would always take female humans for brides. I wasn't saying that you being a created werewolf was a bad thing. From what I hear you are an excellent pack leader."

"At least you're good at giving compliments." she grumbled before opening the wine and pouring a little in a glass seeing him confiscate it. "What…"

"I know for a fact that you aren't old enough to drink."

"I will never be old enough so hand it back. It's not even a lot so I'll be fine. It's not like I'll get drunk since my system burns it off too quick. A hangover for me lasts five seconds." she said and reached for the glass but he held it further away causing her to get too close to him. She glanced up seeing him look down causing her to move away and pull out the second glass to pour another. She poured some and took a sip liking the flavor of it.

"You are really stubborn you know that?"

"Deal with it, I don't plan on changing for anyone." she shot back simply and rose her head proudly only to see him smile at that. She ignored the feeling it gave her and took another sip of wine. She saw him bring out a block of cheese and slice a piece before holding it out to her. Without thinking she leaned down and took a bite seeing him raise an eyebrow.

Elaina realized what she did so she leaned away quickly before taking a bite of the food on her own plate. She saw him slice a couple more pieces and sit them on her plate without a word. Elaina could see him fiddling with her fork as if he had something to say but he remained quiet. Instead she watched him down the wine in the glass in one gulp making her see some trail down his chin.

"Um…you got…" she started but he only looked perplexed so she leaned forward and wiped it away with her thumb. She watched him straighten up slightly so that they were eye level and something in her just had to know so that when he leaned towards her, she found she wasn't able to stop him.

When his lips touched hers it felt like time had literally stopped around them. She felt something strong in her surface instantly and she found herself deepening the kiss. She didn't know why but all she knew was that she needed to be with him. Her breath was frantic but so was his, his touch was gentle but rough, and his lips tasted like sin sent straight from the devil. She felt his arms wrap around her causing her to snap out of what seemed like a dream.

She struggled in his arms as she pulled around seeing him look confused. "Let me go." she said watching him frown about that.

"You're running away from me again."

"I said let me go! Now!" she snapped as thunder rumbled in the once clear sky. She struggled to get free as rain started falling so he released her.

"What are you running him?" Fury demanded after standing seeing her move away from him. She was definitely running from him.

"Just stay away from me."

"You know it's not that easy!" he yelled at her after grabbing her shoulders but she only shrugged his hands off her.

"I don't care! Just leave me alone!" Elaina smacked his hand away from her and ran back to the house missing him pull a small black velvet box out of his coat pocket.

She ran all the way home through the rain feeling it soaking her through to her bones. "Elaina you're soaked!" she heard Tricia exclaim before hurrying off to get a towel but she only headed to her room. She was in the doorway when Fury entered the house. She went to her room and changed into a pair of pajama pants and a tank.

"Elaina are you okay?" she heard Julie ask in confusion but she didn't answer as everyone came one by one to knock on her door.

"Just go away! I'm fine!" she yelled angrily when another knock sounded. After that no one so much as came near her door but it doesn't mean she couldn't hear them talking about her.

When the sun started setting she slipped on the plain flat white tennis shoes as cars pulled up one after another. She walked out of her room and met Tristan at the front door.

"Are you ready?" he asked so she gave a nod and they went into the back yard.

"You three should stay inside, it tends to be pretty frenzied." Connor warned Tricia who gave a small nod so they stayed inside and looked out the kitchen window.

"Tonight we hold the dance of the males. All eligible males not over the age of twenty-six are allowed to participate! So those who want to fight step forward now!" Tristan called and Elaina just stood in the center seeing males remove their shirts trying to look intimidating.

Elaina looked up suddenly when a figure walking forward caught her attention and that's when Fury stepped forward causing her to feel her heart pound. Why would he be doing this!?

"Is that all?" Tristan asked causing them to nod so everyone moved back so she drew a circle around them with Tristan right before they changed and started fighting without another word. They knew the rules so it didn't need to be explained.

She saw wolves get thrown out one by one causing her to look away because she didn't want people fighting over her. It made her sick to see so many willing to fight just to be Alpha when she barely had to fight anyone. She could heard wounded barks and howls of pain as they got injured fighting for the right to be called her mate.

"Go Fury!" she heard his pack cheer so she looked seeing it was Fury and only one other wolf in the circle with him. She stood there seeing the fight go completely vicious as they bit, clawed, dragged, and rolled in the circle. It seems like it would never be over.

"Stop." she heard Tristan order causing them to break apart but at the last second the gray one latched onto Fury's neck and she heard him growl twisting on the ground. "STOP!"

Elaina felt something inside her as the gray one kept going as others around murmured quietly. "STOP IT NOW!" she roared watching it jump away from Fury who had already sank his teeth into the arm. She saw them both change back showing them covered in dirt, blood, and sweat. She felt something coursing through her and realized it was worry. She could see the teeth marks in his neck healing but they had still been bleeding badly causing her hands to start shaking so she tucked them behind her back.

"You are equally matched, the choice shall be up to our Alpha on who she wishes to have." Tristan announced so Elaina stepped into the circle but while the other looked at her as if he deserved it, Fury didn't look at her at all.

Why wouldn't he look at her?

Elaina walked forward and stopped in front of Fury. He looked just as bad as the other. Even more so with the bite marks on his neck that were already healing. "Why did you even enter this fight?" she asked quietly, he finally looked up from the ground.

"You seriously have to ask me that?" he countered like he couldn't believe what she'd just ask.

"I wanted to be sure." she murmured only to see him take her wrists and kiss the inside of each one. She felt heat rise to her cheeks as she watched him do that. She heard girls giggling as the wolf next to Fury seemed irritated that she was only paying attention to him.

"I want to belong to you and only you Elaina." Fury replied causing the one to stand and go to touch her but Fury got between him.

"She has not chosen you." he pointed out and Fury realized he was right. Had he done all of this for nothing?

"Yes, I have." Elaina stated as she looked elsewhere causing the girls to squeal happily. She saw Fury spin around so fast it almost disoriented her. She was pulled directly against him and rewarded with a kiss that caused her feel giddy and excited all at once. She suddenly knew what she'd been searching for in the endless forest that had been her dream as he pulled away slowly.

Him. She had been looking for him all along and now she'd found him.

She suddenly realized there was an odd weight on her left hand. She looked and saw an engagement ring causing her to gawk. "Why…"

"I was hoping I'd be the one you picked. I was planning on asking until I found out about the fight, but I guess I'll ask anyway." he explained as he played with a strand of her hair. "Marry me?"

"Like you left me any choice." she grumbled right before the packs started howling causing her to laugh. She saw Fury nod in Rave's direction causing Rave to nod back before grinning at her. She realized it was probably him who told her aunt to bring them along.

As part of tradition her and Fury turned and took their first run as mates. The stars shone brightly in the sky as the half moon hung lazily in the sky and not a cloud shone in sight. A perfect night for a perfect run.

That's when howls erupted and she looked seeing the pack catching up. She looked to her left seeing Fury next to her and somehow knew that's where he would always be.

Dear Aunt Tricia,

Hey it's me, Elaina. Everything is going great here in Montana. The pack is having so much fun and there is so much to do. I can't wait until you come visit again. Fury even caved and we got a couple horses. (Don't tell Daisy I want to surprise her.) Anyway, we've finally set a date for the wedding, the summer since that's when Daisy isn't in school and you all can stay for a while. This house is way to big for just Fury and myself despite the others always inviting themselves over. Don't worry, I've picked my colors so we can start planning, and like all men Fury looks like he'd rather not discuss it. Men and weddings just don't get along…unless your Rave.

Speaking of Rave, he asked me to have you call him, he's picking out an engagement ring. He wants to have a small wedding, he never liked big events but I told him a wedding only happens once…unless you're a celebrity or someone important then you're bound to have a minimum of two. He's excited about proposing to the point of it making him a little clumsy.

Fury has been a bit disappointed about that because he's always following me around just to mess with me, and when the others are there he pretends not to because he doesn't want them to know about him doing that. It's hilarious because he looks irritated causing the others to get confused but all I can do is laugh. He's a good guy, I don't think I could've found anyone more special which makes me a bit sad that I left in the first place to get away from him. Now it's like we can never be separated, even when he goes hunting he always comes back earlier then he planned cause he doesn't like to be away for so long. It's not like I'm complaining though.

How's Connor and Julie doing, I'm glad to hear about their engagement. Julie has even called and we're even thinking about doing a double wedding so that's it's bigger and all of our friends can be here. Tell Julie I miss her and that I am completely expecting her to come out here during winter break and hang out. Give Daisy a hug for me. Love you. See you soon.

Your Niece,
Elaina

P.S. Fury says hi and wishes that you called more. I think he needs more ideas on how to make up for all of the stupid things he's doing. Last night he tried to check the pipe under the sink and ended up breaking it. I had to call to get it replaced.

About the author:

Born in Enterprise, Alabama, Margaret Yoder now currently resides in Morgantown, WV. She attends West Virginia University where she double majors in Chinese and International Studies and double minors in Japanese and English.

Book Summary:

What do you get when you mix a pack of unruly and annoying werewolves, a couple of vampires, and a near death experience? Elaina's life. Spending most of her life in a wheelchair was easy until she bit a vampire out of defense. The next thing she knows is that she wakes up with a dog bite on her hand, she walks as if she's never spent day in a wheelchair, and her once calm life erupts into a complete chaotic storm of events. Getting her heartbroken she finds herself getting attached to a rogue, Fury. He makes her think of how easy life could be if she just agrees to the pack laws and take a partner to help her run everything. With the help of her friends and her new pack she finds that not all choices are easy, and some are practically deadly.